THE NERVOUS WRECK

JUNE WALKER AS SALLY MORGAN.
OTTO KRUGER AS HENRY WILLIAMS.

THE
NERVOUS WRECK

BY

E. J. RATH

ILLUSTRATED WITH
SCENES FROM THE PLAY

WILDSIDE PRESS

THE NERVOUS WRECK .

CHAPTER I

GAME BUT NERVOUS

DAD MORGAN stood with his shoulders against the top rail of the corral fence, apparently asleep on his feet. The sun had a persuasive warmth, which was good for kinks in the system. He never could decide whether it melted or baked the twinges out of him; but he knew it for an emollient of power and virtue. His figure dropped somnolently. His pipe hung loosely from a corner of his mouth. His eyes were half closed.

But Dad Morgan was not asleep, nor were his half-closed eyes idle. They were watching two riders descend the slope on the far side of the wide coulée in which the ranch buildings sprawled. There was a piebald horse ridden by a girl and a sorrel ridden by a man. They were still somewhat distant for disclosure of these details, but Dad Morgan knew who was coming. The pace of the riders was a walk, and Dad understood the meaning of it.

"I expect he's got himself all chafed up," he

mused. "But he'll put it on his nerves; see if he
don't. Nothin' ever happens to him regular and
natural, except maybe swearin'."

The riders were out upon a green level, and the
piebald horse broke into an easy lope. The sorrel
followed, then checked and settled down to a restless
walk. The girl in front turned in her saddle, glanced
backward, brought her mount to a stop and waited.
When the sorrel had come abreast the two horses
walked again in the direction of the ranch. Dad
Morgan grinned, shifted his position against the
fence and began filling his pipe.

He was smoking lazily when the riders came to a
pause at the corral gate. The girl swung off with an
easy sweep and waved a gauntleted hand.

"Hello, Dad."

"Howdy, Sally? Howdy, Wreck?"

The man on the sorrel made no answer, for he
was engaged in a task. With both hands gripping
the pommel, he raised himself in the stirrups, tight-
ened his lips, and scowled. Then, very slowly, he
fetched his right leg across the sorrel's back. As he
did this he flattened himself forward until the pommel burrowed into the pit of his stomach and his
arms gripped the sorrel's neck in a tense embrace.
Then he slid crabwise to the ground. He stood
there for several seconds, looking at his legs, which
had retained the posture necessary to enclose the
barrel of a horse. Slowly he straightened them, one
after the other. There was a groan in his look, but
he did not give it speech.

He turned a savage and challenging eye in the direction of Dad Morgan.

"I'm fine," he said.

"You're lookin' real well," observed Dad. "Had an idea you might of got lamed up some, but I can't say as I see any signs of it."

The rider of the sorrel stumped stiffly forward half a dozen steps.

"Who—me? Lame? What would I get lame for?"

"Come to think of it, Wreck, I'm durned if I know. I reckon anybody who can set on a flivver for fifteen hundred miles, maybe sixteen hundred, is kind of acclimated. Anyhow, the sheriff says—"

Dad Morgan broke off at a slight but peremptory gesture from the girl, who had opened the corral gate and was accelerating the piebald horse through it with a gentle flick of her quirt.

She was a free, loose-limbed girl, brown in the cheeks and neck, clear and serene of eye—a girl of the open spaces and the rolling range. The wide calm of the big country somehow found its expression in Sally Morgan. But the look that went with the gesture, while it never broke the calm, checked Dad as surely as though it had been an order from Ma herself.

The rider of the sorrel watched his mount follow the piebald into the corral, then straightened his shoulders, set his teeth and stepped off briskly in the direction of the house. He stumbled once, pulled himself together with a wince and hastened his step.

Dad watched him until his figure disappeared through the doorway.

"Now, I'm wonderin' which nerves—"

Sally stopped him again. "Let him alone, Dad. He's game, anyhow."

"I ain't sayin' anything he can hear, Sally. I'm just wonderin' which nerves is responsible. We ain't allowed to lay it on the sorrel, or on the saddle, or on any of the failin's of human flesh. It's got to be nerves or nothin'."

"Well, don't plague him about it. If he wants to blame it on his nerves, why should we care? And I don't think he likes to have you call him 'Wreck.'"

Dad viewed his daughter with a glance of surprise.

"He ain't ever said so," he remarked.

"And would you expect him to? He's a guest."

"He's payin' eight dollars a week to Ma. I ain't sayin' we *asked* him for it. Ma didn't want to take nothin'. But when a man's payin' he's got the rights of free and unlimited speech. And if he don't like—"

"He's a guest, just the same," repeated Sally. "And so long as he stays here we're under an obligation to treat him right."

"I'm treatin' him all right, ain't I? There ain't a single thing about life in these wild and irreverent parts I haven't told him, any time he asked me. Why, all I been doin' the past two weeks is easin' education into him."

Sally smiled.

"And I've picked up considerable about nerves, which sort of makes it an even split," added Dad. "He don't mind my callin' him 'Wreck.' If he was goin' to squeal about it, why would he lay claim to bein' such? You heard him say it. 'I'm a nervous wreck,' he says, sort of proud."

"Oh, well, don't rub it in, Dad."

"Ain't rubbin' it in. Ain't goin' to," Dad looked up suddenly. "Did you say something about his bein' game?"

Sally smiled again and her glance wandered to the crest of the grassy slope and seemed to go beyond it.

"It was awfully funny," she said, "but I was scared for a minute. We rode over as far as the second ridge; I wanted him to see a real piece of range country. He wouldn't admit he'd never been on a horse before. But he did pretty well, although the sorrel was getting nervous from the way his mouth was pulled."

"It's catchin', maybe."

"Perhaps. At any rate, we were standing there, right close to the edge, when a bee lit—on the sorrel. You know what happened. The way he went over that horse's head you'd have thought he'd learned to fly. It carried him over the edge, too, and he went down about twenty feet before he grabbed hold of a bush and stopped himself. I thought he was going all the way."

"I expect you roped him?" observed Dad.

"He wouldn't let me. He got mad as fury when he saw I was going to. He said he guessed he could climb back without any help, and he did. And he wouldn't let me catch the sorrel, either. It must have taken him twenty minutes at least. And then it took him another five minutes to get on. I can't describe exactly the way he did it. It was like shinning up. Of course, he was pretty well scratched and mussed, and his temper was in a frightful state."

"Any language?" asked Dad.

"No; he was too busy, I think. Coming home he nearly fell off twice, trying to ease himself in the saddle. But he never squealed. And he says he's going out riding to-morrow morning. He won't make it, though; he'll be too lame to move."

Dad nodded with understanding. Any dude would be too lame to move under equal circumstances. Yet he was not entirely certain that the Wreck would fail to move, even though too lame; for he had a way of playing the game according to his own rules.

"I'll put on a house dress, I believe," said Sally.

"Sure," agreed Dad. "Bob's here."

She paused for an instant, a look of surprise in her eyes.

"When did he come? I didn't expect him until to-morrow morning."

"He came a while back. He ain't goin' to be able to go with you to-morrow, as near as I can make out."

Sally frowned involuntarily, then shrugged and continued her march toward the house. Dad settled back against the fence and resumed his musing. Sally would be mighty disappointed if she did not get to the train to-morrow; she was all packed and expectant. But he knew that she would not say very much; she was not much of a hand at complaining. Still, it seemed, even to Dad, that it was too bad to postpone everything right at the last minute. He would not mind riding over with her himself, but it was too long a trail for people with twinges and kinks. Sometimes he wished the ranch was a little mite nearer the railroad. But Sally never even complained about that.

There had been no railroad at all when Dad Morgan came into the range country; at least, none within a couple of hundred miles or more. Now there was a main line north of them, only about thirty-five miles on a good trail. It seemed very near to Dad when it first came; but when Sally began going to school in the East, and there were seasonal goings and comings, with the necessity of maintaining communications between city and ranch, Dad realized that it was not very close, after all. So far as he and Ma were concerned, that made no difference. But Sally had grown up, and she had an education, and she knew the ways of places far beyond the range, and—well, Dad understood. Still, even Sally was quite satisfied with the range country, provided she was not quarantined there.

It was not a very large ranch that Dad Morgan surveyed through half-squinted eyes, nor was it a busy one. The air of idleness was everywhere about it; idleness, but not decay. It was simply a ranch taking a long and honorable rest. The busy years were behind it. They had been busy indeed when Dad Morgan and Ma were young and when, coming out of Kentucky, they staked their tiny fortune in a land so big that it gripped them with awe. Time passed, cattle went to market and the ranch prospered. There were others who came into the country and there were new brands on the range. So imperceptibly that he scarcely sensed the change, Dad slid out of the competition. He had all he needed; let the newcomers do the striving. And now there were only a few head bearing the Bar-M brand and scarcely enough work for a single hand.

"I aint got any kick," mused Dad. "I got mine; enough, anyhow. Let the rest of 'em hustle. They haven't come into their rheumatism yet. Only I'm sure sorry that Sally's goin' to miss her train."

So was Sally. But, true to Dad's mental prediction, she did not say much about it, even to Bob Wells, who had ridden twenty miles to explain and would have to ride back again that night. Bob was the sheriff. He was other things besides sheriff; things that were much more important in a material way. He had cattle of his own, and a couple of mining claims that promised, and he owned a general store at the county seat. Dad Morgan said there wasn't a more likely young hustler in all Montana than Bob Wells. And when Bob took to calling on Sally, Dad felt that the future was working itself out in a proper and prosperous fashion.

As nearly as Dad could figure it out, in the absence

of direct information, Sally was going East to see about things for her trousseau. Anyhow, the sheriff seemed to be certain enough about it, and Sally made no denial. She had known Bob Wells since she first rode her own pony, as a little wild thing raised on the Bar-M, and she did not encounter any surprise in the idea of marrying him. It was all very natural and according to the custom of the country.

"I reckon," said Dad, as he glanced up from his supper, "that Bob's got more to lose by your missin' that train than maybe anybody else around these parts."

The sheriff winked as he reached for the coffee pot and helped himself to another cup. He was a large, healthy and well-pleased young man, with a slightly boisterous air, even in moments of repose.

"Bob can't help it," said Sally, promptly, ignoring her father's allusion. "He has a sheriff's job down at Fisher and he has to be back there to-night. It really doesn't make any difference if I wait a few days, only— Well, Milly Field is going to be in St. Paul, and I thought I might spend a day with her before I went on to Chicago. But I can see Milly some other time; maybe I can get her to come out here."

Ma Morgan nodded, but made no comment. Ma was never very talkative; ordinarily she contented herself with confirmatory nods, the opinions and conclusions of others usually being sufficient for her.

"If it wasn't for the fact that there'd be no way

of getting the horse back, I'd ride over alone," said Sally.

"No chance," declared the sheriff.

"Pooh! Why not? Why, Bob, I've done it. I rode as far as the railroad last summer and I know every inch of the trail. And it's only about thirty-five miles."

"Well, I wouldn't let you ride alone. Besides, there'll have to be a pack horse to take your grips. You can't manage everything, Sally."

Sally thought she could, and she felt a faint resentment at the contrary implication. But she had no intention of arguing it with Bob; he was always positive about things.

"Did you want to go to the railroad to-morrow?"

It was the Wreck speaking. All through supper he had been eating with a silent voraciousness that caused Dad Morgan to wonder if there were any nerves in the stomach.

"Why, I'd planned to go," said Sally, "but it seems we can't make it."

"Certainly we can make it," declared the Wreck, with sudden asperity in his voice. "Why not? I'll take you."

The sheriff laid down his knife and stared. The Wreck never failed to amuse him, but this was their third meeting. If Bob Wells had nerves of his own he was unaware of their existence. He had heard of city folks with nerves, but the Wreck was his first personal encounter with such. So the Wreck would take her to the train, would he? The sheriff glanced at Dad and grinned.

"On a horse?" he inquired.

"In a machine," answered the Wreck, shortly.

"Oh-h-h!" It was spoken with gusty good nature, but it carried a volume of scorn. So the Wreck thought, at any rate, for he glared through his horn-rimmed glasses and pushed his plate back.

"Want me to drive you over in the machine?" he demanded, switching his glance to Sally. He flung it out as a sort of sweeping challenge that included even Ma.

"Why, it would be lovely," said Sally.

The sheriff took plenty of time to laugh. He rather expected Dad to join, but Dad merely remained quizzical. Ma and Sally were watching the Wreck.

"Yes, it sure would be lovely," said the sheriff, easing down for speech. "Going to put a flivver over the trail, eh? What are you figuring to do? Run her on two wheels?"

The Wreck made an irritable movement of his shoulders and ignored him. He was still looking at Sally.

"Isn't there a road?" he asked.

"It's a road part of the way," said Sally. "A good part of the way. Yes, it is, Bob; you can drive a wagon over it."

"And what do you do when you come to the mountain?" inquired the sheriff, smiling. "I haven't noticed any road there yet."

"But it connects up with some other road before you get that far; I'm certain of it." Sally was getting interested. "And the other road must go somewhere. There were some people from the north who came through in a car only last spring."

"Well, it's a long, roundabout road, even if you located it," said the sheriff. "I know the people you mean. They had a *car*."

Still the Wreck ignored him.

"Is it country like this around here?" he demanded. "All open and plain sailing?"

"There's plenty of open country," answered Sally, with a faint smile.

The Wreck amused Sally, just as he did the sheriff. But she found something more than amusement in him. There were times when his assurance fairly startled her. Besides, she still liked the idea of making her train.

"Road part way and open country the rest of the way," observed the Wreck. "Anything the matter with that? You don't hear me yelling."

"I'll hear you yelling if you try to make it in a flivver," remarked the sheriff, and he coupled another laugh with it.

Sally was musing over it, and found the idea slightly exciting.

"Bob, I don't see any reason why it can't be done," she said, slowly. "And if we had to turn back, why there's no harm, anyhow."

"Turn back!" echoed the Wreck. "What for? You want to catch a train, don't you? Well, when

I start catching trains, I catch 'em. Want to go?"

"Why, I—"

Sally looked at the sheriff. He shook his head authoritatively.

"Can't be done, Sally. I know what I'm talking about. And besides—"

He paused to observe the Wreck, who had pushed his chair back from the table and risen. Sally nibbled at her lip; there were times when she wished Bob would not be so sweepingly authoritative.

"Any time to-morrow that you're ready, I'm ready," said the Wreck, regarding her with a stare that was almost belligerent. "And anybody who tells you it can't be done is suffering from arrested mental development."

He limped out of the room, but there was something absurdly aggressive in his gait. Dad Morgan eyed his back appraisingly and then looked at the sheriff.

"Wreck's kind of saddle sore," he observed, mildly, "but he certainly keeps chipper."

"He's a nut," said the sheriff. "He can't do it in a million years."

"But he might, Bob." Sally had a look in her eye that boded a desire for discussion.

"What? In a flivver?"

"I've heard," said Dad Morgan—"not that I've got personal experience—but I've heard that folks can go 'most anywhere in them things, except in society."

CHAPTER II

THE ranch buildings were miles back of them; how many, Sally could not exactly tell, for there was no speedometer on the flivver. There was a hole in the instrument board where once a speedometer had been, but it had been taken out for repairs somewhere in South Dakota and the Wreck refused to linger for a week in order that it might be made to register again. But they were fifteen miles from the ranch, at least, and the railroad was still more miles to the north. By the trail which wound high along the eastern flank of Black Top it was about twenty miles, as nearly as Sally could figure. They could not follow the high trail, of course; somewhere a road branched, which they must take, and Sally was intent on watching for the road.

It was an odd sensation, bumping over the trail on wheels; it helped her to forget that there had been words with the sheriff the night before, just as he was saddling to ride back to his job at Fisher. The sheriff did not want her to go, and he made some remarks about the Wreck which, to Sally, seemed perfectly silly. The idea of anybody objecting, she thought; even Dad was willing that she

14

should go, although he predicted they would be back at the ranch before nightfall, and probably afoot.

Now and then she studied the Wreck with a side-long glance. It was rather funny to watch him, tensed over the wheel, his jaw set with an absurd amount of determination and his eyes staring aggressively ahead through his horn-rimmed spectacles. He seemed to make an unnecessary task of the matter, although she admitted to herself that it was a pretty bad trail for anything except a horse. Once she even remarked the fact to him, after he had navigated a detour that carried them around a boulder.

"Bad trail?" he echoed, almost sharply. "You don't call this bad, do you? I call it a boulevard."

The queer part of it was that he seemed to mean it. Most young men, had they been driving in place of the Wreck, would have bragged of an achievement that approximated the impossible. But he had a point of view that was quite different; he was obsessed with a resolve to make the task so childishly simple that the sheriff would eat his words and be overwhelmed with mortification.

The Wreck's name was Henry Williams, and he belonged considerably farther east than Sally had ever been; as far as Pittsburgh, in fact. His coming to the Bar-M had been without specific premeditation; it was merely an incident, it appeared, in a great plan. They first sighted him in the middle of a forenoon, two weeks back, coming furiously up

the coulée, with a radiator that boiled like Old
Faithful and a carbon knock that sounded like the
crack of doom. He brought the thing to a stop in
the dooryard, introduced himself, asked for water,
tarried for lunch, tinkered with the car, stayed for
supper, and then kept on staying.

"I'm a nervous wreck," he told Dad Morgan and
the family. "I've got insomnia and things like that.
I look healthy, but don't let it fool you. I'm a
wreck."

It seemed that his doctor, back in Pittsburgh,
diagnosed him, and he believed the doctor. He had
been working too hard; he was on edge all the
time. He was not very old, but the city was killing
him. Anything that savored of excitement was in a
fair way to put an end to him.

"What you need," said the doctor, "is a long trip
somewhere, by yourself. Cut out the cities; dodge
the towns. Buy yourself a flivver and strike out
for the wild West. That's the only place where a
man can lead a quiet life in these days."

Dad Morgan allowed that the doctor was right;
but the Wreck said no, the doctor was a liar. The
West had not been nearly so quiet as promised.
He had been within three hundred yards of a cyclone
in Minnesota, had three blow-outs in the two Da-
kotas, had collided with a runaway horse—after
causing the runaway—had been arrested four times
for violating speed laws, had been in one fight with
a man who called him a dude and had been held up
two days by a cloudburst. All this was bad for his

nerves, he explained, as he passed his plate for a third helping at supper. It aggravated his insomnia, too. Dad knew that his insomnia must be pretty bad, because he had to stay so long in bed in order to get his sleep. He turned in at nine the first night and they had to call him for breakfast.

But it seemed that the Wreck liked the Bar-M. He stayed and stayed, and appeared to think they ought to be grateful to have a paying boarder. Dad and Ma and Sally were, in fact, glad to have him, for, outside of the sheriff and a few other natives, visitors at the ranch came seldom. Besides, the Wreck was something of a curiosity, and when he did not talk about his nerves he could tell interesting tales of the East, which nobody but Sally believed. She had been as far as Chicago, so that she had something to judge by.

And now the Wreck was taking her to the train, mainly because everybody but Sally said it could not be done in a flivver. Sally was not at all certain about it herself, but she had a curiosity that could only be appeased by the attempt. Besides, it was nice of the Wreck to volunteer, and she did not think it was hospitable to refuse.

The trail got worse, as most of them do. It wound and climbed in a tortuous fashion, simple enough for a horse, but most of it never intended for a contraption with a 56-inch tread. Ordinarily, at the top of the rises, Sally was wont to check her horse long enough for a sweeping view of billowing range, bench land and the stern figure of

Black Top, which was their nearest mountain. Black Top was not a very high mountain, but, standing curiously alone in the range country, was a useful mark for reckoning. Nearly everybody who traveled the neighborhood took bearings from it, even though they chanced to be strangers.

But to-day Sally took no sweeping views when they reached crests in the trail. Rather, she drew deep breaths, looked down ahead of her and gripped the seat; for the Wreck had a trick of taking the down grades with a swoop, they being the only stretches of trail which offered chances for speed. If it had not been for the horn-rimmed glasses, there would have been something positively debonair in the way he plunged into the unknown. He had a habit of hissing triumphantly through his teeth whenever he reached the bottom and found the car still running on four wheels, which Sally found almost as disconcerting as the swoops.

They had come to the end of a long, twisting descent, which he volplaned with amazing abandon, when Sally ventured a comment.

"How do you get it up again when it turns over?" she asked.

It was a look of annoyance and disappointment that he gave her.

"Listen," he said. "Don't *you* start saying it can't be done. I thought you were different."

"Oh, but I think it can be done, Mr. Williams," she hastily amended. "Only—well, you might break an axle, or something. Mightn't you?"

The Wreck brought the machine to a stop and allowed the engine to race in a horrible manner.

"Want to get that train, don't you?" he demanded.

"Why, of course."

"Am I alarming or otherwise annoying you?"

"No, indeed!"

"Have I busted anything yet?"

"I don't believe so."

"All right. Let's go."

He stamped his foot on one of the pedals and they leaped forward along the bottom of a little draw into which the trail had carried them. Sally held tight and smiled. She enjoyed his childish faith in himself; besides, she figured that she could jump clear as soon as it became necessary. Why should she complain? The Wreck had uttered no criticism the day before, when the sorrel pitched him.

They got out of the draw after sliding back twice; he said he could climb a tree with proper traction and she expressed no doubt of the statement. After that the trail climbed and twisted again. It was winding out of the grass country and in among clumps of spruce and wild rose bushes. Also, it was narrowing steadily, but neither the Wreck nor Sally gave any early attention to that fact. Not until it was shrunken to a mere path among rocks and trees did the flivver come to a stop. The Wreck killed the engine, climbed out and went ahead for reconnaissance.

"We'll have to roll a lot of rocks out of the

way," he said when he came back. "Are you good at it?"

Sally fought against a smile, for she was contrite with guilt.

"It wouldn't do any good to start rolling rocks," she said. "We'd be at it till doomsday. I'm awfully sorry, but we've come too far. It's my fault."

"Too far?" he repeated, puzzled.

"Yes. You see, we're beginning to climb the side of Black Top, and you can't get anything up here but a horse. I was so busy watching the trail that I didn't notice our bearings. It was stupid of me, but—well, it's done."

He nodded, then glanced ahead at the disappearing trail.

"If a horse can do it—" He was thinking of the sheriff.

"Oh, no," said Sally, emphatically, and shook her head. "It's useless to think of it. Why, there are some places it just goes along the edge, not more than three feet wide."

He was reluctant to abandon the idea and still stared at the trail with an appraising eye.

"We'll have to go back," explained Sally, "to the place where the road turns off. We passed it."

"I didn't see it," he remarked. "Did you?"

"Certainly not. If I had I'd have spoken about it. But it's there, of course. Don't you remember that we spoke about a road turning off, last night? That's what we had to watch for. It's not much

of a road, I imagine; but a car came through last
spring."

"How far back is it?" he demanded.

Sally could not even guess.

"It can't be far," she said.

The Wreck stood for a moment in gloomy contemplation.

"It upsets my nerves to turn back," he announced.
"I get jumpy and shaky. It irritates me. But—oh,
blazes!"

He reached for the crank and yanked it viciously.
Sally dismounted and stood breathless while he made
a turn. He managed it ultimately, after a furious
charge into a clump of saplings, which flattened
under the attack like wire entanglements before a
tank.

"Get in," he commanded.

They were off on the back trail, leaping and
careening. For ten tempestuous minutes they traveled the down-grade, with Black Top casting a long
shadow before them.

"Keep your eye peeled for that turn-off," ad-
monished the Wreck, as they plunged reeling into
a little green coulée through which a tiny stream
trickled.

"I'm a-watching," said Sally.

She was watching carefully, too. She knew the
proper side of the trail to watch, and wasted no
time with an inspection of the other. But no matter
how closely her eyes searched, they found no sign.

Half an hour had passed when he brought the flivver to a grinding stop.

"Well?" It was plain enough that he was impatient.

"It ought to be somewhere along here," said Sally, standing up for a better general view.

"Didn't pass it, did we?"

"Oh, no. We couldn't have."

"All right."

She sat suddenly as the car jumped into stride again.

"Excuse me," he said, briefly, and attended to his driving.

There was another spell of plunging and bucking and watching. Then Sally raised her hand and there was a halt. This time she climbed up on the seat, and made a long survey.

"It's queer about that road, but I can't seem to find it," she confessed.

The Wreck climbed up beside her and gazed squintingly through the horn rims.

"You see, it goes over that way," she explained, with a gesture. "There isn't any other place for it to go. There's a sort of valley running along this side of the bench over yonder. That's the only way a wagon road can get past Black Top; at least, on this side. Yes; I'm certain it's over there. And, of course, it runs north, toward the railroad."

"Road goes up that valley, eh?"

"It must."

"All right. Where does it start from?"

Sally looked at him with a little frown.

"That's just it. I can't find the start of it," she said.

"I never saw a road yet that didn't have a starting point," he remarked.

"There's no doubt it has one, of course. But, you see—"

"Never mind. Sit down."

She had barely scrambled from her perch when the car moved again, swung abruptly to the left, deserted the trail and started across a level stretch of fine grazing land. For half a minute Sally was too surprised to speak. Then she gasped:

"Where—where are you going?"

"Going to find the road," answered the Wreck, through his set teeth.

"But we're completely off the trail!"

"Well, isn't that the idea? We didn't get anywhere sticking to it. You say there's a road over there somewhere. If there is, I'll find it."

The little plateau dipped sharply into a long slope, smooth enough to the eye, but filled with unexpected bumps that lay hidden in the grass. He gave the flivver its head and charged downward. Twice there was daylight between Sally and the seat, but she landed aboard both times. As for the Wreck, his concentration was magnificent; he was there to drive, not to admire nature. They reached the bottom of the slope, then climbed another. After that it was a series of nicely rounded land billows, up and down, up and down. But all the Wreck saw was a road in his mind's eye, somewhere ahead.

The billows became lumpy and broken. There were some that could not be climbed; they forced him to make detours, a thing that irritated him beyond measure. Sally sat in a half daze. If anybody had told her the thing could be done, she would have demanded the proof. Now she had it. A flivver could actually go across country like a horse—and much more alarmingly.

They dipped into a deep coulée, followed it to the end and found they could not get out of it. The Wreck made a masterly turn, part of it on the two outer wheels, and raced feverishly out of the cul-de-sac. Sally was between a cry of alarm and a shout of laughter. It was all too absurd to be true; it was an extravagant dream, loosely woven out of impossibilities. Yet she knew she was awake; they were roaming the wide range on wheels, no matter how ridiculous such a thing might be.

She glanced over her shoulder, frowned in perplexity, bit her lip, then made a quick survey on all sides, as she clung to the seat. Somewhere behind the wallowing range land Black Top was lost to view. She took a bearing from the sun, and as she did so it broke upon her with a sense of shock that the yellowing disk was dipping close to the earth.

"Stop!" she commanded.

He obeyed with his usual disconcerting abruptness. Sally glanced at the watch strapped to her wrist and caught her breath.

"Do you know that it's after six o'clock?" she cried.

He bent over to examine the watch, then produced his own, which he wore in a pocket.

"Ten after six," he confirmed. "I think we're both a few minutes fast."

"And do you know we're supposed to catch that train at seven?"

Sally's voice had a note of consternation.

"Don't get fussed," he advised. "We'll make it."

He was plunging forward again, but she checked him with a vigorous grip on his arm.

"We're headed in exactly the wrong direction. We're going south, and we ought to be going north."

"Well, we've got to go south until we get out of this what-you-may-call-it," retorted the Wreck. "I can't turn around here."

"But—but—"

Sally was thinking about the east-bound express. She did not know, but she had a feeling that the railroad was still very far away. They had been on the road since noon, and she could not for her life tell how many miles they had wasted—but probably most of them.

"But what?" asked the Wreck, impatiently.

"We'll just never make that train."

"Why not? Who says so? Certainly we will. If there's a railroad there with a train on it, we'll make it. Just as soon as we get to this road you spoke about—"

"But where is the road?"

The Wreck removed his hands from the wheel, folded them in his lap and looked at her.

"You said it was over this way, didn't you?"

"I—I'm not sure. I said it was in a certain direction from a certain place. But I don't believe we've been going in that direction. At least, not all the time."

"We've been going as nearly in one direction as we could," he said, coldly. "Don't blame me if the country is a hodge-podge. Don't think for a moment that I'm standing up for it."

"I'm not blaming you. But we ought never to have left the trail."

"That's blaming me," said the Wreck. "If we stayed on the trail, how could we make the road?"

"What we should have done," said Sally, "was to search until we found where the trail and the road connected."

"All right. We'll go back to the trail, if you'll acknowledge that the road isn't over here?"

He was rather irritating, thought Sally, but it would be ridiculous to quarrel.

"We don't seem to have found the road yet," she compromised. "But we can't stay here; that's certain. We ought to be driving on."

"Sure. We'll pick up the trail again."

"If we can," supplemented Sally.

She realized instantly that it was an unfortunate remark. She had forgotten that the Wreck had nerves, and was sensitive. He had started the car, but now he jammed the brakes again.

"Look here; have you got the idea in your head that I'm lost?" he demanded.

"Please go ahead. It's getting later and later."

"Because if you have," added the Wreck, "I'll remind you that I drove all the way from Pittsburgh without getting lost. And if you think you can lose me in a little two-by-nothing prairie you'll have to guess some more."

"Oh, drive on!" exclaimed Sally.

He did drive on, expertly and furiously. She cast a hopeless glance at the low ridges that seemed to have sprung up on all sides, and frowned anxiously. Perhaps the Wreck was not lost, but Sally was quite certain that she was.

CHAPTER III

"IF YOU START, FINISH—"

NO longer had she any idea that they would find the railroad and the water tank at which it was possible to signal the train. When seven o'clock came she dismissed that from her mind; all that was now left was to get back to the ranch. The sheriff was right; it could not be done, as the Wreck said it could. Sally wondered how the Wreck would handle himself in defeat. She did not think the sheriff would have much mercy, but she knew there would be an explanation from the author of the attempt, who would never admit that the venture had gone against him. He was too proud for that.

The motor stalled on a grade, the flivver slid backward a few lengths and the Wreck dismounted to crank. Sally awoke from her musing. The country was growing different; there were a few scattered trees near them, and down in a deep coulée that lay ahead there was a whole grove. She also observed in the same swift sweep of her eyes that the shadows were attenuated, and she remembered that for some time the sun had been visible only from the tops of the rises.

"I'm sure this it not the way we came," she said.

"I'm taking a short cut," he answered. "Hold tight."

The car tilted almost to the balancing point, then reluctantly settled back to an erect position.

"But the trail is over to the west of us, and we're not going west. We're headed almost east again."

He heard the protest with a look of scorn in his eyes.

"Will you tell me how I'm going to steer west, over that thing?" he asked, with a gesture of finality.

Sally admitted to herself that the ridge immediately to the west of them did not look scalable. They were moving along at its base, apparently barred from the range beyond it.

"What we should have done was to follow our own tracks," she said.

"Tracks!" echoed the Wreck. "Take a look behind us and see if we're leaving any tracks now."

It was true they were not very distinct, and she knew that after the wind had a chance at the grass they would disappear.

"We didn't even start to follow them, when we had the chance," she said, stubbornly. "*I* could have made them out."

"Oh, I suppose so. And the eagle-eyed sheriff, too."

The Wreck's tone was jeering and bitter. It brought a flush to Sally's cheeks, but she conquered an impulse to retort. Bracing her feet solidly against the floor-boards, she sat stiffly back in the seat and kept an eye on their course. She felt a sharp sense of humiliation in being lost on the range; that was a trick for dudes, perhaps, but not for a girl born and raised within half a day's ride. Even Ma would probably laugh. If only she could get a glimpse of Black Top; they could walk to it, even if they had to abandon the flivver. But Black Top had vanished in a mysterious way, somewhere behind miles of hummocks. It surprised her to find that the country was so broken. She had never ridden over here, but from a distance it had seemed quite like the rest of the range.

Sally was making another discovery, too. Things looked differently from the seat of a flivver than they did from the back of a horse. She did not understand why they should, but it was a fact. Perhaps it was because a horse on a trail can take care of himself, leaving a rider free to keep an eye on general bearings; while a car must be constantly guided, with a sharp watch on the immediate rather than the distant landscape. She did not realize, from lack of experience, that a passenger rarely pays as much attention to a route as a driver, because there is no need for the passenger to do so. At any rate, the range had an unfamiliar aspect, and she was now aware that even back on the trail, which she had ridden many times, there was a certain strangeness that puzzled her.

"You'd better keep out of this draw," she said suddenly, breaking a long pause. "You'll get mixed up in those cottonwoods, as sure as a gun."

"Well, where else shall I go?" he asked, stopping the car in order that he might glare at her without, having his attention distracted.

As she glanced on both sides of them she was unable to discover any alternative. All she did was to shrug, and the Wreck drove on again, headed directly for the cottonwood trees.

They rode ruthlessly over a few light saplings, but when they got in among the larger trees the Wreck found it necessary to maneuver in zigzags. Sally gritted her teeth and sat tight. It was a nightmare, sure enough, she thought; things like this did not happen elsewhere. A boiling, steaming flivver, the hideous roar of a red-hot exhaust, and all about them the serene environment of a wilderness, miles from anywhere—it was impossibly fantastic.

"There's water here somewhere," she called sharply. "Watch yourself!"

The Wreck circumnavigated a tree, steered straight for a barrier of young alders and sent the machine crashing magnificently through. The front wheels dropped sharply, the flivver tilted forward at an angle of 45 degrees, plunged, flattened out again and came to a stop, hub deep in a stream.

"There!" said Sally. "I told you there was water."

"I never denied it," said the Wreck.

"Now what are you going to do?"

He stepped out on the running-board and descended briskly into the stream, which cooled his legs pleasantly. Wading around to the rear of the car, he fumbled in the luggage compartment, then appeared with a canvas contraption which, upon being unfolded, was a bucket.

"I'm going to fill the radiator," he said. "Water is exactly what we need."

Sally made a gesture of helpless exasperation and watched him as he went methodically about the task. The flivver drank more than a bucketful and he nodded in a satisfied way when at last it overflowed at the orifice.

"And now what?" she demanded.

"Now we drive on, of course."

He climbed back into the seat, after returning the bucket to its place, and jammed his foot on the pedal that engages the clutch. The flivver trembled, moved, stopped again. There was a terrifying racing of the motor. He did something more to the pedals and the gears were in reverse, but still the motor raced without producing a corresponding movement in the car.

"No traction," remarked the Wreck, as he glanced over the side and watched the rear wheel spinning in the stream.

He stepped out again and tramped around in the water for a while. It was nowhere above his knees. It seemed to Sally that he took a childish delight in paddling about; she wanted to scream. Then she wanted to laugh, he was so solemn and deliberate about it.

"Cold water is great stuff for the nerves," said the Wreck, looking up.

She glanced at the sky, then at her watch, and there was dismay in her eyes.

"Do you know that it will be dark in about half an hour?" she demanded.

He also took an observation of the sky, and nodded.

"And that the train went long ago, and that we're nowhere near any railroad—or anything?"

"I don't admit that we're *nowhere* near the railroad," he said. "We've made a lot of progress. But I'll admit we're not right on top of it."

"Then what are you going to *do?*" she fairly shouted.

He sloshed his legs about in the stream in a tentative, exploratory fashion.

"The bottom's hard enough," he said, "but there's a lot of slippery stones. She won't take hold. And the way things are, I can't get the chains on. She won't go forward and she won't back. She needs a chance to cool out, anyhow."

He seemed to be actually contented, a fact that was no less amazing to Sally than it was maddening.

"Do you mean to say we'll *never* get out, Mr. Williams?"

The Wreck ruffled at once.

"I said nothing of the kind," he retorted. "I didn't even hint it. Certainly we'll get out. What do I carry a block and tackle for? You don't call this trouble, do you? She's been in worse fixes than this—three times. We hauled her out of a regular river once. This is nothing but a trickle."

"Well, you'll never trickle out of it before dark," she said, with all the emphasis of disgust.

"Maybe not," he admitted.

"And after dark you can't run."

"Can't I? You wait till I turn on those road lights. She looks like two locomotives."

"You'd try to keep on running across country— at night?" she demanded, her voice incredulous.

"Certainly. You haven't seen those lights yet."

"Then you'll run without me, Mr. Williams. I'd like to get back to the ranch. I'll take reasonable chances. If I had a horse I could make it. But"— she paused to settle an uncompromising gaze upon him—"I'm not insane."

"Meaning?" suggested the Wreck.

"Meaning, of course, that we're anchored here for the night."

"Oh, in that case," he said, with a shrug, "I guess we are anchored."

Sally stood in her place and glanced up and down stream. The little river was not more than ten yards across, shallow everywhere and brisk of motion, with alders and cottonwoods and fresh green banks on either side. It was beautifully peaceful and sylvan for a picnic, or a camp; but Sally was theoretically aboard a train, headed eastward, and to be stalled in a flivver in the middle of an oasis, no matter how charming, was irritating beyond all patience. Of course, she should have taken the sheriff's advice; Bob knew better than she did. If he had not been so positive probably she would have yielded; but he had thrown out his line of opposition in such a challenging way that he fairly forced her into the adventure.

She climbed out on the rear deck of the little roadster, gathered her skirts and leaped, landing clear of the shore, up among the bushes.

"There's a package of sandwiches in the back of the car. Get 'em out," she commanded. "And hand me my coat, too; I want it to sit on. You might give me the small grip, too. And then I advise you to come out of that water. It may feel good now, but it's liable to get cool after dark and first thing you know you'll have rheumatism. And if you get rheumatism you'll have something real to worry about."

The Wreck did all the things that she commanded. She opened the package of sandwiches, apportioned half of them equally and wrapped up the remainder.

"We'll need the rest for breakfast," she said. "Get your bucket out again and draw some water. I'm dreadfully thirsty. We'll keep that bottle of coffee until morning."

They sat under a cottonwood, ate sandwiches and drank out of the bucket. When it grew dark he waded out to the flivver and switched on the lights. But they were pointed the wrong way, so that the adventurers received only an indirect benefit from the glare. He thought it would be better if they transferred themselves to the other side of the stream, but Sally said she had gone as far as she intended to.

"Do you honestly think you can get that thing out of the water?" she asked.

He snorted scornfully.

"Not that it's likely to be of any particular use, even if you do," she added. "I expect to be walking to-morrow."

The Wreck strode away among the cottonwoods. For once he seemed anxious to avoid argument. When he returned, Sally had curled herself up under the tree, with the coat over her, and was preparing for slumber.

"Better get a coat and find yourself a place," she advised. "We'll need to make an early start."

"You'd better sleep out in the car," he said.

"Why?"

"It's safer. If anything come along—"

She laughed; he was such a ridiculous tenderfoot, with such funny ideas about the West.

"What do you expect? Indians?" she demanded. "No, thank you. I'll stay here where I'm comfortable. I've a gun, anyhow, so don't worry."

"Suit yourself," he answered, and an instant later she heard him sloshing in the stream.

"You going to try to sleep in that car?" she called. "Because you'll never get any sleep, trying to fold yourself up in that."

"I'm not *going* to sleep," came his voice, irritably. "I never do sleep. I've got insomnia. I'm just going to sit here and keep watch, that's all. If you want anything, holler."

"I'll holler," she promised, and smothered a laugh.

A few minutes later, as she was becoming drowsy, she was aware that he had switched off the lights. After that it was very dark under the cottonwoods, and very quiet, save for the cool rustle of the stream, which was ceaseless and soothing. Sally's last conscious mental effort was a dim hope that something would come along to give him a good scare; she wanted to find out how he would react. Perhaps a coyote might bark. But if a single coyote lifted his muzzle and howled within a mile of them, Sally did not hear it. She slept like a healthy young animal.

The Wreck felt something punching him between the shoulders. He straightened up in the seat, slowly opened his eyes, blinked them and found the glare of sunlight dazzling. The thing punched him again, and he turned around. Sally was standing on the bank, prodding at him with a long stick.

"Hi, you!" she called. "Do you know it's after seven?"

"G' morning," said the Wreck. "Why didn't you call me?"

"Call you? I've been fairly yelling at you. I've scared every jack-rabbit in the county, but you never budged. Is that what insomnia does to you?"

"I must have just dozed off," he mumbled, as he yawned and stood up to stretch.

"Oh, yes."

He did not see what she was laughing at as he stepped down into the stream and waded ashore, but refrained from asking any questions.

"The coffee's still hot," she said, as he joined her. "I think we'd better finish it, and then fill the bottle with water. And I think we'd better save half of these sandwiches, too. We may want some lunch."

She watched him slyly as he ate his breakfast, still rubbing the sleep out of his eyes. Evidently he had slept in his wet clothes all night, but he did not appear to be any the worse for it. After the meal he carefully polished his spectacles, put them back in place and scrambled to his feet with the resilience of a youth. The Wreck was a good deal of a puzzle to her. She felt that there was a lot of fraud about him, but that he was entirely unaware of it.

He went out to the car again, found the block and tackle, and then crossed the stream in search of a suitable tree to which he might hitch one end of his line. Sally questioned his purpose immediately. She did not see why he wanted to haul the car out on the other side, because they would never get back to the ranch that way. Why haul it backward? The Wreck made an elaborate show of patience as he explained. The bank over which they had plunged was too steep; there was a better chance to get out on the other side. Anyhow, they wanted to keep on going, didn't they? He didn't believe in going backward. She saw that he knew more about the mechanical demands of the job than she did and let him have his way.

With two of them hauling on the tackle, Sally in the flivver and the Wreck on the opposite shore, they finally worked the thing clear across and half way up the sloping bank. Then he started the engine and the car pulled itself out under its own power. It seemed to Sally almost a miracle of engineering, but the Wreck took no pride in it as he coiled up the tackle and tossed it into the back of the car.

"Now what are we looking for?" he demanded, as he settled himself behind the wheel. "The ranch or the railroad?"

"Are you still thinking about the railroad?" inquired Sally in amazement.

"Why not? We started for it. What's the use of quitting? I suppose there's a train to-day, just as there was yesterday."

"Of course. But— Well, it seemed better to head back to the ranch."

"Thought you wanted to get to Chicago and buy your trousseau?"

Sally colored faintly.

"I never said I was going to buy a trousseau," she observed.

"Well, your father said so, anyhow."

"Did he? Well, I don't know what I'm going to buy yet. Maybe I'll buy a trousseau and maybe I won't. If I see one that I like I probably will."

"Yes; you probably will," said the Wreck. "My

idea is, keep going. If you start out to buy a trousseau, for the love of Mike, buy it. Don't start if you can't finish. Here goes for the railroad. And—"

He paused to regard her critically.

"—if you catch to-day's train, you don't need to say anything to anybody about missing yesterday's —unless you want to."

"Oh, I don't mind telling about it," said Sally, easily. Just the same, she thought it was mighty considerate of him to make the suggestion.

The flivver plunged forward through the cottonwoods, which were more sparse on this side of the stream, and was out in open land again, where it looked fairly level for a considerable stretch.

"The thing to do now is to look for that road," said Sally. "After we find it and see which way it runs, we can tell better what to do next."

He drove in silence for several minutes, heading in a direction she suggested. He seemed preoccupied. She knew that he had something on his mind, and at last it came.

"If you tell the sheriff that I missed yesterday's train, and if he tries to give me the laugh," said the Wreck, "I'll bust his nose all over his face."

Sally greeted this with a joyous shriek.

CHAPTER IV

GASLESS

THE going became better and better, although Sally could not yet discover that the route they followed promised to carry them either to the railroad or to the ranch. But it was a relief to be in open country again, where the undulations were gentle and rhythmic, like a long ground swell, and where the flivver sailed a fairly stable course. Two or three times they found themselves in a cul-de-sac from which it was necessary to make a retreat; but, on the whole, it was much easier than the ride of yesterday, even though it suffered in point of excitement.

With the lightening of his labors at the wheel, the Wreck became almost loquacious. He talked a good deal about Pittsburgh, and all points east. If his conversation carried a note which stressed the inferiority of the West, Sally declined to be drawn into argument. He seemed to be happy and he was doing his best to render a service, and she was willing to be indulgent.

As they crested a long, easily sloped rise she sighted Black Top again. The Wreck, whose power of vision through his thick-lensed glasses was sometimes surprising, saw it as soon as Sally.

"There's your mountain," he said, "right where we figured it."

Sally studied Black Top carefully.

"It's not where I figured it," she said, puzzled. "We've been working east a lot faster than I thought. Why, it's a good fifteen miles away."

"Five," said the Wreck.

"Do you mean that I can't judge distances?"

"Five miles; maybe only four."

"But it's rather absurd for you to say that," protested Sally. "Because I can tell perfectly well just how big it ought to look at any distance."

"Listen: do you know I can't see anything more than five miles away?" he demanded. "If it was any further than that I wouldn't be looking at it. Five miles."

She uttered a little laugh of exasperation.

"Perhaps five miles is your limit back East, Mr. Williams. But you're not making allowances for our Western air. It's very clear, you know."

He threw up one hand in a violent gesture.

"I've been hearing all that stuff ever since I got out here. Even the real estate dealers use it. I've been told that you can see mountains fifty miles, or maybe sixty or seventy miles. 'It's the rarefied air,' they say. All bunk! You people out here operate on the principle that everything's got to be big. You're sort of crazy on the subject. Fifteen miles! Why, I can almost see it without my glasses."

Sally made another survey of Black Top.

"It's nearer twenty miles," she said.

"Now you're trying to get me into an argument," retorted the Wreck. "I'm sorry we ever looked at the fool thing."

"Oh, but I'm not," sweetly. "I've got a better idea where we are. I think we ought to turn more to the right. If we find that road—"

He brought the car to a stop and stared at her.

"You see," she said, pointing, "there's Black Top. We're looking at the eastern slope, where the trail runs. Now, if we take a bearing from that, we get a general idea of the direction of the road."

"You're still looking for that road, are you?"

"Why, of course I am. Aren't you?"

"And your idea of looking for a road is to take a slant at a mountain five miles away?"

"Fifteen miles—yes."

The Wreck grinned in a jeering way.

"Five or fifteen, it's the same idea. Instead of looking for what you want to find, you look for something else. I suppose that's the Western idea. I guess that's the way the sheriff looks for things."

She refused to bridle at that. She felt that the Wreck had something up his sleeve and she was cautious.

"After you've gone and lost yourself a few times out here," she said, "you'll give three cheers every time you see a familiar landmark."

"Landmarks!" he echoed, still with a grin. "Mountains miles and miles away, instead of what you're really looking for."

"Yes, landmarks," she said, stubbornly. "And if you've got any better way of going about it, I'd be proud to know it."

The Wreck broke into a full-sized laugh and rubbed the day-old stubble on his chin. Sally had never seen him so merry.

"My own idea of looking for a road," he said, "it to keep your eye on the place where a road ought to be."

He was staring at Sally as he spoke, but when she matched the stare his glance drifted. Sally's drifted, too. Then she uttered an exclamation, stood up in the car and leaned forward.

"It's—a road!" she gasped.

There was no doubt it was a road. Not a wide, paved road; just a pair of tracks in the grass. But it looked like a boulevard to Sally; she could scarcely believe in the reality of it. She glanced behind the car. The road twisted away out of sight a few rods in the rear. Then she looked at the Wreck. He was lolling back, his finger-tips drumming on the steering wheel, his expression one of triumphant content.

"When did you see that road?" she demanded.

"What road?" drawled the Wreck. "Do you see a road? I thought you were looking at a mountain."

"I—I ought to strangle you," said Sally.

He smiled lazily and began polishing his glasses.

"You just let me go on making a fool of myself, Henry Williams. I bet you saw that road before you stopped the car. I could hate you for that."

"Aw, go on and look at your mountain," he counseled. "The road isn't going to run away. I'll watch it."

Sally sat down again, stared at the road, clenched her fist and then burst into laughter.

"If you ever tell about finding the road," she said, "and they give me the laugh, the sheriff won't be the only person who'll have his nose busted all over his face."

"H'm," mused the Wreck. "Then we'd better make an agreement to lay off."

"You bet."

"All right; we'll let it stand that way."

"How long ago did you see that darn road, anyhow?" she demanded.

"Just the same second I stopped the car."

"Well, it's horse on me," confessed Sally. "But anybody might miss it. It isn't much of a road, after all. You'd have to be looking right at it to see it."

"You'd never see it looking at a mountain."

She had an impulse to box his ears, but she was afraid of breaking his spectacles. The spectacles were of some use, after all; they found a road. She stood up again and studied the dusty tracks as far as her eye could follow them. They showed no sign of recent travel, either wagon or automobile. In spots the grass tufts half obliterated them. On second observation, it did not look so much like a boulevard, after all; it was not a road to inspire any great degree of optimism. But she admitted that it was very much better than nothing at all.

"Well, which way?" asked the Wreck. "Go ahead I suppose."

"It seems to go ahead in a general direction of north," said Sally. "That's where the railroad is. I don't know where it runs in the other direction. I—I believe I'll leave it to you. It's your road."

The Wreck nodded and drove ahead. For a while the road seemed to have no definite objective; it followed the easiest contours, snaking its way along indolently. It topped rise after rise, but it brought nothing into view save more range country. There were times when it faded almost into nothingness, and other times when the ruts burrowed so deeply that they took charge of the wheels and made steering not only unnecessary, but impossible. But Sally observed that, in a general way, it seemed to be working northward, although so furtively that she suspected it of trying to conceal its destination. She kept an eye on Black Top, still remotely visible, although she did not dare let the Wreck catch her doing it. Perhaps Black Top did not help to find the road, but it was still a sort of hitching-post for her dead reckoning. So long as she could see it, she did not feel lost.

Once the road crossed a draw, where it forded a shallow stream. The Wreck watered the radiator again and filled his canteen. Sally was beginning to wonder about the railroad. Certainly they had gone far enough to reach it; much more than far enough, in all likelihood. But she had never so much as heard the whistle of a train nor seen distant smoke against the skyline. It was all endless range, and pretty poor range, at that, with the grass thin and half starved and wide stretches of plain dirt.

The Wreck drove with great deliberation; now that he had a road under his wheels he was not nearly so dashing as when he took the open range at speed. Sally noticed that he did a lot of leisurely coasting, with the engine throttled so low that sometimes it stalled, forcing him to dismount at the bottom of grades and crank. He seemed preoccupied and rather silent, speaking only in answer to her questions. Even during a stop they made for lunch, when they finished the remainder of the sandwiches, he did not have much to say.

In the early afternoon they came to another road, which marked the end of their own. The other road formed the top of a T, along the stem of which they had been traveling. Here the Wreck halted and turned a questioning eye on his passenger. Sally held silent debate with herself. There was no Black Top in sight to help, although she knew fairly well where it lay. The baffling thing about the new road was that it probably paralleled the railroad, and she had no means of telling in which direction it offered the best prospect. It was much more of a road than the old one; it had traces of frequent travel by automobiles.

"I suppose we might wait until somebody comes along and ask," she suggested.

"What's the use?"

"Perhaps there isn't any. It does seem sort of futile just to sit here."

The Wreck nodded.

"Then let's turn to the right," said Sally. "It seems to point to Chicago, anyhow."

He turned to the right and they followed the new road. For a road that suggested the pretensions of a highway, it did not seem to pass anything. The Wreck remarked the fact after they had traveled it for an hour.

"Don't they ever build any houses or towns out here?" he asked, with a touch of his old irritability.

"Certainly they do," said Sally, sharply.

"Well, where are they?"

"Has it occurred to you that Montana is the third largest State in the Union?"

"Is it? Then why in blazes doesn't somebody come and live in it?"

"You make me dog tired," said Sally, ineffectively. "You leave Montana alone."

"Going to."

Both of them were rather cross and both knew it, and after that the silence was long. It continued, in fact, until the flivver came to a stop that had something inadvertent and ominous about it. The Wreck did not even lift the seat to examine the gas tank. He knew. He had, in fact, been expecting it for the last two hours.

For fifteen minutes there was a tremendous boom in conversation. Didn't he know that he was running short of gas? He certainly did. Did she think he was asleep? Didn't he carry an extra five-gallon can? No, he didn't! How in blazes could he, when he had to pack two grips and a lot of other stuff? Why did he waste so much gas rambling over the ranges and getting lost? Why didn't she know where the road was, instead of trying to steer by a fool mountain? Where was he going to get any more gas? Oh, he was just going to stroll down to the corner and have them bring it up from the garage. Well, what *was* he going to do? Sit there and enjoy Montana. Did she think he was going to get out and push it?

After it had run like that for a while Sally climbed down to the road and walked a bit, in sheer desperation. He was unbearable, and he did not seem to care. She knew that if she owned a million dollars she would give it all to be back at the Bar-M. This was worse than being stalled in midstream—for this was hopeless! It was probably miles to anywhere. She would not mind walking those miles if she knew which way to go. As for the Wreck, he showed not the slightest symptom of walking. He had found a bit of shade under a tree, just off the road, and had gone to sleep.

Eventually Sally climbed back into the car, tried to make herself comfortable and succeeded in falling into a doze. When she awoke it was dark and somebody was touching her on the arm.

"It's me," said the voice of the Wreck.

"Wha-what's happened?"

"Nothing yet. We're still in the same place. But there's a car coming down the road and we'll get some help."

That roused her into full wakefulness. She whirled about and looked back over the darkened range. Far away, a mile at least, the twin white lights of an approaching car showed clear. The Wreck switched on his own tail light, and strolled down the road to greet rescue. Sally watched.

When he had gone about a hundred feet he stood in the middle of the road and waited. Presently, as the oncoming car drew nearer, she could see his figure outlined against the growing glare. She saw him hold up his hand and wave it. She heard the throb of a big motor stilled. Then he stepped out of the beam of light, and she could hear voices.

Perhaps a minute elapsed. Then the Wreck stepped briskly into sight again and advanced toward the flivver. There was something in his walk that instantly riveted her attention. It boded things.

"Where's that gun of yours?" he demanded, as he reached her side.

"Gun?" echoed Sally, in a whisper. "What's the matter?"

The Wreck's voice seemed drawn to a fine edge.

"There's something about that outfit I don't like," he said. "Let me have the gun."

Sally had already located it, but she was puzzled.

"Who are they? What do they want?"

"I don't know who they are," said the Wreck. "But I want that gun. Here, get back in the car."

She had started to climb out, but he barred the way.

"If there's going to be any gun-work," declared Sally, "you'd better leave it to me. I know more about it than you do."

He reached for the holster, took it from her hands and possessed himself of the six-shooter that it contained.

"Don't leave this car," he commanded. "I'm going to attend to whatever has to be done. Nobody's going to get hurt. But I'm going to find out something damn quick."

He was gone again, hastening up the road toward the staring headlights. Sally noticed that he carried the gun behind him. She endured a moment of wild self-reproach for letting the thing get out of her hands. He was evidently in a frightful temper; he didn't know how to use a gun, anyhow—and he was nothing but a fool tenderfoot.

CHAPTER V

THE NERVOUS GUNMAN

IT was a big black machine, long and squat and heavy, with luggage on the running-boards, luggage on the rear, three spares, and four occupants, one of them a chauffeur in uniform. The Wreck ignored the chauffeur, although he kept a furtive eye on him. He stepped close to the side of the tonneau and addressed himself to one of the three persons who sat there.

"I'm asking you again for a few gallons of gas," he said. "I've got to have it; that's all. You can spare me some without any trouble."

"And I'm still telling you to go to the devil," answered a heavy voice from the central figure. "We haven't got any gas to spare. And you'd better get busy and roll that flivver out of the road and let me get by. If you need any help, my driver is here."

"I don't want that kind of help," said the Wreck, still controlling his voice. "I want gas."

The heavy voice laughed.

"We're not running a tank wagon. Why don't you carry enough gas with you? That's what other people have to do. You people with flivvers are always running short of something. Move your car."

"We people with flivvers," declared the Wreck, slowly, "are not gas hogs. If I had as much gas as you've got in your tank I could run from here to New York. You're burning about a gallon every three or four miles. That's what I call being a damned hog. It's you birds that keep up the price. All I'm asking is five gallons and I'll pay for it. Do I get it?"

"You do not."

There was an abrupt change in the Wreck's demeanor. He stepped back a pace, pulled his cap close over his eyes and brought to view an object he had been concealing behind his back. Even in the gloom it was possible to get an idea of what it was.

"Stick 'em up!" he barked. "All hands. Be in a hurry now."

There was a feminine shriek from the tonneau, and the Wreck then and there first learned that one of them was a woman. But it was no time for courtesies.

"All up—everybody! You there, in the front seat! That's the idea. I want to see eight hands up all the time. And I don't want to see any funny movements, either."

He had to take it for granted that eight hands were up; he could not count them very clearly in the dark, particularly as his eyesight was none too keen. But that, of course, was something they did not know.

"Listen hard, now," he said, briskly. "When I tell you to do something, do it quick and don't give me any back talk. I want everybody out of that car, on this side of the road. And just keep those hands up; I'll open the doors. It'll be awful good for your health if you bear in mind that I'm nervous. I'm apt to get excited. Everybody out, now; one at a time. Line up!"

The driver came first, his arms stiffly aloft. Then three figures in single file from the tonneau, the last one wearing skirts. The person with the heavy voice coughed nervously.

"We'll give you five—"

"Shut up!" commanded the Wreck. "You'll give me anything I want. You three—" He indicated the passengers with a wave of the gun. "You three step out in front of those lights where I can keep a good eye on you. That's business. Stay there. Now, driver, got a can?"

"Ah—ah—yes, sir."

"Get it—and be careful you don't get anything else."

The man in uniform moved cautiously to the side of the car and unstrapped a five-gallon container from the running-board.

"It's full, sir," he said.

"Full, eh? Carrying extra gas and wouldn't give me a drop, eh? All right, you pick up that can and march—straight up the middle of the road."

For a few seconds it puzzled the Wreck what to do with the trio who still stood with their hands up in the glare of lights. He solved it by ordering them to a point midway between the two cars, where he made them sit down and told them not to budge.

"My partner up here in the flivver," he explained, "is looking at you over a pair of sights. He's a pretty good shot. He's nervous, too."

The man with the five-gallon can walked ahead until the Wreck halted him within half a dozen paces of the stalled car. The Wreck stepped ahead to speak to Sally. He found that she had dismounted and was standing by the roadside, beyond the beam of light.

"You crazy—"

He placed a hand roughly across her lips.

"Shut up!" he whispered. "Stay where you are and say nothing. I'm running this."

Sally was boiling, but she obeyed. It seemed the only way to keep him from some other wild folly.

The Wreck called to the man with the can and, as he reached the flivver, told him he would find a funnel on the floor.

"Pour that stuff into the tank, and see to it that you don't spill any of it."

It gave him a small thrill of satisfaction to find himself smartly obeyed. Then he marched the chauffeur ahead of him, back to the big car. As he passed the group in the road he tossed them a cheerful word of caution.

"My partner," he said, "noticed one of you didn't keep his hands in plain sight. He says he wouldn't like to have it happen again."

The Wreck and the driver went directly to the rear of the gas-eating monster.

"How much in that tank?" demanded the Wreck.

"About fifteen, sir."

"Pet-cock in the bottom? You'd better have, if you don't want me to shoot a hole in the tank."

"Y-yes, sir. We got a pet-cock."

"Stick that can under it and let her go."

Presently the driver announced that the can was full, and the Wreck verified the statement.

"All right. Dump it out in the road."

The driver stared through the darkness.

"Dump it out!" And the Wreck executed the order himself by kicking the can over.

"Now fill it again," he commanded.

The second filling was accomplished.

"That'll do. That leaves you five gallons. It's too much for a hog, at that. Come along with the can, now."

They made a second trip to the flivver and emptied a second dose into the tank under the seat.

"Now we go back again," said the Wreck. "And when I tell you to do something, I don't want any questions asked."

"N-no, sir."

Once more at the side of the big car, the Wreck ordered his servant to lay aside the five-gallon can.

"Got a tire pump on that engine?" he inquired.

"Yes, sir."

"Rotten luxury. But it's going to save your back a lot of work. Get busy now and let the air out of those tires. All of it!"

The driver hesitated, from bewilderment rather

Courtesy of White Studio, N. Y.

THE HOLD-UP FOR GASOLINE

Scene from the Play.

than insubordination. But he jumped to the task
when the Wreck prodded him with the muzzle of
Sally's six-shooter. The tires flattened themselves
under the wheels, each with a long, shrill sigh.
"Open up those valves on the spares," directed
the Wreck.
The spares also sang a swan song.
"There. That'll keep you busy for a while. Come
along."
They joined the group of sitters in the middle of
the road. Standing with his back to the headlights
and carefully shielding his own face from illumination, the Wreck contemplated his victims for a
moment.
"You!" he said, suddenly, with a significant gesture of the gun. "The big one who didn't want to
sell any gas. Stand up!"
The owner of the heavy voice rose slowly to his
feet, looking slightly anxious. Most of the belliger-
ence had departed from him.
"I've a good mind to give you a trimming,"
said the Wreck, "but I haven't got time to do it
right. I've met all kinds of hogs in my time, but
you're in the blue-ribbon class. Maybe you don't
know you're getting off light, but take it from me
you are. If you think a flivver is funny, I'm going
to give you a chance to play with it. Hump yourself!"
He urged the large man in the direction of the
flivver, leaving the remainder of the group behind
him. Sally had climbed back into the seat, and the

Wreck joined her. He switched on his headlights and took the wheel, but he still had the gun in his hand.

"Now, you just lay hold of that crank and get to work, hog."

The gentleman with loud signs of wealth seized the crank and yanked it violently.

"Spin it," ordered the Wreck.

He spun it, but there was no answer from the engine.

"Spin it some more."

Not even a sputter.

"Spin it again—harder."

Still there was no response. The large man panted heavily and wiped his forehead.

"You going to keep me here all night?" demanded the Wreck. "If you don't spin that crank—"

There was another furious spell of whirling. Sally pinched her companion.

"How can he start it when you haven't turned on the ignition?" she said.

"He can't," said the Wreck. "Doggone it, what did you butt in for? I wanted to see him spin it."

He reached over, threw the switch, and the engine was off with a night-splitting clatter. The big man staggered wearily toward the side of the road. His gait was accelerated when a mud-guard nudged him roughly as the flivver sprang into life. They heard him shout something; it sounded like a threat, although they could not catch the words. Then the

Wreck took a solid grip on the wheel and began to drive.

Once Sally looked behind her. The headlights of the motionless car had faded to small points. She glanced at the Wreck. It was not possible to see his face clearly, but she could imagine the expression. He would be gritting his teeth and staring truculently at the road, quite in his glory. It was five minutes before she spoke, and then she cut loose.

"You've done it now!" she exclaimed. "You sure have fixed the pair of us this time. Have you gone stark mad?"

"Don't argue," advised the Wreck.

"Don't you know what you've done? Don't you realize anything? Do you think you can get away with a thing like that? Why, you've committed a crime!"

He shrugged impatiently. How women did talk!

"A crime!" repeated Sally, dwelling on the sinister word. "Do you know that people have been shot for things like that, or strung up, or sent to prison for life? Haven't you any sense at all? And you dragged *me* into it!"

"Didn't. I told you to keep out of it."

"But I was there, wasn't I? And I heard you tell them that I was holding a gun on them. What difference does it make that I wasn't? You've had me just as guilty as you are yourself. And if they catch us—"

She left the sentence unfinished, for it was leading to things too awful for contemplation.

"Who in blazes is going to catch us?" he demanded. *"They* won't. It'll take them half an hour to blow up those tires, and they'll burn pretty nearly a gallon of gas doing it. That'll leave them about four gallons, and after fifteen miles or so they'll go dead, like we were. Don't you worry about getting caught."

Sally shook her head in despair.

"You seem to think you can stick your head in the sand like an ostrich," she said. "You don't seem to grasp anything at all. I actually believe you don't realize that you've committed a highway robbery."

"Call that a highway robbery?" sneered the Wreck. "If that's a highway robbery, then everything out here must be getting very much on the pink tea."

"We don't stand for criminals, if that's what you mean. We run them out of the country, or send them to jail—or hang 'em."

He was rather pleased at the information that they might hang him. It jibed with his mood, which was one of deep disgust and resentment. You couldn't please women, no matter what you did. They cried for something, and when you got it for them they did not have gratitude to thank you. Why, they actually reproached you for it! Well, they would wait a long while before he did anything else for them, decided the Wreck. He included the entire sex, too.

"Why, we'll be caught before daylight!" exclaimed Sally.

"Bet you five dollars."

"To-morrow, anyway," she went on, ignoring his challenge. "And they'll have a perfectly good case against us. You held them up with a gun—*my* gun."

"They ought to have been held up. They had it coming to them. They ought to have been shot full of bullets," said the Wreck, fiercely. "Traveling around the country with all the gasoline in the world and wouldn't give a drop to anybody. That's the last time I'll ever start anything by being polite. You only get the laugh. I guess we'll do some of the laughing now."

"If you think I am going to laugh," said Sally, "you're all wrong. I'm not going to cry, either. But I'm just trying to make you understand that you've done a very, *very* serious thing. And all you do is to go on raving about your rights, as if you were actually proud of what you did."

He decided to have no more argument with her; she was absolutely impossible. But the sense of outrage was too deep and sharp for his resolution. He thrust his spectacles close to her face and glared at her through the gloom.

"Will you stop bawling me out?" he demanded. "First you bawled me and bawled me because I ran out of gasoline, and because I didn't get out and walk a couple of hundred miles looking for it. Then when I produce the gasoline, you bawl me out for getting it. You holler if we stay in one place and you holler if we go on. You're just bound to holler, anyhow. When I put you on that railroad train you'll still be hollering. You needn't think you can maul me around. I'm not the sheriff."

Sally was red with anger, but of course he could not see that. She sat with her fists clenched and her lips set tight. Every time he said anything about the sheriff he sneered. And he had no right to! Besides, he talked as if she were a common scold—when she was only trying to bring him to his senses.

"I'm trying," she said, with a show of dignity, "to explain things to you for your own good. But all the thanks I get—"

"For heaven's sake, cut it out!" His voice rose to a shrill falsetto. "Doggone it, you'll get me so fussed I can't do anything. Just as everything is going all right, you start in making me nervous."

Sally found herself speechless from amazement. Nervous! He had held up four people at the point of the gun, robbed them of gasoline, subjected one of them to the indignity of cranking his flivver, and then left the whole outfit stranded in the middle of Montana. He had done it with all the aplomb of an old hand. And when she wanted to make him understand the enormity of the thing, he complained that she made him nervous!

The flivver went on steadily through the night.

She had not the least idea where they were going, but she was thankful they were going somewhere. She wanted to get very far away from the big black car and its four passengers. Occasionally she stole a glance behind, guiltily apprehensive that vengeance was already on the trail. She did not yet appreciate how thoroughly the Wreck had performed his mad work.

The road rose and fell and meandered, but it was too dark to obtain much information about the country. Sally had a strong impression, however, that they went uphill more than they did down, and that the land was steadily rising and growing rougher. But the road was very good and the flivver was setting the best pace she had yet seen.

"Hungry?" demanded the Wreck, suddenly, after an hour of silence.

Sally roused herself and prepared for battle. Of course she was hungry; she was starving. But there was no decency in reminding her of it. She had been doing her best to forget it.

"Eat this," he advised, without waiting for an answer.

He took a somewhat tattered sandwich from his pocket and handed it to her.

"Go on and eat it," he said, sharply. "I had mine a while back. I held out a couple of them at lunch time."

The Wreck was lying. He had held out one sandwich, not two, and with the very idea that he was now putting into execution. Sally had a suspicion

that he was lying; she was certain he had not eaten
anything for hours and hours. But she recognized
a sort of peace offering in the dry and crumbly
object, and wrath suddenly melted out of her.

"I'll split it with you," she said, preparing to
divide it.

"Eat it all. I don't want it. I wouldn't have
it. For Pete's sake, *eat it!* Have I got to jam
it down your throat?"

Sally ate it, smiling in the darkness.

CHAPTER VI

I T was after sun-up when he aroused her by a touch on the arm. Sally's eyes blinked rapidly as she straightened in the seat. The flivver was moving along at a slow pace, intended to promote the comfort of a sleeping passenger.

" 'Morning," said the Wreck. "Sorry to wake you, but I wanted your expert opinion."

" 'Morning," yawned Sally; then shook herself into full wakefulness and inspected him. "Have you been driving all night?"

If he had, she was prepared to acknowledge a tremendous respect for his endurance, for he was not flying any signals of weariness. But he shook his head with a grin.

"I stopped for a while, after you got asleep. I didn't need any sleep; I just can't sleep. But I let the engine cool out. There wasn't any hurry, anyhow."

"Nobody—passed us?" She asked it anxiously.

The Wreck shook his head and laughed. He was in fine spirits for a man with guilt on his soul.

"What I wanted to ask you about was this wire fence," he said. "We've been following it for a couple of miles. What's it mean?"

65

Sally inspected the fence, which followed the line of the road.

"It's somebody's wire, of course," she answered. "It means there must be a ranch around somewhere."

"Do they have breakfast at ranches?"

"They better had!"

"My idea, too," he said. "Whereabouts would this ranch lie, reckoning without the aid of any mountains or other visible landmarks?"

That brought a smile to her face. Plainly, the Wreck was in excellent fettle this morning. He was disposed to be almost playful.

"I'd say it's on the same side of the road as the fence," replied Sally. "And if we haven't passed any gate yet, we'd better keep on until we hit one. There's sure to be one."

He nodded and continued to drive, while Sally studied the country. It was not mountainous, but decidedly hilly, and she knew at a glance that it must lie at a considerable distance from the Bar-M. There was nothing within a wide radius of the Bar-M that looked like this. In the draws it was well wooded, but there was a lot of open range and twice she had glimpses of water. She decided that they were very much to the eastward of Black Top, although she had no idea in which direction the Wreck had been driving during the night.

Presently her thoughts returned to the big car and its passengers, and she caught herself looking backward over the rolling road, wondering what had become of them.

"Here's a gate," said the Wreck.

There was more than a gate. There was a plain road, running under it and off into the hills beyond. Without waiting for a consultation, he climbed down, opened the gate, then drove the flivver through. He was going straight ahead when Sally stopped him.

"Always close the gates after you out in this country," she said, jumping out. "They're put there for a reason. Cattle."

"I was in a hurry for breakfast," he explained.

The private road was a long one, as Sally judged it would be; she knew something about the size of ranches. If you were a stranger and stuck to the public road, you never saw half of them. It was nearly a quarter of an hour before they came within sight of anything but hills and hollows.

Then the ranch buildings flashed abruptly into view as the road emerged from a patch of young spruce. Sally studied the picture with a professional eye. The ranch house, the stables, the outbuildings, the corrals, all classified themselves swiftly under her survey.

"That's a pretty big house," she commented. "Looks sort of new, too. They've got a nice location. See the way those hills rise, off yonder, back of the house. Pretty, isn't it?"

"I can't see anything but bacon and eggs," said the Wreck.

"Here's hoping you see them."

"Well, if I don't—"

Sally checked him.

"See here, Henry Williams," she said, "don't you start anything this morning. You've done enough for a while. You'd better talk very small and be mighty polite. You're still in the State of Montana."

"I'll behave, if you don't rile me," he promised. "But I've certainly got to be fed."

"And when they ask questions, we're a couple of tourists. Don't forget that," said Sally, significantly. "I'm supposed to be a dude, too."

The flivver came to a stop in the dooryard, just as a man emerged from the house. He was a tall, lean man, with a scraggy mustache, and he stood studying them for several seconds, in evident surprise, before he approached.

"Good morning," called Sally, with a wave of her hand.

" 'Mornin', ma'am."

As he walked over to the car he was still scrutinizing them with a pair of steady blue eyes.

"Are you the proprietor?" inquired Sally.

She knew better than that, but she was trying to play a part.

"I'm the foreman, ma'am."

"Oh! Well, I'm sure you're the very person I want to see. Can we get breakfast?"

The foreman rubbed his chin and gave her a further appraisal.

"It sort of depends," he said. "Can you cook?"

"Yes!" It was a chorus from two in the flivver.

For a few seconds the foreman transferred his gaze to the Wreck, who seemed to have acquired sudden interest in his eyes.

"It happens, ma'am, that we ain't furnished with a cook. We had a Chinee, and a Chinee helper. But they blew on us yesterday. But there's plenty of grub, and if you want to cook it, help yourself."

He waved a hand in the direction of the kitchen. There was a scrambling exodus from the flivver. The Wreck beat her to the kitchen door by a couple of yards. The foreman followed.

"I'll show you where everything is," he said. "Tell you the truth, I'm kind of hungry myself. The boys had to rustle their own breakfast this mornin', and they didn't make out none too well. I et some of it and I know what I'm talkin' about. So if you don't mind, ma'am, while you're cookin' up something, make it liberal in quantity. My name's Charley McSween."

He looked expectantly at the Wreck.

"My name's Williams," said the Wreck, taking the hint.

The foreman shook hands and glanced in the direction of Sally, who was already clearing a place on the stove.

"My wife," said the Wreck.

"Pleased to know you, Mis' Williams."

Sally had whirled about, her cheeks suddenly pink. She shot an amazed glance at Henry Williams and received a look of warning in return. Charley McSween laughed.

"I've seen honeymooners before," he said. "I was married once myself. It ain't nothin' against anybody."

Sally opened her lips to say something, broke into a queer laugh and turned to the stove again.

It was the kind of a breakfast that comes once in a long, long time, when you are ready for even the meanest and find yourself sitting down to the best. The Wreck ate with a concentration that was appalling. Even the foreman, who was accustomed to all sorts of appetites, watched with an admiring eye. Sally and the Wreck were still eating when Charley McSween pushed back his chair.

"I'm sayin' that was a regular breakfast," he declared, as he wiped his mouth. "The lady sure knows how to fry bacon. I kind of like to have my eggs flopped over; but that's nothin' against her, because I didn't say so. Coffee was A-1. I can't say as I usually eat toast, but I've got no objections to it. Can you make biscuits, ma'am?"

"Of course I can," said Sally. "But I couldn't wait for them this morning."

"I figured you could make 'em," nodded the foreman. "Can you cook meats? I don't mean plain fryin', but all kinds of ways?"

"Quite a number of ways," she smiled.

"I bet you can do tricks with eggs, like makin' omelettes and scrambles and things like that."

"I can do some tricks," she confessed.

"I bet you can," he said admiringly, as he arose from the table. "I sure did enjoy that breakfast.

If you folks will excuse me for a little while, I've got some things to do. Just set around and make yourselves comfortable. In case you feel like cleanin' up—"

He glanced at the pile of dishes in the sink.

"Of course we'll wash the dishes," said Sally. "We'll be glad to."

Charley McSween nodded and sauntered out of the kitchen. Sally looked the Wreck in the eye.

"I suppose you thought you had to say that," she remarked.

"Only reason I said it," he answered, returning her look, "couples touring around in flivvers are supposed to be married."

"Reckon you're right," she admitted. "Oh, well, it's not important. You might bring these breakfast dishes over to the sink. I'll wash and you wipe."

He was not very dexterous at wiping, but he got through it without breakage. She put an apron on him, much to his irritation; but he submitted because she explained that it was a sort of regulation in kitchens.

"I don't suppose you've noticed things around here very much," she said, "but this is a pretty swell kitchen for a ranch. That stove cost a lot of money; look at it. And running water in the sink. There isn't anything around here that isn't high grade. Did you see that other cupboard over there? It's full of china—not crockery, but china. I don't know where he gets his bacon, but

I never saw that quality served out to ranch hands before. They must live high."

The Wreck wiped the last dish, escaped from the apron and glanced at his watch.

"Only nine o'clock," he said. "We've got all day to make that train."

"I'd clean forgotten," declared Sally. "But we'll find out all about it from Charley McSween."

Charley reentered the kitchen presently, tilted a chair against the wall and sat down.

"We'll have a little talk," he announced. "Better set down."

Sally drew a chair for herself, but the Wreck propped himself against the table. He wanted to be ready for emergencies. Somebody might have spread an alarm.

"Do you believe in acts of Providence?" asked the foreman, after a moment of thought.

The pair from the flivver exchanged glances.

"No," said the Wreck.

"Yes," said Sally.

"That makes it fifty-fifty," declared Charley McSween, "which is a pretty fair break. As for myself, I believe in 'em. I'll tell you why."

He paused long enough to light a pipe and get it going properly.

"As I said a while back, we had a Chinee cook here and a Chinee dishwasher. Ordinarily we don't run to fancy cookin'. But I got that pair of Chinks for a special reason. I'm expectin' the boss. As near as I can make out from his letter, he's about due to-day. He don't come often, but when he does he has to be fed right.

"But these here Chinks jumped on me yesterday. Some of the boys got to foolin' with 'em and scared 'em 'most to death. So they jumped and left me flat, with the boss comin'. What was I goin' to do? You can't run out and pick up cooks like jack-rabbits. And when you do get 'em they're mostly very plain workers. I said to myself, 'Charley McSween, you're in a hell of a fix. You ain't got a cook and you ain't got time to go and fetch one.' And all the time I was rememberin' how particular the boss is about his meals."

He spent a few seconds in thought and resumed.

"Maybe you can see why I asked you about acts of Providence. Only this mornin' I said to myself, 'Nothin' but an act of Providence will replace them unutterable Chinks.' And right then and there Providence steps up and says, 'Here's a lady that can cook rings around any Chink that ever grew a pigtail, along with her husband who can wash dishes fit for the most particular kind of royalty to eat off of.' I'll leave it to you if it ain't so."

Sally smiled, but the Wreck's face had a suggestion of grimness.

"Are you suggesting," he asked, "that my wife and I go to work in your kitchen and get meals for your boss?"

"You've got the idea," said Charley McSween. "Meals for the boss—and the boys."

"Well, get it out of your head. Nothing doing."

The foreman turned to Sally with a slightly pained expression.

"I don't think your husband grasps it, ma'am. He don't seem to quite lay hold of the situation. Here I am with the boss comin', and no cook. Somebody's got to get those meals. I can't cook 'em. There ain't one of the boys can cook good enough. They can rustle things for themselves, but they don't know any city tricks. I've *got* to have a cook."

Sally smoothed her apron and smiled again.

"It's too bad," she said. "I can see what a fix you're in. You've been very kind to us. We've had a wonderful breakfast and we'd just love to oblige you. But we happen to be catching a train. We're—going East. In fact, we're really behind our time now. So I don't see how we can, Mr. McSween, although otherwise we'd be glad to help you out. Wouldn't we, Henry?"

The Wreck eyed her critically.

"It doesn't make any difference whether we would or we wouldn't," he said. "The point is, we don't."

The foreman drew at his pipe for half a minute and stared at the floor.

"I'm sure sorry you feel that way about it," he mused. "I sort of figured you were just honey-moonin' around, with nothin' particular to do, and that you'd kind of pitch in. I'll pay you good, understand. I'll pay you regular Chink wages. I ain't makin' any distinctions because you don't happen to be professional to the business."

"Can't be done," said the Wreck, with an impatient gesture and another look at his watch. "We happen to be catching a train just now. Speaking of paying, of course we'll pay for our breakfast."

Charley McSween dismissed the idea with a gesture, and studied the pair with reflective eyes. Then he sighed.

"It ain't for me," he said, "to go flyin' into the face of an act of Providence. I'm a believer in meetin' Providence half way when she turns up a card for you. I'm sorry—I'm plumb sorry—that you, ma'am, and your husband don't feel like you ought to stay. But we'll make it as pleasant for you as we can, and we won't keep you no longer than is necessary."

Sally arose to her feet with a gasp of surprise and sought the eyes of the Wreck. He was boring a glance in the direction of Charley McSween.

"Let me understand you," he said. "Are you talking about keeping us here, whether we want to stay or not?"

"That's the unfortunate idea," said the foreman, regretfully.

The Wreck laughed nervously.

"You'll be quite busy keeping us," he said. "Come on, Sally."

Charley McSween unlimbered himself from his chair and stood up.

"You don't get it all yet," he said. "You don't either of you understand the workin's of Providence. Now, it seems that when Providence fetched you here, and the lady proved that she could cook, and the gentleman proved he could wash dishes and dry 'em, it wasn't for no ordinary human being to set himself up to say, 'No.' So I says to Providence, 'What are we goin' to do to persuade these young married folks to take hold of this here emergency job and see it through?' And Providence says, 'Leave it to me.'

"Now, it seems Providence knows how to operate one of these flivvers. So Providence takes that flivver and runs it down into one of the sheds. Havin' done that much, Providence conceives the idea of takin' off one of the front wheels, which is also done in a workmanlike manner, with no damage to parts. Said wheel, havin' been removed from the shed, is hid elsewhere, nobody but Providence knowin' where it was put."

Charley McSween spread his hands with an eloquent gesture.

"Now you get an idea of the way Providence works," he said.

The Wreck stepped to the door of the kitchen and looked out into the yard. When he came back he was removing his spectacles.

"I can lick you," he said to the foreman.

"No, you don't," said Sally, as she stepped in front of him. "Not yet, at any rate. Mr. McSween, kindly leave the kitchen. We want to have a little talk about things."

Charley McSween moved hastily toward the door.

"The cook's always the boss in the kitchen," he said.

CHAPTER VII

IN LIEU OF CHINKS

THE Wreck wanted to follow Charley Mc-Sween outside, but Sally had a grip on his arm that he could not loosen without being rough. She dragged him to a chair, pushed him into it and stood on guard.

"You listen to me before you do anything else," she said. "You're going off half-cocked all the time, and I won't have it."

He eyed her savagely.

"Are you suffering from the idea that I can't lick him?"

"Maybe you can, Henry Williams. I never said you couldn't. But you're not going to start in now."

"What's the reason I can't start now? I'm not going to take up a lot of time at it. Do you want me to wait until he gets his gang around him?"

Sally regarded him severely; he seemed so much like a bad little boy that sometimes she despaired of getting anything reasonable out of him.

"You're always ready to fight somebody," she said. "And there isn't any sense in it. Besides, what good would it do us right now? Suppose you do whip him; if it makes you feel any better I'll admit that you can whip him from his feet up. But suppose you do—that doesn't help to find the wheel he took off the car, does it? We'd have to stay around here anyhow until he got ready to give it back to us. You can't run a flivver on three wheels."

"I might," he said, stubbornly.

"Well, if you could, I wouldn't ride in it, so that settles that. It might give you a lot of satisfaction to get into a fight with him, but it wouldn't get us anywhere. It would only make a lot more trouble, and we've got enough now."

"It doesn't bother me any."

"That's just it," said Sally. "It doesn't seem to make any difference to you how much trouble you stir up. But we can't afford to have any more right away—and we're not going to have it."

The Wreck regarded her with a look of intense disgust.

"Do I look like a dishwasher?" he demanded. "Do you think anybody can *make* me wash dishes?"

"Suppose I asked you to wash them?"

He shook his head irritably.

"You haven't got any right to ask me."

"Yes, I have. I'm in this thing as much as you are and I have just as many rights as you have. And if it's necessary for you to wash dishes, then you ought to be glad to wash them, for the general good."

Sally puzzled him. She appeared to be abandoning herself to a situation that was preposterous and intolerable. It did not seem like Sally at all.

"What about your train?" he inquired.

"The train's got to wait for the present," she answered, with a shrug.

"You mean to tell me you're going to stick around here and take orders like a trained seal? You're going to cook for this outfit?"

She reached for a chair and seated herself opposite him.

"Do you realize, Henry Williams, that I'm trying to save you? I don't claim any credit for it, because I'm trying to save myself, too. Have you forgotten what you did last night? Do you want to go roaming out on the road again, to be picked up and sent off to jail? Well, if you do, I don't. We've got to hide somewhere until this thing blows over. And if you can think of any better place than this to hide, I can't."

"I only took a little gasoline," he said, impatiently.

"And you only held them up with a gun, too. And scared the life out of them, and made them sit in the road, and humiliated them, and let all the air out of their tires. And you didn't pay for the gasoline, either; so that's stealing. You'd better take it from me, you've done something to hide for. I know Montana, if I don't know much else. You can't do things like that any more."

The Wreck scowled at the floor.

"How about a bird who steals the wheel off your car? Can he do things like that?"

"No; he hasn't any right, of course. But it's done, and I'm not sure but that's also an act of

Providence, as Charley McSween says. I have a hunch that what we need right now is a hide-out, and this gives us one without hunting for it. Besides, we can eat here."

"And how long do you think we're going to stay parked around here, Sally Morgan?"

"Oh, not long. That depends. I'm sure we'll get the wheel back for the car by the time we ought to start."

He pondered the prospect gloomily. The thing to do, of course, was to lick Charley McSween; no man was expected to endure what Charley had inflicted. If he did not have Sally Morgan on his hands he would do it in a minute. But the Wreck had a sense of guardianship and responsibility. It was not a conscious sense, perhaps; rather, it was instinctive. He was responsible until he put her aboard that train, or until he carried her back to Dad Morgan's ranch. After that he would be free to settle scores with anybody he pleased, but until then he recognized certain restraints.

He was not so entirely a creature of impulse as Sally believed him. There was a streak of calculation in him; it could not be called caution, but it involved a certain degree of premeditation and reckoning of consequences. He could see Sally's point about the hide-out. It irked him to acknowledge that it had merit; he would not publicly admit it. But he was honest with himself. His fundamental urge was to thrash Charley McSween until he produced the missing wheel and then to rush Sally away to the nearest point on the railroad, where he guaranteed to stop any transcontinental flier that might happen along, even if he had to stall the flivver in the middle of the track. But it might not be the quickest way of getting Sally out of a mess. Perhaps it might be better to think things over a bit; not that he wanted to, but that it might be his unpleasant duty.

"There's a telephone here somewhere," he said, looking up suddenly. "I saw the wire."

"Yes; most of the ranches have phones," nodded Sally.

"You could use it, if you wanted to."

"What for?"

"I thought you might want to talk to your folks."

"I wouldn't for a million dollars," said Sally, emphatically.

It was plain that he did not understand.

"Why, don't you see, they think I took the train day before yesterday. And if they find out I'm still in Montana they'll be worried, and they won't understand. Ma would just sit and fret and say nothing, and Dad would go around telling everybody he met. No, indeed; they'd better keep on thinking I made the train. Besides, I couldn't tell them everything, anyhow."

"Why couldn't you tell them?"

"Well, I couldn't tell them about the hold-up, could I?"

"You didn't have anything to do with it."

She regarded him with astonishment.

"But I was there," she declared. "And I hope you don't think I'm a squealer."

The Wreck studied her with fresh interest. No, of course he hadn't thought she would squeal. But he knew that she did not approve of the hold-up, and he had a fixed notion that she did not approve of him, either.

"You bawled me out for it," he reminded her.

"Of course I did. I think it was a terrible thing for you to do. But that was just between the two of us. You don't suppose I'm going around shouting about it to anybody else? I haven't any doubt I'll be bawling you out some more, about other things; but that doesn't say I'm going to run and tell."

There was a slightly offended look in her eyes. She could not conceive how he got the idea that she might desert him, or give him up to the law, just because he had done something foolish.

"I'm much obliged," he said, awkwardly.

She recognized that as a combination apology and tribute, but it made her smile. He never knew what a ridiculous person he was. She felt that what he needed was a keeper, a guardian, a mother and a stern parent, all rolled into one.

"I'm not worrying about myself one bit," she assured him. "I'm worrying more about you."

The Wreck bristled.

"What in— Why in blazes would you worry about me?"

"Well, you were expecting to go back to the ranch, weren't you?"

"That's nothing. I told them I might not be back the same night."

"I know," said Sally. "But it's the second day after that. And you haven't got me to the train yet. And then you've got to find your way back to the ranch—and I don't believe you ever can."

He flung himself into a two-armed gesture of protest.

"Anywhere I've been once I can go again," he said. "I could drive from here to Pittsburgh with my eyes shut. Don't worry about me."

"But Dad and Ma will think you're lost."

"Then let Dad and Ma do the worrying."

"We'll have to get you a road map, if there is such a thing, before you start back," said Sally, "because you'll have a terrible time if you try to cut across country again."

"Oh, I'll take a bearing from Black Top," observed the Wreck, wickedly.

He grinned and Sally smiled. She was glad that he seemed to be in a better humor. But even at his worst, she had never succeeded in getting really angry at him. Several times she had thought she was, only to discover that her anger was tempered with a half-amused tolerance. And she knew that the Wreck himself, in his most violent moments, showed a strain of chivalry that was not to be mistaken. What he might be back in Pittsburgh she had no idea, but here in Montana he was a source of incongruous entertainment.

Sally was not concerned very much about her

own predicament. It mattered very little that she failed to get the train on a particular day; it was just an annoyance. It would not be an overwhelming catastrophe if she had to go back to the Bar-M. Everything could be explained as soon as the present trouble blew over. What gave her real worry was the Wreck himself. She had assumed an attitude toward him almost identical with his own attitude toward her, although she was more keenly conscious of it than he. She had a sort of guardianship responsibility. It would never do to let him suspect it; he would have a paroxysm at the mere suggestion. But the sense of duty burdened her, none the less. He was a stranger in a strange land, absurdly ignorant of its ways, and he was under the protection of the Bar-M, even if he did not know it. As the sole representative of the Bar-M, Sally Morgan shouldered it all.

The Wreck was headed for the door when she called him to a halt.

"Where are you going?" she asked, suspiciously.

"Just for a look about the place."

"You're not going to hunt up Charley McSween?"

"I'm not going to dodge him."

"Well, you're not going to fight with him," she said, firmly.

"Not if he leaves me alone."

"It doesn't make any difference whether he leaves you alone or not. You're not going to fight; not to-day, anyhow. We can't afford it."

"I'm no door-mat," he grumbled.

"Certainly not. Nobody thinks you are. But—Henry, you are *not* going to fight."

It was not the fact of her quiet emphasis that most impressed him. It was being called "Henry." Back at the ranch they called him "Mr. Williams," and "Wreck," and "Mister," and "Henry Williams" and other things. It had never occurred to anybody to admit him to the comradeship of "Henry." Coming at last, it made a rather favorable impression on him. It was the first time anybody had called him "Henry" since he left Pittsburgh. He did not feel quite so far from home.

"Oh, all right, maw," he drawled, as he went through the door. "I ain't goin' to fight."

Sally sat in a chair and screamed. She had not suspected the Wreck of a teasing sense of humor. Why, he was actually making fun of her!

"There's hope for that dude," she said, as she got control of her laughter. "But he's altogether too wild for this country."

She busied herself for a while in the kitchen, confident that he would keep his promise. There was a lot of tidying up to be done; the boys had evidently left the place without a thought of straightening things out, after they had rustled their own breakfast. Sally was a good housekeeper; even better than Ma, for, while Ma was practical, Sally was both practical and scientific. The kitchen was well arranged, with all sorts of conveniences; in some respects it was better than her home kitchen, which had made considerable modern advance over most ranch kitchens. She liked housekeeping, when there was not too much of it, and, best of all, she liked to cook. Charley McSween had imposed less of a hardship than he suspected.

When the kitchen satisfied her, she started on an exploration of the rest of the lower floor. There was a pantry, with more china in it, which caused her eyes to widen.

"This *is* a swell outfit," she murmured. "H'm! Limoges! Well, now, what do I know about *that?*"

There was a dining-room, too, that did not appear to be used for any purpose except serving meals. Of course, the boys did not eat there; they had their grub in the kitchen. A dining-room implied a sort of effete exclusiveness that impressed her deeply.

Beyond the dining-room was an enormous living-room; it occupied at least half of the area of the ranch house. She liked it at once, not only for its spacious dimensions, but for the comfort, even luxury, with which it was furnished. There was a great stone fireplace, and curtains at the windows, and Navaho rugs, and furniture with leather cushions, and lots of pictures on the walls—mostly pictures of Indians, and cowboys, and other things that she knew about. But best of all, there were books—books scattered about on the tables and whole shelves of them against the walls.

She roamed about the big rooms as Alice roamed in Wonderland; not amazed at anything she saw, but marveling that it should all be there in the middle of the range country, where most living-

rooms run to plainness and simplicity, and too often
to drab barrenness. She studied the pictures, she
examined the titles of the books, she sat on the
leather cushions, she absorbed the atmosphere of the
place, gratefully and deliberately.

"This," she told herself, "is what I'm going to
have some day, only mine will be exactly my own.
I'm not critical, but I can do even better."

Finally she picked up a book that she did not
believe would be disappointing, dragged one of the
big chairs close to a window and curled herself into
a knot of luxurious comfort. She followed the
story for a chapter or two, forgetting the Wreck and
the flivver and the train going East. But after a
while her mind became pleasantly dull and hazy, and
a gentle weight on her eyelids closed them. She
was aware only of the fact that she was going to
take a nap and she found joy in it.

Probably she dreamed. But she was never quite
sure of it, because if it began as a dream it ended
as something that really happened. There was a
rhythmic throbbing in her ears, and as she came
slowly and reluctantly to consciousness it grew steadily louder. There was a mechanical regularity about
it that reminded her of the windmill at the Bar-M,
but she realized an instant later that she was not in
her own home. And it wasn't a windmill, either; it
was more like an engine. Her eyes were blinking
now. Why, it was an automobile!

Sally uncurled herself and straightened up in
the big chair. If Henry Williams had resurrected

that flivver, if he had found that wheel, if he had been in a fight with Charley McSween—well, then he was going to have some first-class trouble on his hands. Her ears were sharper now; she was completely awake. She listened a second or two longer. No; it was not the flivver. It was a different kind of an engine, more orderly and dignified—wealthier.

She leaned forward and pushed aside a corner of the curtain. The thing that made the noise had just come to a stop outside. Sally stared at it with round eyes.

"Why, I believe— Oh, it is!"

She flipped out of the chair with the sudden speed of a cat and raced in the direction of the kitchen.

"They've trailed us!" she gasped, as she ran.

CHAPTER VIII

HIDING OUT

A S Sally charged into the kitchen by way of the pantry, the Wreck was coming in through the door that opened on the yard. He stared at her in plain surprise; he did not know she could run so fast.

"What's the hurry?" he asked, mildly.

"We're trailed!"

"Trailed? What do you mean?"

"Have they seen you?" she panted.

"Who? What are you talking about? I haven't seen anybody but some horses down in a corral."

"Well, we're trailed all right, Henry Williams. They're out in the front now!"

"Who's out in front?"

"The people you stuck up—the big car!"

The Wreck lifted his eyebrows, looked thoughtful for an instant, then began squaring his shoulders.

"Oh, all right," he said. "We'll stick 'em up again."

Sally groaned.

"We've got to get out of here," she said, sharply. "We've got to make a getaway. We'll get a couple of horses down at the corral before they see us. You'll just *have* to ride."

It was a despairing thing to contemplate the Wreck on horseback, but it seemed the only chance.

"Oh, I can ride," he said. "I can ride anything. Only it's easier to stick 'em up. Here's what we'll do." His eyes glistened. "We'll take their car!"

Sally shook her head angrily.

"No, you idiot!" she cried. "We'll take horses, if we get a chance at them. Hurry!"

She had seized him by the hand and was dragging him in the direction of the door when in walked Charley McSween. Sally stopped and eyed him appraisingly. If the Wreck insisted on whipping him, this seemed to be the chosen time. And if it was necessary, she would help.

"I was just lookin' for you," said Charley, addressing the Wreck. "I want a hand with some baggage outside."

"Huh?" inquired the Wreck.

"Baggage," repeated Charley. "The boss is here."

Sally and the Wreck exchanged a slow glance. Then she pinched his fingers tightly, and he knew it was meant to be some sort of a signal.

"Where are your men? Can't they handle baggage?" she demanded.

"The boys ain't here, ma'am. So I'm askin' him," with a nod toward the Wreck.

"Well, my husband doesn't handle baggage."

Again she pinched the Wreck's fingers.

"What's the reason he don't handle baggage?" inquired Charley. "Ain't it dignified?"

"He's—he's not strong," said Sally.

The Wreck began to squirm and look truculent.

"I admit he ain't exactly powerful lookin', ma'am. But a while back he said he was goin' to lick me, so I thought maybe he could rassle a couple of trunks without sustainin' any personal damage."

"No; you'll have to get somebody else," said Sally.

Charley made no effort to conceal the disgust in his soul. He inspected the Wreck from his horn-rimmed spectacles to his shoes, following the examination with a gesture of contempt.

"Seein' as your wife won't let you," he remarked, "I suppose me and the chauffeur 'll manage."

The Wreck never knew how he managed to maintain any self-control, but he blamed it all on Sally. All he did was to shout:

"If you think I'm a baggage-smasher, you just wait and see what happens to your dishes."

Charley went out with a remark to the effect that he did not have to pay for the dishes. The Wreck and Sally stared at each other.

"You—you stuck up the owner of the place!" she wailed.

"He was a hog," said the Wreck, with fine simplicity.

He was not worrying about the owner; his mind was occupied with plans to revenge himself for the insults of Charley McSween.

"Of all the awful luck," continued Sally, in an awed whisper. "To think that we walked right into his hands. I knew there was something queer about this place the minute I took a look around the house."

"Well, what do we do now? Swipe the horses?"

Sally considered, then shook her head slowly.

"No; I think we'd better wait now. I don't believe it's quite as bad as I thought. You see, they didn't trail us here, after all. They were coming, anyhow. Probably they don't know we're here; if they did, we'd have heard from it before this. We've got to figure this thing out now—carefully. The main thing is to keep them from seeing you. That's why I wouldn't let you go out to help with the baggage."

He was not a good hand at playing a waiting game, and said so. He was still in favor of going out and taking the big car, a feat which presented to him no considerations of dismay. But Sally sharply ordered him to put the idea out of his head.

The situation bewildered her, but she did not think it had yet reached a crisis. Nobody in the car had seen her; it was very unlikely that they even knew their hold-up man had a girl with him. So long as she could keep the Wreck out of their sight and as long as the flivver remained locked up in a shed, there was still a chance to figure something out. But how utterly exasperating it was! Just when she was satisfied that they had blundered into a safe hide-out, she discovered that they had really walked into the lion's den.

"What worries me right now," she mused, "is that Charley may say something about the way we came in this morning. That might easily get them asking questions."

"He won't," said the Wreck, sourly. "He isn't going to let his boss know what a close squeak he had in the kitchen. I'll bet money on that."

"Hope you're right. But Henry, if they ever do discover us—"

"Fireworks!"

It comforted her a little to observe that he was still the same confident Wreck, although she might have remembered that he was always thus and that it did not necessarily signify anything. He was confident when he first mounted the sorrel horse, but the horse had at least an even break, if not the better of it.

"The thing to do, of course, is to keep them from seeing you," she said. "You'll have to stay in the kitchen all the time, I'm afraid. I don't suppose they'll come in here."

"They're not going to coop me up in a kitchen," he growled. "Besides, it was dark last night, anyhow. They didn't get a good look at me. I had my cap pulled down."

"It's the glasses, Henry. They mark you."

"I can't help it if I have to wear them."

"Oh, I don't mean that," she said hastily. "But they identify you. Nobody could miss them."

"Make me look like an owl."

"Nonsense. Don't be so sensitive. They look very well, but—"

"They don't look well," said the Wreck, harshly. "They look like the devil. Don't you start soft-soaping me, Sally Morgan."

"Oh, all right; they look like the devil," she retorted, desperately. "But just the same, they're one of the reasons why you've got to lay low. And you've got to keep out of trouble for a while; I mean fights, and arguments. You can't go milling around every time somebody says something you don't like."

He showed sulky symptoms, and Sally hoped he would keep on being sulky for a while; it might keep him quiet. If she was going to pull him out of this mess, thought Sally, she would have to humor him; for she saw the situation as one demanding shrewdness and finesse. As for the Wreck, he was brooding over restraint. If he was going to get her out of this hole, it was an affair that called for action. They had the same goal in view, but the methods were hopelessly divergent.

Charley came into the kitchen again.

"We got that baggage in, thanks to nobody that washes dishes," he said. "And now, ma'am, I'll have to ask you to hustle dinner. They're real hungry."

"They'll have dinner just as soon as I can get it," said Sally, promptly.

The Wreck regarded her with a look of amazed disappointment. Was she going to turn to and

cook for a hog? It was enough to be drafted as
cook for an unknown, but to do chores for your
enemy was humiliation. He was about to speak
when she stopped him with a look.

"Seems they didn't get any regular breakfast,
except crackers, which they had with 'em," explained Charley. "That leaves 'em kind of hungry.
They got hung up on the road. In fact, they got
held up."

"You don't mean it!" exclaimed Sally, who was
digging into the flour barrel, as a first step in the
direction of making biscuits.

"Oh, it don't seem like it was serious, ma'am.
That is, there wasn't anybody got shot. Feller just
took watches and valuables and left 'em flat without
any gas."

Sally ventured a look at the Wreck. He seemed
to be curiously elated.

"It's been done before," said Charley, who was
slightly bored. "It ain't anything to what they used
to do. Only the boss is pretty well stirred up,
which maybe is natural enough. He comes from the
East, where they don't know anything about such
things."

The Wreck was standing near a window, polishing his spectacles. It was Sally's first conscious
glimpse of him without the horn rims. He gave
her a swift impression of being another person.
But there was no time to study him; Charley was
too interesting.

"Who is the boss?" she asked, trying to be in-
different.

"His name is Underwood," said Charley. "He's
from New York. It's funny the way those New
Yorkers buy themselves places that take such a
pile of travelin' to get to. And he don't come here
oftener than once a year. This time he drove all
the way. It don't sound reasonable, but he did.
He's got his boy and girl with him. I expect
he'll stay a few weeks."

Charley watched her as she began to mix the
flour.

"His bein' from New York is why I was so particular about the cookin'. I had Chinks here last
year and they did real well. So I went and got
another pair this summer; but, as I told you, the
boys got kind of juvenile with 'em and they lit out.
It seems that a Chink expects you to take him serious.
It beats hell."

"The boss must have money," suggested Sally.

"Yes, ma'am; he's lousy with it. He raises fancy
cattle, only that ain't the way he made his money.
He took it from somebody in Wall Street. But
there ain't any finer cattle in Montana. They don't
know how he made his money. They don't care.
I can't say that I care anything myself. I'm liberal
in my views. If I were you, ma'am, I'd sort of
give 'em plenty to eat, but I'd make it look as
much like New York as I could."

"Oh, I'll give them lots," said Sally. "Don't
you worry, old—"

It slipped half way from her lips—"old timer." It was awfully hard to play tenderfoot when Charley was around. But Charley gave no sign that he noticed anything.

"That's right, ma'am; feed 'em liberal and fancy. I can see you're goin' to make an awful hit with the boys."

He went out again, satisfied that dinner was under way and that Sally would be a credit to his discrimination in cooks. She was flying around the kitchen like a marionette on wires, attending to three or four things at once, but without the least trace of confusion.

"Poke that fire up, Henry; put a lot of wood on it and get it going. I want a hot oven. There's a pile of wood outside the door. Fill the kettle over at the sink pump and put it on. I've got fifty things to do, and you've got to help with some of them. Better put your apron on, too; you'll get all mussed up if you don't."

The Wreck went about his task with a scowl.

"The big lying hog," he said. "I never touched their watches and valuables."

"They're just excited," explained Sally, as she hunted for a rolling pin. "People always exaggerate. Charley doesn't suspect us, anyhow, so there's that much gained. Don't fill the kettle too full; it'll boil over."

"I'm not. I'll be hanged if I'd break my neck cooking for them."

"That's nothing. I've cooked for lots of people.

Besides, we're stalling for time. We're going to give them the best meal we know how."

"Chinamen's work!"

"It would be a good thing for us if we were Chinamen," said Sally, blandly. "Then we'd have a complete alibi."

He grumbled his way through the chores, but she could not complain that he was inefficient. Although he seemed constantly at the point of disobedience, the Wreck followed his orders. He even kept a faithful eye on the stove, while she went into the dining-room to set the table. She took a swift peep into the living-room while engaged in this task, but the Underwood family was evidently up-stairs.

"Underwood?" she mused. "Can't say that I remember hearing the name around here. Fancy cattle, eh? I've heard of somebody around here who raised prize Herefords. I'll bet it's the same one. But if it is, we're a long way from the Bar-M. We haven't any neighbors like that."

She fussed over the table as though she were a hostess; she set out the best china in the pantry, polishing the plates lovingly and carefully.

"Wall Street," she said. "No wonder he's fussy about his meals."

There were footsteps on the staircase that came down into the living-rooms, and Sally, with a final look at the table, fled back into the kitchen.

"They're coming down," she informed the Wreck. "We've got to hurry. Thank Heaven, biscuits don't take long. You keep an eye on that coffee, and don't let it boil. Stop it just when it starts. I haven't time to cook any meat; besides, I don't know where they keep it. They're going to have an omelette."

It was a very large omelette that she made, fluffy and thick, a rhapsody in yellows and golden browns. The Wreck eyed it with jealous disapproval, but she did not give him to time to express an opinion. She had him opening a can of soup and pouring it into a saucepan for heating. There was time for that much, anyhow.

"I'll cook them a regular meal next time," she promised. "But this will have to do for short notice."

Her enthusiasm for the odious task depressed him.

"Don't work your head off," he advised. "You'll get no thanks for it."

"Oh, I've got lots to do yet," said Sally, cheerfully. "For one thing, I've got to wait on the table."

The Wreck nearly upset the coffee pot in his anger.

"You will *not!*" he exclaimed.

"Of course I will."

"I'll not have you waiting on hogs, Sally Morgan. They can wait on themselves."

"Don't be ridiculous. They don't eat in the kitchen. Somebody's got to carry it to them."

"All right, then. *I'll* carry it to 'em."

She stared, then shook her head vehemently.

"You can't. You've got to dodge them as long as you can. There'll be a blow-up, as sure as a gun, the minute they see you."

"Well, I'm going to wait on them, if anybody does," he said, doggedly. "What's the use of dodging around? We may just as well find out now as any other time."

"See here, Henry Williams! If you—"

She stopped, studied his face with a new interest and remembered something. Reaching out, she lifted off his spectacles, then stepped back a pace for another inspection. Her scrutiny lasted several seconds.

"It makes you look tremendously different," she said. "Can you see anything without them?"

"I can see you," said the Wreck, blinking.

"Wait a minute."

She ran to a closet and came back carrying a starched white jacket.

"It must have belonged to one of the Chinamen," she said, "but I think it will fit you. Put it on."

She managed to get him into it, after fierce protest. Then she viewed him again.

"I really believe," she said, slowly, "that you can get away with it. With that, and the apron, and no spectacles, you don't look the least bit like a nervous wreck. You don't look like a hold-up man, anyhow. And if you're sure you can get around without falling over things, I believe I'll let you try it. But be awfully, awfully careful about your voice. Try to disguise it, if you can. Don't forget yourself and *bark* at them."

"I never bark."

"You did then. But you mustn't. Just keep remembering that we're still hiding out. I think they're at the table now. You can take in the soup, and don't forget to serve things from the left."

He picked up a tray and began navigating cautiously in the direction of the dining-room. Sally watched him anxiously. It was an awful risk, she thought; but if he passed the test she would feel a lot safer.

CHAPTER IX

THE FOUR-IN-ONE BANDIT

THERE were two persons in the dining-room when the Wreck entered with the tray. He could make them out with reasonable clearness as he drew nearer to them. One was the girl, Underwood's daughter. If you liked colorful blondes, she was just the right sort; slim, with a delicate prettiness that belonged to the city. Opposite her sat a youth who appeared to be a year or so older. He was well set up and rather good-looking, even if there was a surly set to his features. He was drawing things on the table-cloth with the tine of a fork.

In the living-room there was a table, close to the dining-room door, and on the table was a telephone. Somebody with a heavy voice was using it; the Wreck identified the voice instantly. It belonged to the large man who would not share his gasoline. The girl and the youth were listening, and the Wreck, putting down his tray, listened also, pretending to be busy by wiping the soup plates with a napkin.

"Well, you've got to get him," said the heavy voice, with a note of irascible authority. "I don't care if you have to try every place in the county.

He ought to leave word where he goes. This is Underwood talking. What? Yes, certainly. Oh, you understand now, do you? Well, you get him. Leave word every place you try that he's to call me. He knows who it is. And you tell him it's important, see? Tell him it's the most important job he ever had. I don't call people up for nothing. Get busy."

There was the snap of a receiver roughly replaced and the creaking of a chair.

"Haven't they located him yet, father?" called the girl.

"No; and I don't believe they're half trying." Underwood was entering the dining-room. "First they thought he was over at Fisher. Now they think he's gone back to the county seat. I don't care where he is. I want him."

The owner of the ranch seated himself at the end of the table. The Wreck observed that he lowered himself into his chair with a slight stiffness of movement. It pleased him to think that he knew the cause. The mudguard of the flivver showed a tell-tale warp, where it had nudged him violently. There was no mistaking Underwood, even without the aid of spectacles. The Wreck had seen him in the white glare of road lights, toiling desperately at a crank, and the heavily jowled face was forever marked in his memory.

"I don't see why you can't have Charley call in the men and start them out on the road," observed the youth.

"They've got work to do here," growled his father, as he spread a napkin. "And it's not their job, anyhow. It's a sheriff's job."

The Wreck, who was ladling soup at the serving table, never spilled a drop. He merely prolonged the task, as he listened.

"It seems to me he ought to have some deputy you could get hold of," suggested Harriet Underwood.

"I don't want his deputy. I don't do business with deputies. I want the man in charge. Lord knows, I pay enough taxes in this county to get a sheriff when I want one. He must be a fine sheriff to let a state of affairs like this go on."

"Well, I guess you could get another one elected, if you wanted to," remarked the young man, with an effort at lightness.

His father glared at him.

"Don't be an ass, Chester. What we want now is a sheriff—on the job. We're not running next year's election."

The Wreck, having ladled soup into three plates, picked one of them up and turned toward the table. This was the crisis, and there was no longer any use in trying to postpone it. He laid the plate in front of Miss Underwood, and then, for the first time since he had entered the room, he seemed to attract family attention.

The girl gave him a casual look and picked up her napkin. Chester's examination was equally brief. Servants were a matter of no great interest,

"THE WRECK" HEARS OF THE DESPERATE HOLD-UP.

Scene from the Play.

either to himself or his sister. But the scrutiny of Jerome Underwood was more prolonged. The Wreck blinked painfully and wished that he had his glasses; he wanted to read the big man's expression more accurately.

He had fetched a second plate of soup and laid it before the ranch owner before a word was addressed to him.

"You didn't work here last summer," announced Underwood.

"No, sir."

It was a bitter wrench, but the Wreck kept his voice low and respectful.

"What's your name?"

"Williams."

"Where are you from?"

"Pittsburgh, sir."

"Just working here for the summer?"

"Yes, sir."

Underwood nodded and picked up his spoon. The Wreck moved off toward the serving table and got another plate of soup. He felt as though he were treading on air. He did not believe he was going to mind waiting on the hog, after all; it was so much satisfaction to fool him.

The head of the ranch ate his soup with purposeful speed, pushed back the plate and began drumming on the table with the tips of his thick fingers.

"It's a fine telephone service we get out here," he grumbled. "I suppose that girl hasn't bothered her head about it since."

"But of course it may take time to locate him, father," said Miss Underwood.

"It ought not to. What's a sheriff for? He's supposed to be within call, if I know anything about his business. Here's a bunch of highway robbers running around the country, and I dare say he's never heard about it. And they talk about improving the roads for tourists!"

Jerome Underwood's voice trailed off in a low growl and he continued to drum with his fingers.

"Well, I wanted to take a shot at the one in the road and you wouldn't let me," complained Chester.

"That would have been fine business, wouldn't it?" observed his father. "He'd have shot every last one of us before you could lift your finger. You never had a chance after you got out of the car. If you wanted to take a shot at him, why didn't you do it before you climbed out?"

"But it was just a bit unexpected, father. We didn't think—"

Underwood silenced his son with a gesture.

"Of course we didn't think. We didn't think that the country was running wild, with a lot of desperadoes doing as they damn please. But we found out differently, didn't we? *You* shoot at him! Why, there were three more of them up by his car. I *saw* them."

"Timothy said he didn't see anybody else," said Miss Underwood.

"Timothy's a blind ass. What do you expect

of a chauffeur who is scared so stiff that he forgets how to work a tire pump? I say there were three men, lined up at the side of the road—with guns. Why, if it hadn't been for them I'd have had the other one."

The Wreck collected the soup plates and piled them carefully.

"You could have jumped on him while he was trying to get his car started," observed Miss Underwood, with a nod.

Her father mumbled something that did not appear to be a reply. The Wreck was feeling jubilant. He would not have missed waiting on table for the world. Now he knew how deeply he had bitten into the pride of Jerome Underwood; for even in the intimacy of the family circle Underwood had not confessed his humiliation at the crank of the flivver. He had been hidden from the family sight as he toiled, and now he was hiding the story. Too bad, thought the Wreck, that he had not marched the whole family up where they could see.

He carried the soup-plates back to the kitchen, where he found Sally standing in the middle of the floor, her hands clasped and an anxious look on her face.

"Is it all right?" she whispered.

"Sure it is," he said.

The grin on his face meant more than his words. Sally breathed deeply and exhaled a long sigh.

"I was getting anxious," she said. "You were

gone so terribly long. Didn't they ask you a lot
of questions, or anything?"

"They're too busy telling each other how they
were held up by four men," he observed.

"Four?"

"Yes—the liars. Four desperadoes, Underwood
says. Me—" The Wreck peered down at his white
jacket and apron and smiled wryly. "Me—I'm four
desperadoes."

Sally did not join in the smile. She was ready
to admit that he was one desperado, at the very
least.

"Tell me everything they said, Henry."

"I've got to go back. Give me the next tray-full.
I'll tell you about it afterward. I'm getting some
information now."

Sally hurried with the tray and the Wreck went
back to the dining-room. Underwood was still
drumming on the table. He glanced at the tray as
it passed him, ceased drumming and riveted his eye
on the omelette. Even a dyspeptic, which the boss
of the ranch was not, would have viewed it with
attention. The Wreck was actually proud to carry
it, for not only was it an object of beauty in itself,
but Sally had found things to garnish it with, so that
it was art in a frame.

Two minutes later Underwood looked up from
his plate and fixed his glance on the Wreck.

"Say, who made this omelette?" he demanded.

"The cook, sir."

"Biscuits, too?"

"Yes, sir."

And the coffee?"

"Yes, sir."

The large man helped himself to another mouthful and lingered over it.

"Not the same cook who was here last summer," he announced.

"No, sir."

"Who is he?"

"It's a lady, sir—my wife."

The Underwood family sighed comfortably, in unison.

"At last, father, we've got somebody who can cook," said Harriet. "Remember how awful it was last summer?"

The boss of the ranch nodded and reached for the omelette platter.

"Tell your wife that she's a good cook," he said. "Tell her to keep it up. Tell her to have fried chicken to-night, and browned potatoes, and beans, and corn, if she's got any—and more biscuits. Understand? More biscuits. Coffee, too. And I want her to make some pie. If she hasn't got stuff to make pie out of, we'll send for it. And tell her to cook a lot of everything."

Harriet Underwood frowned and glanced at her brother.

"Remember, father, the doctor said—"

"The doctor's in New York," interrupted Underwood. "What he doesn't know will never get into his bill. Don't forget, Williams—whatever you said your name was—have your wife keep right on cooking."

The Wreck, passing the biscuits again, acknowledged the command with a nod. He was hungry himself and he hoped there would be something left of the omelette, although he could see that the chances were against him. He did not need to be told that Sally Morgan could cook; he knew it before they did, back at the Bar-M, where Sally often shooed her mother out of the kitchen and ran things to suit herself.

"People can eat more out in this country," observed Underwood, apparently talking to himself. "It's the dry air and the altitude. Back in New York—"

There was an uncertain tinkle of the telephone bell in the next room. He lumbered hastily out of his chair in answer to it.

"Yes; this is Underwood. Got him, have you? . . . All right. Put him on. . . . That the sheriff? Great Scott! you're a hard man to get. . . . Never mind. This is Underwood. Get me? What? . . . Yes; that's right. Off in the northeast corner of the county. Now, listen:

"I was held up last night in my car. About thirty miles from the ranch, I should say. West of it, on the main road; there's only one road. We didn't come here direct; drove around by way of Duncan. The road's better. Had my son and daughter with me, and a driver. Are you getting this? . . .

"Four men. . . . Yes; four! Blocked the road

with their own car and held us up. We never had
a chance. Took watches, valuables, money. What?
. . . Took everything we had that was worth carrying off. Stole all the gasoline out of our tank and
left us flat on the road. Let the air out of our
tires with a knife. How's that? . . .

"How the devil can I give you a description? It
was pitch dark. They had handkerchiefs over their
faces. I'm not supposed to furnish a set of Bertillon
measurements, am I? You didn't expect me to take
fingerprints, did you, with a gun stuck under my
nose? You're what? . . ."

There was an inarticulate rumble from the living-
room, then a booming of the heavy voice.

"You're surprised?" roared Underwood. "You
didn't think there was anybody working the road
over this way? Well, if you're surprised, what
do you think I am? Doesn't a property owner get
any protection in this county? I'm no tourist. I've
got a place here. If you want to know whether I
pay any taxes just look up the books. What? . . .
Oh, you know about me, do you? Well, I'm damned
glad somebody knows about me. Now, the best
advice I can give you is to get busy. . . . How's
that? . . .

"How do I know what direction they went in?
They started east when they left us; that's all I
know. I want action—understand? I'll pay any
reward and any expenses that are necessary, but I
want action. I'm going to find out whether a tax-
payer in this county has any protection against high-

waymen. . . . All right. You're getting on the
job at once; is that it? . . . Yes; I'll be here for
some time. I'll expect to hear from you without
much delay. Your name is Wells, isn't it? . . . All
right."

The Wreck, who was pouring coffee for Chester,
spilled some into the saucer, but recovered himself. So the sheriff's name was Wells!

Jerome Underwood came back into the dining-
room, wearing the expression of a man who has
achieved a stroke of business.

"Made it pretty strong, didn't you, father?" suggested his son, with a faint smile.

"Strong? Certainly I did. You don't suppose
I wanted to give him the idea that it was a tea
party, do you? When I've got a hand I play it
to the limit. I don't want him loafing around
and taking things easy. I want him on the job. He
knows who I am. If he doesn't it won't take him
long to find out."

He made another dive at the omelette.

"Says he'll get a posse on the road at once. Well,
he'd better. A posse! What they need out here is
a few New York policemen."

The Wreck, seeing no immediate need of his
services, disappeared through the pantry in the
direction of the kitchen. He had a queer look;
as much a look of triumph as anything else.

Sally jumped up from a chair by the window and
shot a glance of inquiry at him.

"Where are my spectacles?" he demanded. "My eyes hurt."

She found them and the Wreck began to look like himself again.

"Now tell me everything," she ordered.

"He's been at the telephone, raising the county against four desperadoes," said the Wreck. "He's made a regular yarn of it by this time. I guess they'll hang us for sure, Sally."

"They'd better wait till they catch us."

The Wreck contemplated her for a few seconds. He wondered just how she was going to take the news.

"He's a good liar; he piled it on. And he pulled all the old stuff about influence, and how much taxes he pays, and all the New York dope. He made me thank God I came from Pittsburgh."

"Could you get any idea of what's being done about it?" asked Sally, with the practical aspects uppermost in her thoughts.

"Oh, there's a posse getting on the job," said the Wreck, wearily.

"A posse," mused Sally, nodding. "Yes; I'd imagine that. Who did he have on the phone?"

"He was talking to the sheriff."

"The sheriff. Uh-huh. Well, that means—"

Sally stopped and stared at the Wreck. Something had startled her.

"What county are we in?" she demanded.

He shrugged. He never tried to keep track of counties and he did not know. But she read something in his eyes that caused her to clutch at his arm.

"Henry Williams! He wasn't talking to—"

"Yes, he was. That's exactly who he was talking to."

She walked back to the chair by the window and sat down, suddenly limp. For half a minute the Wreck was unable to figure just what sort of reaction she was having. It seemed to him that every possible emotion flashed into her face, one succeeding the other so rapidly that all was a confused blur. And then, with her head tossed back and her eyes wide with merriment, she began to laugh.

"Oh!" she gasped. "Oh, Henry, did you ever hear of such a joke? Bob Wells; Bob—out with a posse—to catch *me!*"

"I'll admit it's a joke," said the Wreck, cheerfully.

"Why, it's a perfect scream! I might have known we were in the same county; it's so terribly big. But I never even thought about it. And now he's got the sheriff—Bob Wells!"

She passed into another spasm of laughter while the Wreck watched. Any time they wanted to laugh about Bob Wells the Wreck was a willing listener.

"I start out for a trousseau, and I get turned into a hold-up man, and I'm chased—by *Bob Wells!*"

"It's great," he affirmed, solemnly.

Then he saw that another change was coming. She was getting control of herself and the laughter was fading. There was a questioning look in her eyes, a chewing of her under lip.

"H'm. It's rather ambarrassing at that," she said, slowly. "I don't know that it's so funny, after all. It complicates things. Bob Wells is an awfully good sheriff. When he goes after people he's a perfect bloodhound. He got a murderer last year that nobody ever dreamed he could get. And if he should ever find us—"

She broke off and plunged into another period of reflection. Presently she was frowning, and the Wreck saw that she was clenching her fists.

"Henry Williams," she said, standing up and facing him, " I don't like it. I don't like it one bit. Bob Wells hasn't got any business to be chasing me!"

There were times when even the Wreck could be just to a foe.

"But, Sally, how does he know who he's chasing?"

"Doesn't make any difference. I said I didn't like it, and I don't. I won't stand for it. Bob Wells—chasing *me!*" And she again clenched her fists.

The Wreck had never been able to make anything out of women, and now he knew that he never would.

CHAPTER X

THE WRECK FIGHTS

SALLY did not get her emotions sorted out and classified in an orderly manner for the rest of the day. They insisted on mixing themselves up; they refused to stay where she tried to put them. Ordinarily she was of a temperament quite serene and obedient to her will, except, of course, when the Wreck charged into it like a frisky steer. Even on those occasions her departure from a normal calm was brief and largely superficial. But the news that Sheriff Bob Wells was going out with a posse upset her poise; it struck deeper, and affected her in so many different ways that she seemed to be spinning like a weather vane in a whirlwind.

She laughed, she was serious, she was scornful, she was angry, she was incredulous, she was alarmed —all these and other moods took possession of her, one giving way to another, only to come back and repeat itself after a while, so that the final result was to leave her in a very uncertain state of mind.

It did not help her that the Wreck seemed to be singularly unmoved by the news. He treated it as if it were a matter of small consequence. But Sally was not in the habit of steadying herself by leaning

on Henry Williams; she could only account for his
calmness by attributing it to a failure to realize the
situation. He did not know what it meant to have
a Montana sheriff and a posse hard on his heels,
but Sally did.

Even at that, she did not believe they would be
caught. Surely, she told herself, there would be a
way out of things. It was not pursuit and possible
capture that disturbed her and awakened every
absurdly conflicting emotion that lay within her;
it was the fact that Bob Wells was the instrument of
the law. That jarred her in a most illogical but
effective fashion. Any other sheriff might do his
duty without protest from Sally; but Bob Wells—
why did he go and run for sheriff, anyhow? He
had plenty of other things to keep him busy. If
he had not hustled around and got himself elected
sheriff, he could have ridden over to the railroad
with her and she would have been on the train long
ago. It was a fool trick for him to get into politics,
thought Sally.

"Don't let it worry you," said the Wreck.

"It doesn't worry me; I'm perfectly calm," retorted Sally.

"You're nervous, anyhow."

"I'm *not* nervous."

"I'm an expert on nerves," he said. "You can't
fool me. I've spent my money on specialists and I
know. Right now you're more nervous than I am—
and I'm a wreck."

There was a good deal of that kind of conversation all afternoon. The Wreck had an idea that if he could get her really angry she might forget about the sheriff for a while. But the only times she got angry were when she thought about Bob Wells, and then she was just as likely to be laughing again the next minute. As for getting angry at the Wreck, she refused. It was a form of comfort that was denied her, for some unaccountable reason.

"Bob Wells ought to have more sense than to let anybody fill him up with a fool story about four highwaymen," she said, as she sat down to peel potatoes for supper. "Why, there isn't any such thing as even one road agent, nowadays."

"We even have 'em in Pittsburgh, Sally."

"Pittsburgh! I'm tired of hearing about Pittsburgh. You'd think the sun rose and set in Pittsburgh."

"Not if you lived there," said the Wreck.

"Well, don't be holding it up as a model, anyhow. It sounds—provincial."

He refused to be irritated, which did not help Sally at all.

"But you'll see the sun rise and set there before I get through with it," he remarked, with a confident jerk of his head.

"Now, what do you mean by that?"

He explained, with a sudden enthusiasm that surprised her, that as soon as he had his process finished he was going to take the smoke out of Pittsburgh and take a lot of money away from the corporations that made the smoke. It was the first time

Sally ever heard him talk much about himself, except the nervous part. They knew he was a chemist, and that was about all. Dad Morgan, not being qualified in chemistry and regarding it as something that existed only in text-books, had never pressed inquiries. He assumed that the Wreck was some kind of a professor and let it go at that.

But it seemed that the Wreck was a chemist who did things in steel plants and he had picked up a lot of information about smoke, as well as a good deal of smoke itself. He was going to make Pittsburgh as smokeless as though it were run by electricity. It was only a question of time and patience and a little more research, he said. He explained the whole thing to Sally, with a lot of words that she did not understand; and while he was talking about Pittsburgh and what he was going to do to it, she also learned that he was born in Yonkers, New York, had three sisters, was a graduate of a college, had been to Europe twice, had lived a year in Australia, could play golf, hated the movies and was thirty-two years old.

"H'm," said Sally, who actually forgot about Bob Wells for a few minutes. "I thought you were older than that."

"That's because I'm all shot to pieces," he said, gloomily.

"What rank nonsense."

"Wait till you get insomnia."

"Bosh. You only think you're sick. Whatever made you nervous, anyhow?"

"Women."

She stared.

"Women?" she echoed. "Henry, are you joshing me?"

"It's a fact," said the Wreck. "I can't stand women. There's a pair of them in the laboratory. And three of them in the office. And seven in the boarding house. And thousands of 'em, going to work, and coming home, and butting into you, no matter where you go. I haven't got anything against 'em, but I just can't stand 'em."

Sally continued to stare.

"Did you ever take one of them to a movie?" she asked, curiously.

"Once. But she got sore at it and cried."

"Did you ever learn to dance?"

"No!"

"Did you ever sit on a front porch and talk to one of them?"

"Not unless they nailed me."

"And you think you're a woman hater?"

He looked at her in surprise.

"I didn't say I hated them. I don't. I just can't stand them. They make me nervous. They act so—" He stopped and appeared to discover that she was a woman. "I—excuse me."

"Certainly I'll excuse you," said Sally, "because you're a big idiot. Put on an apron and help me with these potatoes."

He was obeying her when Charley McSween came into the kitchen, burdened with two medium-sized grips and a ridiculous little bag that belonged to the Wreck.

"Seein as you've got convictions against rasslin' baggage," he said, "I fetched it up myself. Now, about accommodations." He scratched his ear. "When we have Chinks here, we sleep 'em off in a corner of the bunk house. But your wife ain't a Chink. We'd have plenty of room in the house, only the boss and family are here. There's one room left up-stairs, but she's awful small and I don't figure that she'll do for two people. Looks to me like Williams here—what's your first name, anyhow?"

"Henry," supplied Sally.

"Well, it looks to me like Henry 'd have to take the Chink corner of the bunk house. How about it, Henry?"

The Wreck said it would suit him exactly.

"The boys ain't like to bother you any, seein' as you're white," added Charley.

"They won't bother me," said the Wreck, significantly.

Sally was not so confident; she knew how "the boys" sometimes behaved when they had a dude on their hands. But she hoped that Charley was right, because the Wreck was not a patient young man and there was no telling what might happen if they started to haze him.

Four of the boys came in at supper time; there were three more who were out having a look at the fences and Charley said they might not be back for a couple of days. The quartet took one look into the kitchen and then made a quick start for the bunk house, where there was more scrubbing and shaving within the space of half an hour than Underwood's ranch had known since Charley could remember. Then they drifted into the kitchen and hung around.

Sally was always good to look at, even when she wore a big apron. If she was not downright pretty, she did not miss the mark by any noticeable distance. There was a smooth fluff in her brown hair that even Harriet Underwood might have envied. There was a steady, friendly look in her brown eyes, which were as fine and long-lashed as any pair that might have been found in the face of a beauty. Her lips had a pleasant curve when she smiled, showing strong, beautifully even teeth which even the Wreck had observed to be white beyond a fault.

The boys at Underwood's ranch even fell to cleaning their finger nails as they watched her. Somehow, without even so much as suggesting it by word or look, Sally had a way of creating in others—men, usually—an impulse to be neat. She did not mind having the boys sitting around the kitchen, even though they did not belong there until they were told to come and get supper. There was, however, one feature that bothered her. She had chosen to be from the East, like the Wreck, and it was not easy to play the part. There were lots of things that a tenderfoot was not supposed to know, or say, and it kept her constantly on guard to remember the fact. She found it safer to confine herself to "Yes," "No," and "Really?" so far as it was possible. The boys laid it to shyness, although that was not one of her traits.

Just as she feared, they found the Wreck amusing. A good deal of the conversation centered around his spectacles, which he wore, except for excursions into the dining-room. But some rare policy of restraint seemed to have settled upon him; he calmly ignored most of what they said, and when he did answer it was with an apparent good-nature that surprised Sally. She knew, however, that he was not bearing it as easily as he seemed to be; he was simply holding himself in. Evidently she had made him understand the need for caution, and for that she was thankful.

He spent most of his time in the dining-room, while the boys were having supper in the kitchen, where Sally did all the table-waiting that was necessary. It was during supper that Sally confirmed an idea which came instinctively to her when the boys first entered the kitchen. One of them, they called him "Mort," was a cow-puncher by occupation and a lady-killer by way of diversion. There was no denying his good looks; certainly Mort would not have denied them. He was young and slim and straight, with a bold, slightly amused look in his eyes and a small black mustache of which he made a great deal. He was a graceful youth, a little too confident, but obviously efficient. She could see that to Mort a sort of deference was paid by the other boys, particularly when it came to a matter of women. Probably without realizing it, they stood aside for him and gave him a clear path when petticoats came to the ranch.

She had seen other Morts in her young time, but always when she could control circumstances to suit herself. The covert way in which his glance constantly followed her was faintly irritating; she was conscious of it even when her back was toward him. His gestures and his speech were meant for her, and her alone, and she did not welcome the exclusiveness. Given the freedom of her true Montana status, Sally would have handled him without the least trouble in the world. He would not have bothered her at all; at least, not more than a few minutes. But being a temporary tenderfoot hampered her, and took away most of her natural weapons. Probably, under other circumstances, she would not even have taken the trouble to dislike him; but now she disliked him frankly.

One by one the other boys deserted the kitchen after supper, but Mort stayed. There seemed to be a tacit understanding that the field belonged to him, growing out of the futility of competition. He sat there, watching and talking with practiced ease, as she went about her work. Now and then the Wreck came in from the dining-room, where the Underwood family still sat in the thrall of Sally's first real meal. The Wreck, donning his spectacles, would eye him narrowly, but say nothing. As for Mort, he now ignored the Wreck completely, having made it clear some time earlier that he regarded him merely as a passing source of polite amusement.

Sally fidgeted. She did not want to lose her temper; she felt that there was enough trouble on her hands. She kept an uneasy watch upon the Wreck, not that she expected or wanted him to do anything, but rather fearing that he might attempt something beyond his scope. There were times when she even wished that Bob Wells might walk into the kitchen, because everything would then be simplified and settled. Bob knew exactly how to handle them. But there was nothing to do but play a lone rôle. She scorned to ask anybody for help.

The Wreck observed a flush in her cheeks when he came out of the dining-room for the last time and cleared a place for himself at the end of the kitchen table, at which he sat. He did not ask any questions; he merely observed a fact, and then went gravely about the business of eating his supper. Mort was laughing quietly. The presence of the Wreck did not seem to disturb him in the least degree; he did not seem to know that he was there.

"But you're goin' to like me a whole lot," said Mort, persuasively.

He was evidently reverting to a discussion from which the Wreck had been absent.

Sally made no answer. She was busy piling dishes in the sink and her back was turned toward the lady-killer.

"By and by there'll be a moon up," continued the cow-puncher, as he rolled himself another cigarette. "I'm a sort of an expert on moons, and walks, and things like that. I reckon we're goin' to have a look at that moon."

Sally continued to pile dishes. She was afraid that she was going to get angry, particularly with the Wreck sitting there and listening. She imagined him writhing on the edge of his chair. If she had turned around to look at him she would have been astonished and dismayed to observe his stolidity.

So whole-heartedly was the Wreck minding his own business that Mort did not even waste a glance on him as he rose languidly from his chair and strolled in the direction of the sink. But the Wreck was watching the lady-killer. He seemed to be studying the graceful swing of his walk and the youthfully arrogant tilt of his head as he approached Sally Morgan, as if they were something to be envied and almost admired.

"There ain't a reason in the world why you ain't goin' to like me," said Mort, softly. "Now, for instance."

There was skill and experience in the arm that slipped around Sally's waist. She leaped aside with a swift movement and faced the owner of the arm, her eyes blazing.

Simultaneously, the chair in which the Wreck had been sitting went over backward with a crash. But the Wreck did not go with it. He seemed, as nearly as Sally could figure, to arrive at the spot where Mort was standing at about the same time the back of the chair touched the floor. One of the finest china platters in the Underwood pantry was in his hand.

The platter rose and fell and splintered musically, all in a breath, its pieces falling in a sort of cascade around the lady-killer's head. But the Wreck did not pause to observe results. There were other things to be done, and he did them.

If Sally had attempted to analyze his style, even she might have regarded it as unethical. It was fettered by no observable rules. It was free and loose and versatile, rather than orthodox, and its dominant characteristic seemed to be speed. That, of course, made it exceedingly difficult to follow. Likewise, it made it difficult for Mort to establish successful competition. He did not happen to be wearing a gun; but that occasioned him no dismay, for he was correctly accounted to be a smart young man with his fists. What bothered him was the total irregularity of the affair and the fact that the Wreck seemed to be careless in his methods.

Part of the time the Wreck had both feet clear of the floor, the result of a climbing tendency. The lady-killer found it peculiarly disconcerting to be climbed by a wild man who wore horn-rimmed spectacles. The impact of the platter was merely a passing discomfort. It was the things that followed that really counted. He was cramped for room; he could not get his arms into action. He felt as though a large bee had picked him out as a thing to swarm upon. The bee clung amazingly.

Perhaps the Wreck did use his fingers and his

elbows, as well as his fists. Perhaps he even used a knee, now and then. It may have been that the top of his head more than once came in violent contact with the lady-killer's nose. It never occurred to him to break from the clinches, or to restrain an instinct that sent his hands searching for a wind-pipe to throttle. His sole idea was to remain at close quarters and do his work within the confines of an embrace.

Naturally, it could not last very long. Even a healthy young animal like Mort can be taken unaware and overwhelmed by a lawless fury from Pittsburgh. The lady-killer was suddenly tripped and went over on his back, and the Wreck finished it on the floor. When he arose he was gasping for breath and there was a cut on his cheek that bled in healthy fashion. But his spectacles were still in place and his gray eyes gleamed through them with fanatical fire.

Mort lay for half a minute, blinking slowly, while he tried to orient himself. He was not very pretty to look at; all the time he had spent in shaving and scrubbing was thrown away. His dazed glance fixed itself on Sally, then moved uncertainly in the direction of the Wreck. Presently he hitched himself wearily to a sitting posture and began the job of climbing to his feet. He was approximately erect, although swaying, when the Wreck closed in again. Sally gasped. Heavens, wasn't he satisfied? *She* was.

But the Wreck closed in not to fight. He merely

wanted to remove any further incentive to combat. He stooped, jammed one shoulder into the lady-killer's stomach and folded him over it. Staggering to the door, he pushed his way past three of the boys and Charley McSween, who had been standing there staring in, and chucked his burden half a dozen paces from the threshold. Then, without pausing for examination of his handiwork, he walked grimly back into the kitchen and resumed his place at the table.

"Do I get any coffee?" he demanded, irascibly, glaring at Sally.

He certainly got it.

CHAPTER XI

—AND RIDES

SALLY had very little speech with the Wreck that evening, and such words as they exchanged dealt with routine trivialities. He was not in conversational mood, finishing his supper in almost complete silence, but with excellent appetite. She waited upon him in an awed daze. There were a thousand things she wanted to say, but she could not bring herself to the point of breaking in upon his reverie. She would have liked to wash the cut on his face, where the blood had dried, but feared that he would resent attention.

When he finished supper, he mumbled something about taking a walk, and left the kitchen, plainly with no desire for company. It worried her a little when he did not come back; in fact, she did not see him again that evening. She did not know, of course, that the Wreck was haunted with the fear that she would try to thank him for something. He did not want to be thanked. Or, if it was not a case of thanks, and she wanted to scold him, he was in no mood to endure a reprimand. So he escaped.

A couple of hours later, as she sat outside the kitchen door, studying a landscape half lighted by

the moon, she glimpsed a figure against the skyline of a low ridge, and she thought, of course,
that it was the Wreck in search of lonesome con-
solation. She sighed and was sorry for him. She
did not learn until next day that the figure was
probably that of the lady-killer enjoying the moon
by himself, for it appeared that the Wreck had
been sound asleep in the bunk house for more than
an hour.

As she went up to bed her mind was still filled
with wonder and not a little apprehension. He was
altogether too unexpected and disconcerting, she
thought; he never gave anybody warning. If it had
been somebody else, there would have been words;
even Bob Wells would have said something before
he began the thrashing. She smiled involuntarily
as she recalled an earlier wish that Bob might walk
into the kitchen in order to save a situation. It did
not appear that there had been any urgent need of
his services.

"Nevertheless, Henry Williams is going to get
himself into trouble," she mused. "He just won't
learn to restrain himself, and I don't seem to be
able to do a thing with him. But it was dear of
him, all the same. My, how he can fight!"

She found him in the kitchen next morning, with
a fire started and a kettle set to boil, and looking
as nearly contented as he ever did. She did not
want him to think she was ungrateful, so she forced
herself into an expression of thanks. The Wreck
merely grunted and changed the subject by telling

her how poorly he was sleeping, which relieved her because it was a sign that he was normal again. After a while he disappeared, to get the dining-room ready for breakfast.

Charley McSween came in cautiously.

" 'Mornin', ma'am."

"Good morning," said Sally.

He sent a glance slowly about, then breathed like a man relieved at the failure to find something.

"Where's the Bengal tiger, ma'am?" he asked, respectfully.

"He's setting the table, I believe," and she smiled.

"I was kind of afraid he wouldn't shrink back to household chores, Mis' Williams. But I'm sure glad he's on the job. I reckon you've got the trick of handlin' him, although offhand I'd say it must be kind of complicated."

Sally was not at all sure she had the trick, but said nothing.

"Mort, he's gone off ridin' fences," said Charley, after a pause. "He's feelin' sort of set back. I didn't see the start of it, but I come runnin' when I heard the crockery. Mort, he's a pretty fair hand, but he ain't very intelligent in his head when it comes to women bein' around. I'm sure sorry. He got what was comin' to him. Seemed to me like it was done efficient and prompt, although Mort was tellin' a couple of the boys afterward that it was on account of all civilized rules bein' ignored and obliterated."

"Was he hurt much?" asked Sally.

"Not bodily, ma'am; nothing permanent. He just sort of had his pride tromped on. It was a kind of sudden thing to look at, if I do say it, and I've seen various kinds. The boys say Mort is talkin about askin' for his time. I sure hope the Nubian lion has finished his rampagin' for the present. I'm gettin' short-handed."

Sally bit her lip and looked in the direction of the pantry.

"The part of it that puzzles me," said Charley, "is whether I didn't quite understand you right yesterday, ma'am. I been goin' round with the idea that you told me your husband wasn't very strong."

"Why, he—" She did not know exactly what she wanted to say. "There are times when he has nervous strength, Mr. McSween."

Charley nodded thoughtfully.

"I reckon that's it," he remarked. "I hope he don't get nervous too often. Might I ask, ma'am, if he's got different styles of killin' cow-hands, or is he always partial to climbin' and clingin'?"

"I'm afraid he's rather versatile," said Sally.

"That's what I told Mort, so he wouldn't feel like any improper advantage had been seized and acted upon. Mort claimed if it had been regular rules he would have won. But the boys and me sized it up from all angles possible and figured different. We allowed that the Tasmanian devil was liable to wallop him any style, regular or volunteer."

The Wreck came into the kitchen and found Sally laughing. He looked suspiciously at Charley McSween.

" 'Mornin', Henry," said Charley.

"Good morning."

"You're lookin' excellent." There was a look of puzzled respect in Charley's eyes.

"Feeling all right," said the Wreck, shortly.

Charley hesitated for a few seconds, with a thought in his mind, but somewhat uncertain as to the expression of it.

"If it's just the same to you, Henry, we'll sort of keep the late unpleasantness confidential between us. The boss and the family would be liable to get the idea we ain't got the right kind of discipline. They've just come through an experience that has harrowed 'em some and they're kind of jumpy. I'd like to keep things as smooth as possible, barrin', of course, such times as questions of personal honor arises."

"You don't hear me saying anything," observed the Wreck.

Charley nodded.

"That's the right idea, Henry. That sure is satisfactory to me. And—oh. Come to remember, Mort told the boys that there wasn't anybody tipped him off the lady was married. It sort of surprised him when he found out what was the movin' spirit in bringin' about his downfall. He seemed to be kind of upset at not havin' due notice of matrimony."

"What good would that have done him?" inquired the Wreck, coldly.

"Mort says he'd have laid off if he had only knew."

The Wreck shook his head.

"I was going to lick him anyhow," he remarked. Charley eyed him with renewed interest.

"Kind of a personal antipathy, I reckon," he mused.

"Kind of."

"H'm. I hope it don't happen, Henry, that you've took any wild longin' to overcome and abolish a humble instrument of Providence?"

The Wreck grinned, and Charley nodded his head, reassured.

"I'm old in sin and misdeeds," he said, "and it ain't likely I'm ever goin' to show any noticeable improvement. But somehow I ain't ready to be repealed. You young folks just keep on washin' dishes and cookin' and honeymoonin' for a while, and I reckon everything's goin' to come out nifty and proper."

Charley was drifting out the door when he remembered something.

"The sheriff phoned in a while back. It seems he's gettin' under way. The boss has sure got him stirred up."

Sally and the Wreck exchanged a long glance, she pursing her lips tightly.

"I suppose I'm silly," she said, "but I don't like it, just the same. Bob's an awfully smart sheriff, everybody says. He finds out all sorts of things."

"Stop worrying," said the Wreck.

"Oh, I'm not. It doesn't scare me the least bit. Only— Oh, well, of course he isn't supposed to know. He'd never dream of it, naturally. But it's not very nice."

There was a troubled look in her eyes all forenoon, but the Wreck did not know it, for he disappeared after the morning dish-washing. He hated
to wash dishes; his very soul rose in rebellion. The
only reason he endured it was because Sally would
have to wash them herself if he did not. Women
were always imposing obligations on people even
without making any demands, he reflected irritably.
You had to do things for them, or you felt mean
inside. The lesser evil was to do things.

Sally's day did not brighten until afternoon, when
Charley made a suggestion. The Underwoods had
ridden back into the hills to see some of the prize
cattle; they might not be back until late. If Sally
and the Wreck wanted to take a couple of horses
and looked around a bit they could have their pick
of what was left in the corral. Charley thought he
could find a riding skirt for her; there were always
some outfits for possible guests.

Sally jumped at the chance, but looked doubtfully
at the Wreck.

"Henry is not very fond of horses," she said.

"I'm crazy about 'em," he retorted.

They discovered when they went down to the
corral that Charley was going with them. It suited
Sally, who felt that he would be useful if the Wreck
got himself into trouble. She did not know that
Charley's precaution lay in another direction; he
was running no chance of losing a cook and a cookee.
The Wreck merely scowled as he climbed grimly
into the hated saddle. Perhaps there was a ray of
sunshine in the fact that he was not riding a sorrel,

but he was not very hopeful that grays behaved any better. Charley, however, said the gray was gentle and that anybody could ride him—that is, anybody within reason. It was plain that he was not optimistic as he watched the Wreck mount.

Setting off across a bit of undulating grass country, they were presently climbing gradually into the hills. Sally was athrill; she loved to ride and Charley had given her a mount that was beautifully gaited. But the Wreck rode with a single passionate determination—not to fall off. One hand tightly gripped the pommel, and he pulled leather even at a walk. All this was quite as Charley expected; he had seen them from the East before, and most of them were alike.

Sally, however, did not fit the picture he had fashioned in his mind. He kept an eye on her for some fifteen minutes before he said anything, watching the easy and confident sway of her body, the manner in which she used her hands, and all the unconscious tricks of people who are bred to the range.

"I reckon there must be quite a piece of ranch country around Pittsburgh," said Charley.

"Ranch?" echoed the Wreck, who was riding in the middle, with Charley bringing up in the rear. "Not within a million miles."

"Honest, now? Watchin' your wife, I'd have been ready to swear to it. It's queer how quick people can pick some things up."

Sally turned an inquiring glance, swinging about in her saddle as she did so.

"I been watchin' you ride, ma'am," explained Charley.

She flushed slowly, then faced to the front again. "I've been West before," she called. "And, of course, there are *some* horses around Pittsburgh."

"Yes, ma'am; I figured you must have been West."

She might have known he would, if she had stopped to think anything about it. But it was rather annoying to be caught unawares. Perhaps it did not make any difference, although it might awaken the suspicions as well as the surprise of Charley McSween. She was beginning to see how difficult it was to play parts; she had never tried, until now, to be anything except exactly what she was.

"When I was a little girl," she added.

"Yes, ma'am. That's the time to learn things, when you're little. Now, Henry, here—"

The Wreck's horse recovered himself from a stumble, and the rider recovered, too, but after an alarming lurch.

"Just kind of hold yourself loose," advised Charley. "As I was sayin', Henry, not bein' broke to it in early youth, is liable to be a little mite slower pickin' up all the habits and customs to which horseflesh is addicted. But he's doin' real well. I ain't claimin' he can ride like Mort— S-h, now!"

The Wreck had brought the gray's head up with a savage yank and was trying to turn in his saddle.

"Easy on him, Henry. I wasn't meanin' to cast any reflections. I reckon you'll be ridin' as well as

Mort in no time at all. I was only considerin' the differences in human upbringin'. Now, as for fightin', free style and unrestrained, there ain't any legitimate comparison. It's kind of like a prairie dog tryin' to commit felonious assault on a çoyote, Mort bein' the first named. But you got to admit that even a prairie dog knows *some* things. I reckon Henry—"

Sally interrupted with a question about the size of the Underwood ranch, and after that she kept up a flow of questions. She wanted Charley to let the Wreck alone, and after a while Charley took the hint, though reluctantly.

Up in the hills they met a couple of the boys, who pulled off the trail and made room for them, bowing to Sally and casting upon the Wreck glances of solemn but curious deference. If they had grinned at his horsemanship there was no telling the consequences; but they were wholly respectful until he passed by, and then their offense was nothing worse than a wink at Charley.

The Wreck did not enjoy his ride. He never did, although it would have been useless to expect him to admit it. The gray horse was as bad as the sorrel; all horses were bad. If only he knew where Charley had hidden the front wheel of the flivver he could laugh at every horse in Montana. But just now there was a certain method in his grim purpose to stay in the saddle. If things came to the worst, he and Sally could steal horses, and with that event as a possibility he was behooved to learn something about this painful and primitive method of travel.

Sally had just suggested that they turn back, certain that by the time they reached the house the Wreck would have enough for the day, when they encountered the Underwoods—father, son, and daughter. It was her first close glimpse of the family, and she studied them with interest, especially Harriet. Charley performed the introduction.

"Mis' Williams here is the lady who does our celebrated cookin'. There ain't anything further that needs to be said. Henry I reckon you've all met. He is likewise expert in his chosen line."

The Underwoods did not pay much attention to the Wreck, but they were frankly interested in Sally. Even Jerome Underwood was disposed to be gracious, for he was not unmindful of the dishes that came to his table. It was his first experience with a woman cook at the ranch, and it suited him so well that he had forgotten all the admonitions of his New York specialist.

Charley and Sally and the Wreck trailed along with the Underwoods on the homeward ride. The three members of the family rode well, and the Wreck found a new reason for hating them. The only thing that gave him any satisfaction was the fact that nobody appeared to notice his horn-rimmed spectacles. Beyond that, he did not enjoy himself at all, even though Harriet Underwood, with all her blond charm, happened to fall in beside him as they followed the trail.

He was in no mood for appreciation of Harriets, for the saddle galled him and his legs ached and the gray horse had a viciously disturbing canter. Harriet herself was unaccustomed to gentlemen who washed dishes, even in the freedom of the West; but at that she would have been willing to chat with him if he was so inclined. But he rode silent and scowling, knowing that he was a grotesque figure—preferring to brood rather than to converse.

Underwood and his foreman rode together, talking of the ranch. That left Sally and Chester Underwood paired. Chester found himself in a state of agreeable surprise. He did not know that cooks were young and good to look at, and knew how to sit in a saddle. He did not know that they could laugh and talk and be unaffectedly interesting at the same time. But he discovered all these things, and he forgot that the ranch bored him. He had quite a gay time of it all the way home. People from the East always had an interest for Sally; she liked to hear about things of which she knew very little, being possessed of a healthy and enthusiastic curiosity. She led him to talk as much as he would, and found him willing.

Watching from the rear, the Wreck's brooding turned into a morose channel. Why was it that he couldn't talk to a woman in that fashion? He knew that he had none of the graces; he scorned them. But why were they given to the stripling sons of rich men? How did it come that he was always clumsy and ill at ease whenever a woman was about?

Even Sally Morgan bothered him. If she bothered him, why didn't she bother Chester Underwood? But she didn't; not a bit. Nor did Chester

Underwood bother her. But Henry Williams did; the Wreck knew it. She was on an easy footing of comradeship with the newcomer in five minutes; it was always the same way with ranch hands, or anybody else. But with himself he felt that she was constantly under a constraint, even though she tried to mask it. She never understood him; sometimes she laughed at him; sometimes he was certain that she had a sense of pity for him, a realization that fairly sickened him. What the devil was the matter with him anyhow? And with her?

When the ranch house came into sight, some idiot urged his horse to a gallop. The Wreck assumed that it was Chester, but he could not be sure. He was too busy. The gray galloped also; he had a brainless way of imitating other horses. Everybody galloped. The Wreck survived the gallop by some astonishing trick of fortune, but he did not survive the sudden stop at the gate of the corral. He went right on for a little distance, reaching the ground on all fours. As he slowly arose he became aware that Chester was grinning down at him.

His hands rolled themselves into fists automatically, and he took a step forward. Then Sally was at his side, gripping him firmly by the arm.

"Let go of me," he said savagely. "I'm all right."

"Why, of course you are, Henry." And then, in a whisper: "You come with me. You're not going to do any fighting to-day. I'm ashamed of you. Henry Williams, you're worse than a locoed steer. I don't know what I'll do with you."

CHAPTER XII

THE SHERIFF ARRIVES

WILD, and yet wilder, were the tales that came from the Underwood family concerning the short and simple incident of borrowed gasoline. Even Charley McSween conceded that the West must be reverting to halcyon times. Jerome Underwood stuck to his four bandits with a tenacity worthy of the best possible imagination. Harriet Underwood, at first disposed to be literal and to report only those things which she saw, remembered that she was clever enough to slip her rings down her neck, where they scratched but were otherwise safe. She had held her ringless fingers out for the inspection of the man with the gun, and he growled at her.

Chester confirmed the four bandits, because he had wisdom enough to see that his father might appreciate confirmation. There was a note of repressed heroism in Chester. Several times he had been about to leap; all that restrained him, it appeared, was a fear that when the shooting began others than himself might fall as sacrifices in the horrid fusillade. He told all this to Sally during the ride back to the house, with a gay nonchalance that surprised her. She had an idea that resourceful lying rarely came before middle age, so that she was driven to believe that Chester was either precocious or prematurely advanced in years. Chester was a large, strongly built youth, doubtless capable of bandits as well as football; but, knowing him for a liar, she found herself filled with an ungracious undercurrent of doubt concerning the precise status of his nerve.

The most surprising development involved Timothy, the Underwood chauffeur. Timothy had begun by being literal. He had been heard to say that there was but one bandit. But he multiplied by six, perhaps inadvertently, perhaps because he drew inspiration from higher sources. At any rate, he did not spoil matters; he magnified.

He ran the chance of denunciation by a determination to be with the progressives rather than the conservatives. There were six bandits, and even Jerome Underwood admitted that Timothy might be right; for chauffeurs had good eyesight, else they would not be employed as such. Six bandits, of whom Timothy personally observed five at close range and sensed the presence of another, standing in the gloom at the side of the road, with a sawed-off shotgun in the hollow of his arm and a disposition that yearned for provocation.

Sally and the Wreck discussed these matters when they were certain that nobody eavesdropped. The Wreck did not view the situation graciously.

"Liars," he said.

"But don't you forget yourself and say it," warned Sally.

"What do they need to lie for?"

"What difference does it make? And it's better for us, isn't it?"

He jerked his head in a familiar, irascible way.

"Four!" he said. "Six! They talk as if somebody turned out the army."

"Let them talk. I hope they run it up to a dozen."

"It makes me writhe."

"Well, stop it. You don't see me writhing. Henry, I believe you're jealous. I believe your nose is clear out of joint because they don't stick to just one. Why, I honestly believe you want to be *accused*."

He made a gesture of angry dissent.

"You let them have as many as they want," advised Sally. "And if you've got any pride about what you did, swallow it. It 'll only get you into trouble—both of us. Anyhow, you ought to take it as a compliment. They've got you equal to six men."

"I hate liars," said the Wreck.

"Well, we're liars," she declared cheerfully. "Yes, we are. We've lied about ourselves by not telling the truth. That's the worst kind of lying. It's sneaky."

The Wreck stiffened.

"All right. We'll go and tell 'em," he said.

Sally shook her head.

"Oh, no, we won't. We'll just stand pat. If it

was just you, you could do as you pleased. But part of it's me. And if you've got a New England conscience bothering you, I haven't—right now."

"Pittsburgh's not in New England."

"Yonkers, then."

"Nor Yonkers, either."

"Oh, stop arguing."

But they argued nevertheless; not in a very dignified way, Sally was ready to admit. It impressed her as being juvenile. Argument, however, seemed to be the only common ground on which they could meet. She despaired of ever getting Henry Williams to agree with her about anything. His own frame of mind was exactly the same. There was no logic in her. Neither of them realized that it was inaction that galled, rather than suspense.

Timothy, the chauffeur, ate his meals in the kitchen. He was a respectful creature, although he came from New York. He always said "sir" and "ma'am," until Sally was in fidgets over his deferential speech. He had a mild glance that followed her wherever she went, which the Wreck observed, and of course mistook. So he formed a dislike for Timothy, who did not exactly cringe under his obvious displeasure, but who met it with a patient submission that was worse than defiance. There was no harm in Timothy; he merely lied through force of higher example. And if he admired Sally, he was not alone. So did the boys who worked on the ranch, although they were careful to remember what happened to Mort. Dudes were fair game, and the Wreck was one; but they observed a caution born out of a memory of what happened to the lady-killer. They needed no word of advice from Charley McSween. Mort was out on the range somewhere, recovering his beauty, and they remembered it every time they looked at Sally.

Most annoying of all the people at the ranch, so far as the Wreck was concerned, was Chester Underwood. Chester, having discovered Sally on horseback, was rediscovering her in the kitchen. If he had any previous ideas on the subject of caste, he forgot them in the democracy of Montana. He kept drifting in and out, on pretexts, and sometimes he sat down and watched her as she worked with her sleeves rolled up on brown arms. To Chester the Wreck was merely a person who washed dishes, waited on table, and fell off horses—quite uninteresting and not a claimant for notice.

The washer of dishes found himself growing surly, without knowing why. The able-bodied heir of Jerome Underwood was not worth bothering about, so long as he stuck to his own business and did not annoy the Wreck. He could talk to Sally, if he chose, and if Sally chose to talk to him, which it seemed that she did. He could even sit around and tell lies, glibly but clumsily, and there was no real reason for interfering with him. But he was an irritant, nevertheless, although the Wreck never clearly identified him as such. He thought that he was ignoring Chester, not realizing that his subconscious self was constantly aware of him.

Sally was growing restive. The labor of cooking for a large household did not dismay her, although it was not exactly recreation. She did enough cooking at the Bar-M, where there were not so many mouths to be fed. It was the fact that she seemed to have settled into a routine that apparently led nowhere. She wanted to be moving again, although the time and the means had not presented themselves. She did not know whether she wanted to go on to Chicago, or back to the Bar-M; but she wanted to go somewhere. It was her duty to be cautious; she did not forget that. But no matter how necessary it might be to remain in hiding, it was also irksome. Being young, she did not have the patience that comes with years. But she kept a grip on herself because there did not seem to be anything else to do.

Anything that broke the routine, however, was welcome, even an invitation from Chester for a ride over the hills. She went, and there were just two in the party. Nobody had invited the Wreck, and as it was not Sally's party, he could not fairly expect it. She did not believe that he cared to go, anyhow, for he hated horses. As she and Chester rode off he stood leaning against the frame of the kitchen door glowering at them. It would not have been a good time for anybody to offer him pleasantries.

He felt unaccountably lonesome as Sally's horse disappeared over a rise. All the way from Pittsburgh to the Bar-M he never suffered from lonesomeness, although there were days when he scarcely exchanged a word with anybody. But now it seemed that the world conspired to isolate him, and he resented the conspiracy. He knew that he could not ride a horse, and he did not want to try; but he hated to have anybody else recognize the fact. Not that he wanted to have a woman hanging around him, for they always made him uncomfortable. Even Sally disturbed him, and he felt that he knew her better than any of the others. But she was an involuntary partner in certain affairs, and he had an uncomfortable sense of being deserted as she rode away.

He went back into the kitchen after a while, where Timothy sat in a corner reading a magazine. There were some dishes that belonged in the pantry, and the Wreck started thither with them. His foot tripped against a chair leg, and two of the dishes slid off the top of the pile and splintered on the floor. The Wreck stood scowling at them until he heard a snicker from the corner. Timothy was grinning with good-natured amusement.

"Huh?" demanded the Wreck.

"Comes out of your wages, I guess," observed Timothy. "I bet you must bust quite a lot."

The Wreck placed the remainder of the dishes on the table and selected the top one.

"I'm going to bust more," he said.

As Timothy dodged the dish he uttered a yell of surprise. It hit the wall just behind his chair. A second one was not so well aimed, for it went through a window. But Timothy did not wait for any improvement in the marksmanship. He bolted for the door, which he reached while the fourth dish was in the air. It crashed against the jamb and most of the pieces fell outside.

The Wreck surveyed the marks of his achievement, shrugged his shoulders, lifted the pile of dishes from the table, and resumed his journey to the pantry.

"Damn that Underwood pup," he said.

Timothy had not personally figured in the matter at all, so far as the Wreck was concerned. He was merely a symbol.

Late in the afternoon the Wreck went for a walk. He could have taken a horse if he wished, but he scorned such things. Horses were only to be ridden as a matter of necessity. His impulse was to take the trail that led back into the hills; it was in that direction Sally and Chester had ridden. But he sternly compelled himself to follow the wheel tracks that went toward the main road. Let her stay out riding as long as she liked; it was no affair of his.

He did not pay much attention to the trail. His mind was concentrated on the problem of where Charley McSween had hidden the wheel of the flivver. In odd hours he had been searching furtively, but without the least satisfactory result. The flivver was locked in a shed, into which he could have easily broken; but he knew that it was useless to search there. Charley would not have made things quite so simple as that. The wheel was somewhere else, and it would be time enough to break into the shed when he located it. Several times he considered the advisability of trying to thrash the truth out of Charley, but Sally always vetoed the project. She had respect for his prowess, but she was by no means sure that he could whip everybody on the ranch. Even if he did, there was no certainty that Charley would tell.

He was still walking slowly, his eyes staring at the ground, when a drumming sound caught his ears. Instinctively, he paused to listen. Horses. They were coming nearer, too. Probably Sally and Chester had been circling around through the hills, he thought. Well, if that was the case, he had no desire to meet them. He did not want Sally to get the notion in her head that he was eavesdropping or that he had the least interest in anything that she did. So he stepped off the trail.

There were clumps of young spruce on every hand, and he moved around behind one of them, where he could not be readily seen. The hoof-beats continued to grow louder, and the Wreck, crouching, peered through his screen for a view of the trail.

Only one horse, after all, he decided a few seconds later, but it was moving briskly. Then, around a turn in the trail, it appeared. It was a big, black animal, with a long stride, and the man who rode it was also big. A rifle in a holster hung suspended from the saddle. The Wreck, staring curiously, also had time to note that there were two guns at the belt of the rider. Then the black horse drummed on, out of sight.

"Doggone!" said the Wreck aloud, as he stepped from behind his spruce shelter and stared down the trail.

The rider was Bob Wells, the sheriff.

Not long did the Wreck stand in dismayed consideration of his discovery. He clenched his fists and set off at a dog trot toward the ranch house in the wake of the black horse.

He did not attempt to analyze the situation very closely as he ran. There would be time for that later, if indeed it ever reached the point of analysis. The obvious thing to do was to get back to the house as rapidly as possible, and he was doing it. There was Sally to be warned, if ever he got there in time. He groaned as he thought of Sally suddenly confronted by the sheriff. If everything was coming down in a crash he wanted to be there when it happened.

The Wreck found himself running with a steadiness that surprised him. He did not try to sprint. He could not overtake the black horse, anyhow, and there would be nothing to gain if he did. Not being able to guess just how far he had walked, he conserved himself. Step after step he plugged away, slowing a bit on the up-grades, letting himself out on the down-grades, and fighting hard for his second wind. The main thing was to get there as soon as he could. After that it would be time to see what there was to be done about Bob Wells.

When the trail emerged at last from the spruce he came to a halt, panting sharply as he stared in the direction of the ranch buildings. The land was open all the rest of the way to the house, and there was no concealment, if he needed any, so he deemed it wise to make a reconnaissance. He had no notion of being headlong about anything, for his mind was cool, despite his anxiety about Sally Morgan. If she had returned from the ride there was no telling what might have happened.

He could see no sign of the sheriff or the black horse; probably they were around at the front of the house. He could not see anybody. So he struck out at a bold walk to cover the few hundred yards that intervened between himself and the kitchen door. By the time he reached the goal he had recovered his breath.

The first thing he did was to peer cautiously into the kitchen. Nobody in sight, not even Timothy. There was no kettle on the stove, which meant that Sally was still away. He was tempted to steal through the house and see if the sheriff was out front, but abandoned the idea, because he could see nothing to be gained, even if he made the discovery. After a moment of thought he turned his steps in the direction of the corral.

The black horse was there, still saddled. The Wreck stared grimly at the beast, which he had seen before at the Bar-M, and of which he knew the sheriff was uncommonly proud. Bob Wells was undoubtedly up at the house, talking to Underwood and hearing new lies about the hold-up. Sally was still somewhere out on the trail with Chester Underwood. There was nothing for the Wreck but waiting.

He sat on the grass and propped his back against the corral fence, keeping watch upon the trail that led back to the hills, and also upon the house. If he saw the sheriff coming for his horse he would disappear behind the nearest shed. If Sally came first he would be there to warn her. He found little comfort in inaction, but it was the only course for the present.

Half an hour later, still huddled against the fence, he thought he saw a dust cloud on the back trail. Polishing his spectacles, he restored them to his nose for another observation. Sure enough, there were two riders coming. They were coming at a gallop, too, and soon they were so near that he could identify Sally beyond any mistake. There was a fine grace and confidence in the way Sally handled herself in a saddle, and it was not lost even upon the Wreck, poor horseman that he was. She could ride rings around Chester Underwood.

He climbed to his feet as Sally swung herself out of the saddle, and she saw him for the first time. She flashed her quirt in salute.

"Hello, Henry. We've had a bully ride."

"Uhuh," he answered with a nod.

When she saw the look in his eye she knew instantly that something was going to happen. She hoped that he was not going to be so foolish as to have a quarrel with Chester. She knew exactly what he thought of young Mr. Underwood, for he never

made a point of concealing emotions. But a quarrel
would be senseless. Besides, she had a right to go
riding if she chose; kitchen hours were long enough,
Heaven only knew.

The Wreck, however, was paying no attention to
Chester. His gaze remained fixed on Sally. He
was trying to give her a warning before she might
betray herself into an indiscretion. Not being adept
at expressing his thoughts, save in words, the best
he could do was to fashion his features into a queer,
baleful grimace. Sally was puzzled, and she showed
it by a wrinkling of her forehead, which signified
inquiry. What on earth was he trying to tell her?

Chester slid off his horse, so that for an instant
his back was turned. The Wreck quickly laid a forefinger against his lips and jerked his head in the
direction of the corral.

Sally looked, then stared, her mouth opening
slowly. She knew the black horse out of a million.
Bob Wells! Swiftly her glance swung in the direction of the house.

"Well," said Chester, "shall we go up to the
house? I'll see you all the way home, you know."

Sally recovered herself and smiled.

"You go ahead," she said. "Thanks ever so much
for the ride. I want to talk to Henry for a minute."

CHAPTER XIII

A WOMAN'S PLACE

WHEN Chester was beyond ear-shot she turned to the Wreck and almost smothered him in an avalanche of questions. He told it rapidly, while Sally kept an anxious eye on the house. When he finished she sent another glance in the direction of the black horse, who was unconscious of having created a sensation profound and disturbing.

"You don't suppose he's tracked us?" mused Sally.

"How could he?"

"I don't see how he could either. But Bob's awfully smart when it comes to being sheriff. If he knows we're here, the jig's up, of course."

Scorn and defiance shone in the eyes of the Wreck.

"It's a hundred to one he doesn't know we're here," he said. "It's a thousand to one he hasn't any idea who he's after. He's probably come for some more information. And they're all lying so hard that he'll never find out anything."

"Hope so," said Sally doubtfully. "How long do you suppose he's going to stay?"

"Haven't an idea. Not long, I guess, unless he's loafing on his job."

"Oh, Bob never loafs. He's too active. He's a real sheriff."

The Wreck was tired of hearing the sheriff's virtues related, but he side-stepped an argument on the point.

"Well, what are you going to do?" he asked. "Go out in the hills and hide?"

"No-o. We can't do that. But do we dare go up to the house?"

"If we don't, who gets the supper?"

"Oh, I suppose we do," she said wearily. "But if Bob should happen to walk into the kitchen—" She finished it with a gesture.

"He won't. He's busy with Underwood. Got to take a chance, anyhow."

"Yes; we've got to."

They walked briskly to the house, praying that the sheriff would stay somewhere around the front until they reached the kitchen. Sally did not breathe comfortably until she made certain that the kitchen was empty. The Wreck moved over to the pantry door and bolted it.

"Only one door to watch now," he said.

"Unbolt it, Henry. Suppose he comes in the other way? I'm going through that pantry in one jump. And *vice versa*, if he comes in from the pantry. I'm not going to be bottled up."

He unbolted the door and Sally went nervously about the work of getting supper.

"You'd better be careful there's nobody in the

living-room when you set the table," she warned him. "Take a good look first."

It happened there was nobody in the living-room. As nearly as the Wreck could judge, the sheriff and Mr. Underwood were sitting out front. Every minute or so Sally went to a window that commanded a view of the corral to see whether the black horse was still there. It always was. She was overcoming her first dismay, and in place of it was growing angry.

The old unreasoning resentment against Bob Wells was returning. It made no difference if he did not know who he was pursuing; from the standpoint of Sally it was no less unpleasant. Nor was she any too certain that he would abandon the chase if he knew, for he was conscientious to the leaning-backward point—a regular bull-dog. He had a habit of talking about enforcing the law impartially against all evil-doers; he even boasted about it. She remembered when it seemed to sound very well; but that was before she had a posse on her trail. She wondered how far Bob Wells would really go, if he learned the truth. She was none too sure.

When Charley McSween came in she jumped at the sound of his step and a fork clattered on the floor.

"That's company," said Charley. "And it happens we've got company, ma'am. The sheriff of this sovereign and God-fearin' county has dropped in to get a little mite more information about these desperadoes that he's expectin' to exterminate. I just eased in to tell you he's stayin' to supper. Set another plate in the dinin'-room, Henry. He's goin' to eat with the family."

"One more doesn't make any difference," said Sally with an effort at lightness.

"It does with the sheriff, ma'am. He's a powerful eater. I've seen him work. He's a powerful talker, too. He's been workin' up a real good appetite, talkin' to Mr. Underwood. It seems he's aimin' to do great things in the line of makin' the county safe for democracy. He's been tellin' quite a lot about some of the things he has done already, and the samples is impressive. He's got a posse down the road a piece, waitin' for developments. To-morrow, as near as I can make out, they're goin' to raise hell among the wicked."

Sally winced inwardly. Charley was putting things in his own words, of course; but somehow it sounded strangely as if Bob Wells himself were talking.

"So you'd best get plenty, ma'am," concluded Charley, "for he sure has talked himself empty."

All of this brought a grin to the face of the Wreck, which Sally observed, but did not dare resent. But she turned to him abruptly when Charley went out, her mind filled with another thought.

"If he stays to supper, that means you can't wait on the table, Henry."

"I'm not kicking."

"Maybe not.   But who's going to take your place? *I* can't."

"I should say not.   I guess we can get one of the boys."

Sally shook her head.   She knew cowpunchers.

"Timothy!" said the Wreck suddenly.

"But I wonder if he will," she mused.

"He will; don't worry."

"Have you been fighting with Timothy?" and she eyed him suspiciously.

"Lord, no!   Timothy won't fight anybody.   But he'll wait on the table."

She knew that something had passed between the Wreck and Timothy.   She might have guessed if she had counted the dishes.

"There'll have to be a reason for it," she said. "You'll have to be sick.   You'll have to go down to the bunk house and stay there."

"And suppose this sheriff comes in while you're up here alone?"

"Oh, I can take care of myself."

He did not like the idea of leaving her to face possible consequences, but he could see that it might be necessary.   It would take a real reason to avert any possible speculations in the mind of Charley McSween, who still had a way of reverting to the fact that Henry Williams was not "very strong," and who always grinned faintly when he mentioned it.

The Wreck found Timothy in the shed where they kept the big car.   He was passing the time in grinding valves. There was a faint look of alarm in his eyes as he beheld the thrower of dishes.

"You're to wait on the table to-night," said the Wreck bluntly. "Better go up to the kitchen now."

"*Me* wait on the table? I never did. I don't know how. What for?"

"Because I'm sick."

"You don't look sick," said Timothy. "And you didn't act sick a while back."

"I'm sick," repeated the Wreck. "How I look has nothing to do with it. It's nerves. One of my spells is coming on. It was beginning this afternoon —just beginning, you understand?"

The look that he gave Timothy bored him like an auger.

"I tried to walk it off, but I couldn't. It's coming on again. It gets worse. If I don't get to bed there's no telling—"

Timothy began wiping his hands on a ball of cotton waste.

"I'll wait on the table," he said gloomily. "Only if I don't do it right they haven't got any license to bawl me out. You better go get into bed right away."

The Wreck went off to the bunk house, where he stretched himself on the blankets and tried to get interested in an old magazine. He felt like a man who had retreated under fire, but he knew there was nothing else to do. What worried him most was the possibility that Sally might face a crisis alone. If anything happened he wanted to be there.

Sally did not find Timothy particularly deft, although he seemed to be willing enough, once she had an apron on him. She instructed him in some of the rudiments, and had him practicing at the kitchen-table, with imaginary guests to be served.

"It's only for this evening, I'm sure," she said. "Henry is almost certain to be better in the morning."

Timothy said he hoped so, because the boss was always fussy about how his meals were served, having lived in New York most of his life.

Sally felt easier in mind when he reported that the family and the sheriff were at the table. It gave her a breathing spell. She knew that Bob was not likely to get up from the table so long as there was anything more to be served. Eating, to him, was a pleasurable job of stoking, as she had learned from plenty of experience at the Bar-M. He was even slightly vain of his achievements as a trencherman; Charley had been entirely right about it. So she kept Timothy busy between kitchen and dining-room, carrying things that made him so hungry to look at that he could scarcely wait for his own turn.

In fact, he did not wait, for on one of his trips back to the kitchen Sally observed that he was munching something. He brazenly admitted that he had been "snitching" a biscuit or two.

"They look so good, ma'am," he said with an apologetic smile. "And I'm pretty empty. Besides that, it gets on your nerves to hear 'em boosting the food when all you're supposed to do is to carry it round."

Of course she could not be angry.

"Who is boosting it?" she asked.

"The boss and the sheriff are both doing it," said Timothy. "But you've got to admit they make good everything they say, by the way they lick into it."

It did not surprise her to hear that Bob Wells was enjoying himself. What a joke it was! If he only knew! It was some satisfaction to know that you were doing a good job, even if you were conscripted.

Timothy kept her informed of the progress of supper, and also made a report of the conversation.

"It turns out," he said, "that other parties beside us have been getting held up. The country gets awful wild when you're this far from New York."

"Other parties?" said Sally.

"Yes, ma'am. The sheriff has been telling the boss about it. There were two other automobiles stuck up somewhere around here within the past couple of weeks. As near as I can make out from what the sheriff tells the boss, it's a new sort of game. First they had Indians out here that scalped people; that was quite a while back. Then they ran the Indians out, or civilized 'em, and things went along all right until they had road agents holding up stages. Well, they got the best of the road agents after several parties had got killed, and the business sort of died out.

"And then—the sheriff has been going right into

the history of all of it—there was a new bunch got to working on the trains. I can remember reading about them in the papers myself. They used to go through the trains and take everything that everybody had, and anybody that didn't give up got shot. It took quite a while to get rid of all the train-robbers, but finally they did and everything looked peaceful. And now they've begun again on the automobiles."

"Really?" exclaimed Sally.

"Yes, ma'am. I don't mean the same bunch, understand? They hung most of the old ones. It seems, the sheriff tells the boss, that in the last two or three years there's been a lot of automobiles coming through this way; mostly rich people from the East, like the boss. They go clear on out to the coast and then drive all the way back again. Some of 'em carry quite a lot of valuables and these new hold-up gangs sometimes make a pretty good profit. The sheriff says they didn't get into his county until quite recent, but he's heard about their goings on outside of it.

"But now they've got into his county and he's quite stirred up. We're the third car in about two weeks. I guess the business is getting good, because it seems the gang is taking on new members. There were six of 'em that stuck us up, you know."

He said it so blandly that Sally was half persuaded he believed it.

"Six," repeated Timothy. "The boss claims only four, but there was two more that he didn't see. I didn't like to contradict him in front of the sheriff, but there was six, all right. I'm going to tell the sheriff when I get a chance, because he ought to have all the clues, so he can get to work right."

"Certainly," said Sally in an absent way.

She was pondering over the surprising intelligence from Timothy and wondering how it affected the case of the Wreck and herself. If there was really a gang at work in the county—and, of course, Bob Wells would not say so unless it were true—it seemed to make their own case much simpler. The exploit of the Wreck would naturally be blamed on those who were in the business for a living. It began to look as if they were hiding from nothing at all.

It seemed to her that this was an important development, although she did not yet see how it facilitated their getaway from the Underwood ranch. She wanted to find out more about it, if there was anything to be learned.

"You stay here in the kitchen, Timothy," she said. "I've got some things to do in the pantry, and if they want anything in the dining-room I'll attend to it."

She slipped into the pantry and closed the door behind her. At the farther end was the other door, that opened into the dining-room. It was a swinging door, with a half-inch space between the edge of it and the frame. She tiptoed forward, brought her ear close to the crack and stood there breathing softly.

Underwood was talking, but not about bandits. He was talking about Sally's apple-pie.

"I'm going to take her back to New York with me and fire my French cook," he announced. "I don't know what sort of a job her husband can fill, but I'll find something for him."

Sally raised her eyebrows, for this was news. And then she heard the familiar, boisterous voice of Bob Wells.

"I don't blame you," said the sheriff. "The lady can certainly cook. You don't get a good cook once in a lifetime. When you get 'em the thing to do is to rope 'em and brand 'em, and then don't let 'em outside the corral. Cooking is a woman's natural job, but they don't all get to be experts. But now and then, if you keep your eyes open, you can find one. Why—"

He paused to chuckle comfortably.

"The fact is, I'm going to marry one," he said.

"Congratulations," remarked the heavy voice of Jerome Underwood.

"That's the way I look at it," said the sheriff lightly. "The fact is, *Mr.* Underwood, when I sat down here to supper I began to think of her right away. You know how ideas get associated. Well, that was the point. I saw what you had on the table and I tasted it, and she just naturally flashed into my mind.

"You take a lot of girls nowadays and what they don't know about cooking would make even a cow-puncher swear. Of course, your daughter understands I'm not saying anything that touches her. She's in a different position. But out in this country a girl that can't cook isn't worth a hurrah. It's her duty to cook. It's downright important and necessary. A man's got to be fed if he's doing much work out here, and he ought to be fed right."

Sally scarcely breathed.

"You take that chicken, those biscuits, that pie —I've got a girl who can cook every bit as well as that. Understand me, she can do a lot more than cook. She's a smart girl and she's pretty, too. But when it comes to cooking she doesn't have to take her hat off to anybody. After all, it's the main thing. It's the foundation."

"Absolutely," said the voice of Underwood, out of a full mouth.

"And I'll tell you another thing," promised the sheriff. "When it comes to putting up preserves—"

Sally, however, did not wait for a report on the preserves. She was tiptoeing back toward the door that led into the kitchen. She was afraid to trust herself in the pantry any longer.

Timothy looked up from his meal.

"You look all warmed up," he remarked.

"It is a little warm," said Sally.

He helped himself to another piece of chicken, then reached for a biscuit.

"You certainly can cook, ma'am."

She turned upon him with a blaze in her eye that startled him.

"Cook!" she cried. "Well, is there anything

extraordinary about that?   That's what I'm here
for, isn't it?   That's what I am—a *cook!*"

"I didn't mean any offense, honest.   But I just
thought—"

"Don't think.   Don't bother me.   Go ahead and
eat—but don't *talk* about it."

Timothy shrugged and attended to his business.
He indulged himself in the original thought that
women were funny.   He could not see that he had
said anything out of the way; for there was no doubt
about it—she could cook.

CHAPTER XIV

"THE SON OF A GUN!"

THE Wreck, who had been keeping vigil from a window in the bunk house, saw the tall figure of the sheriff striding down to the corral just as dusk was settling. Next he saw the black horse and its rider headed along the trail that led to the main road. He could hear the sheriff whistling; there was a complacent sound about it that made him scowl.

He waited until the man of the law passed from sight among the distant spruce, then set off at a rapid pace for the ranch house. Timothy was still at his supper in the kitchen and Sally was busy at the sink. She flashed him a glance that signified a crisis had been passed without disaster.

"Feeling better?" asked Timothy.

The Wreck nodded as he sat down and reached for a plate.

"Let me tell you something," whispered Timothy, leaning closer. "Don't say a word about the cooking."

The Wreck looked at the giver of advice with suspicion, then filled his plate and went to work. He was hungry. After a minute or two he glanced up at Timothy.

"Well, what's the matter with the cooking?" he demanded.

"S-sh!" Timothy made an urgent sign for caution. "That's just it. There isn't anything the matter with it. Only—"

He glanced significantly in the direction of Sally, who heard, but did not turn her head.

"If there isn't anything the matter with it, what's the idea?" inquired the Wreck.

"S-sh! Lay off. I don't know what the idea is, but your wife bawled me for saying she could cook."

The Wreck studied the set of Sally's shoulders and decided not to press inquiries. Evidently it was not a matter of importance, anyhow; Timothy had probably made an ass of himself and got what he deserved.

Sally had very few words for anybody during the evening. The Wreck vainly tried to maneuver her into a private conversation, but she kept aloof from him. He wanted to hear all she knew about the sheriff's visit, and it puzzled him when he discovered that she was deliberately dodging. Probably she was mooning about things, he figured; women had a way of getting sentimental when there was absolutely no sense in it. He was willing to bet she was half sorry that Bob Wells had not discovered her, although she had been in a wild flurry for fear that he would. It would be just like her. Sentimentality! She wanted her sweetheart, and she didn't want him. If anybody could figure out what a woman really did want, the Wreck was willing to listen.

A couple of the boys drifted in for a late supper, along with Charley McSween. Timothy hung around the kitchen. The Wreck finally gave up the job and went out. He'd be hanged if he'd wash the dishes; let Timothy have a fling at it.

Sally finished her work and went off to bed. She was still angry. "Listeners never hear any good of themselves," kept running in her head. That was not exactly true in her own case. Probably the things she overheard were compliments; she had heard them before and always so regarded them. But—

"So Bob Wells is marrying a cook, is he?" she muttered as she turned off the light in her room. "I'm a smart girl, and I'm pretty; oh, yes. But the cooking is the main thing. It's downright important and necessary; it's the foundation. Oh, wait till I see him!"

Downstairs in the big living-room there was an earnest conversation in progress between Chester Underwood and his father. It dealt with a discovery. Chester, roaming about after supper in hope of a word with Sally Morgan, and failing to get it, had drifted idly down among the outbuildings. He had observed before that one of the little sheds, commonly used for storing tools and various odds and ends, was locked. It was unusual to lock anything around the ranch, but he had paid no particular attention to the fact. Now it aroused his curiosity.

The padlock would not yield to a pull. He tried

several keys, but none of them would manipulate the lock. Then he picked up a stone and began hammering at the hasp. Eventually it loosened under the attack and he managed to wrench it out of the wood. Rusty hinges groaned as he swung the door back.

A dusty flivver stood inside the shed. He stared at it for a while, wrinkling his forehead and trying to remember whether anybody at the ranch possessed such a thing. He stepped into the shed and walked slowly around it. The place was getting rather dark, which was not favorable for detailed observation. So far as he could see, however, it looked just like any other flivver. But no; there was a front wheel missing, on the left side. A soap-box had been placed under the axle. He looked around the shed, but could not find the wheel. It struck him as peculiar that anybody should put a flivver under lock and key, particularly one that had only three wheels.

Presently he stepped outside again and paused for another view of the rear end. His glance rested upon a license-plate and became fixed there. There was a vague stirring in his memory. Then, with a look of astonishment on his face, he hurried off in the direction of the ranch house.

All this he had been relating to his father as they sat in the living-room, and Jerome Underwood had been shooting questions at him that began in incredulity and developed into genuine curiosity.

"You say you can remember the license-plate?"
demanded his father.

"No; I didn't remember the number, of course.
I never took any note of it; I wasn't near enough
the other night. I didn't notice the State, either.
But it just has the general look; I think maybe it's
the color that stuck in my mind."

"And it's a one-seater?"

"Yes."

"H'm! Well, there are millions of them, of
course. You ought always to remember license
numbers in any kind of an emergency."

Excellent advice; but Underwood himself had
omitted to follow it, and he actually had his hands
on the bandit car.

"Get a lantern," he said. "Let's go down and
have a look at it."

Chester fetched a lantern from the kitchen, and
they went down to the tool-shed. Jerome Underwood examined the mysterious flivver with more
attention than he had ever given to his own imported
car. He studied the license-plate with a searching
eye, trying to make himself believe that it awakened
recollection. He could not be sure, but the more
he looked at it the more familiar it seemed to be.
Unconsciously, he was creating a memory of it,
which might, after all, serve just as well.

The missing wheel baffled him. He could not
invent a reason for it. Had there been a smash-up
which crumpled a wheel, there would almost certainly be other marks on the car. But all it showed

were a few ordinary dents and a myriad of scratches, common to hundreds of thousands of other flivvers all over the world. Standing there on its three wheels, with a soap-box serving as a crutch in place of the fourth, the dusty thing possessed an uncanny faculty of annoying him. He was aware of a feeling of resentment toward it. He had hated flivvers always; the people who drove them, as he saw them, never had any road manners. It was useless to pass them on the highway and leave them sputtering in your wake, because there was always another one ahead. Now it seemed that his diffused hatred came to a focus on one solitary specimen out of all the millions.

He led the way back to the house, swinging the lantern and trying to make something out of Chester's discovery. When they entered the living-room he did the obvious thing.

"Go get McSween," he said. "And let me do the talking."

Chester found the foreman in the bunk house, getting ready to pull off his boots. Charley was a believer in going early to bed when there was nothing else to do. He went up to the ranch house, wondering what the boss wanted.

Mr. Underwood always tried to make it a practice of getting immediately to the point, particularly with subordinates.

"Who owns the car that stands in the tool-shed?" he asked.

"What car?" asked Charley.

Then and there he passed a Rubicon, and realized it. Probably he had passed it foolishly, too. But the question had taken him by surprise, and his own question in return had snapped itself out automatically. That was the worst of speaking without due reflection. Why hadn't he said that the car belonged to Mr. and Mrs. Henry Williams and let the truth have its way?

"There's a car down there, a three-wheeled flivver," said Underwood. "Who does it belong to?"

"A three-wheeled flivver?" repeated Charley. "I reckon that's a new kind. It ain't any wonder they keep takin' chunks off the price."

Mr. Underwood stared at his foreman.

"Mean to say you didn't know there was a flivver in the tool-shed?" he demanded.

"First I ever heard of it," said Charley promptly.

Having inadvertently set a course for himself he proposed to sail it. He had a superstition about turning back. And what was all the fuss about anyhow?

"Well, we found one there. My son and I have been taking a look at it. Do you know what we think?"

"U'm! No, I can't say as I do, Mr. Underwood."

Charley was becoming cautious and curious. He scratched his chin and resolved to be deliberate.

"We think it's the same car that was used by the gang that held us up."

"Well, I'll be *dog*-goned! 'And standin' down

there in the tool-shed? Why, I'll just be damned, that's all!"

"And you mean to say you don't know anything about it?"

"But I'm a-goin' to," said Charley. "I'm a-goin to have a look."

He seized the lantern and hastened out of the room before Mr. Underwood could utter another question. Down near the shed he paused for thought. There was no need to go and look at the Wreck's flivver; he knew all about it. What he wanted was a little time.

Twice within the space of a minute he had been surprised, and he proposed to get himself in order before they did it again. It had never occurred to him that any member of the Underwood family would take the trouble to discover the flivver. That was the first surprise. It was entirely unnecessary, too, he reflected; he might as well have left the thing in the open. Nobody could use it, anyhow. But the other surprise—the suspicion that this was *the* flivver!

"The sons of guns!" he muttered. "The *sons* of guns! Stickin' up the boss and then buttin' into his own ranch and askin' for breakfast! I ain't sayin' they did! I ain't convinced. I'm always in favor of preservin' a judicial mind and bein' fair to all concerned. But when you come to think of it—h'm! There's Henry Williams now. It's always been puzzlin' me to figure him. Accordin' to his wife he's a kind of invalid. But accordin' to

Mort, and things which I've seen with my own eyes, he's a rampagin' rhinoceros. I wouldn't pick him to be in the stick-up business, and yet I wouldn't say he don't possess qualifications. The main thing is, he's got all the required nerve. The son of a gun!"

Charley stood tweaking his ear and frowning at the tool-shed.

"Admittin' the indictment—which I ain't necessarily, but admittin' it for the sake of argument—what am I goin' to do? I said I didn't know there was any flivver here. If I go back and say I did, I'm a liar. There ain't anything I hate to be accused of worse than that. Besides, if I admit I knew all about it, and it turns out that Henry lives up to what may be justly expected, then I'm makin' myself a sort of accessory after the fact. Which ain't true and is damagin' to my reputation. I may be rough and untutored, but I ain't any Henry Williams—the four-eyed son of a gun!"

He picked up the lantern, turned toward the ranch house and paused again.

"Furthermore, here I've been tellin' the boss how I got him a prize cook from out East, along with her obligin' husband. He's liable to form a kind of poor opinion if I admit he came near havin' no cook at all. It's a reflection on foresight and management. And it's too late, anyhow. I can't tell him it's Henry Williams's flivver. I can't tell him it's mine. I can't admit havin' any guilty knowledge appertainin' to it. It looks like I had to keep right on bein' innocent, which is one of my best points. But—the son of a gun!"

Deciding that he had been away long enough, he went back to the house, where he found Underwood and Chester waiting for him in the living-room.

"Well?" demanded the boss of the establishment.

"She's a flivver all right," remarked Charley as he set the lantern on the floor. "She's just what you said, a three-wheeler."

"And you don't recognize it?"

"No, sir. It's a new sight to me. It's an amazin' visitation, so far's I'm concerned."

"You mean you didn't know there was a car locked up in that shed?"

Jerome Underwood's eyes were fixed in a glare of incredulity, but Charley McSween gazed back with mild steadiness.

"Didn't know she was there. Didn't know the shed was locked. Hadn't been any call for anything that was kept in the shed."

"But—damn it—how could it get there?"

Charley looked thoughtful.

"I've been tryin' to think," he said. "If she had four wheels I'd say she got there in the regular way. But she's only got three wheels and a soap-box. That puts her in a class by herself. I can't figure her."

"Anybody around this ranch own a car?"

"No, sir. One of the boys had a motorcycle

once, but he couldn't learn to stay on the seat. We ain't had even a bicycle around here since."

Underwood continued to regard him with unwinking amazement.

"You're supposed to know what's going on around here, aren't you?" he demanded.

"Yes, I reckon I am," said Charley. "But it's a fair-sized ranch, and sometimes I'm travelin' around it."

"Do you want me to understand that a hold-up gang can use my place as a headquarters without my foreman even knowing it?"

"No, sir. I don't aim to be perfect, but I don't aim to be too careless either. I take it you're feelin' pretty certain it belongs to the gang?"

"I am now. I only thought so before, and so did my son. But when I'm told that you don't know anything about it, then I'm convinced."

"It looks reasonably convincin'," admitted Charley.

"What went on here the night before I arrived?"

"Nothin' that I 'specially recall. I reckon we all turned in pretty early."

"Could they have run a car in here without your knowing it?"

"Looks like they did, Mr. Underwood. It certainly makes me feel kind of foolish, bein' such a sound sleeper. But there she is, settin' there on three wheels and a box. There ain't any argument about that."

Charley knew that he was looking sheepish, and felt it was the right way to look.

"What gets me," he said, "is why anybody brought the damn thing here at all. What's the idea? And how did they get it here on three wheels? There ain't anything reasonable about any part of it. There ain't anything you can get a good start on for figurin'. Odd times I've seen things that surprised me. But this has got me laid sort of flat out."

Underwood made a restless gesture of impatience.

"I'm sorry the sheriff got away so early," he said. "He might be able to make some sense out of it. It seems that nobody around my ranch knows anything at all about anything."

"I reckon we all look stupid," confessed Charley. "I ain't denyin' you've got grounds for thinkin' so. If I was the boss, and anything like that happened around my place I'd just naturally take a few folks apart until I got the answer. That's the way I'd feel."

Underwood finished a calculating study of his foreman, then waved an arm in dismissal.

"We'll talk about this again in the morning," he said. "I wouldn't like to think there has been anything worse than stupidity."

"I wouldn't want to think so myself," said Charley. "Good night."

He went out with the lantern, passed through the dining-room and pantry and entered the empty kitchen, where he sat down and began filling a pipe.

"Well, I've made a high-grade ass out of myself," he mused. "I got started that way and there wasn't anything else to do. How in blazes was I goin' to tell him that I picked up the first stick-up gang that came along and turned 'em into a cook and dish-washer, without askin' for references? And me believin' that Providence sent 'em!"

He tipped the chair against the wall and hooked his heels in the rungs.

"I lied the only way that was befittin' the occasion. If I'd lied excited and brazen it wouldn't have held good overnight. So I lied calm and foolish. I ain't so sure that I got by either. I was always brought up believin' that a lie well stuck to is as good as the truth. But I ain't sure. It's sort of discon-certin'."

He fell into a long reverie, which came to an end when he muttered earnestly:

"The *son* of a gun!"

CHAPTER XV

COAXING—OR COERCION

BY morning, after he had snatched a few hours of sleep in the bunk house, Charley McSween had given much thought to the affair of the flivver and the Henry Williamses. He could not afford to lose a good cook and dish-washer. That would make more trouble with the boss than holding him up on the road. And if he let them ride away as they had come, it signified a confession that implicated him as deeply as any of the principals.

The problem of keeping them on the job was really simplified. Charley had a certain allowance of conscience; he was tolerant and good-hearted. He had admitted to himself that the conscription of a pair of honeymooners was a mean trick, even in the face of dire necessity. But now he knew something, or believed he did; and it amounted to a justification. It removed scruples, or at any rate made them slumbrous. He not only knew it, but he felt that he could profitably use it. It was neither blackmail nor duress, but merely persuasion. He could show them what the consequences of an attempted getaway might be.

For some reason that probably went back to instinct, he had never taken the hold-up of Jerome Underwood and his family with any deep feeling

182

of shock. It had not seriously disturbed his moral sense. Now, with Henry Williams in the picture, he regarded the affair even more lightly. Besides, there was Sally to be considered. She was a mighty fine girl, he had decided almost from the first; he looked upon her as one of his own people. If she had married a bandit, it was unfortunate, of course. But had she? He had his doubts about Henry. He could not figure him accurately, or even approximately; but it was hardest of all to figure him as a bandit, according to the evidence.

There was one more consideration in the back of his head—the sheriff. There was nothing personal about it, in the sense of a specific grievance. He could not have explained it any better than the versifier who did not like Dr. Fell. But he did not like Bob Wells, and he did not see any reason for throwing business in his way, particularly when it did not impress him as being of a really serious character.

He took the earliest opportunity to interview the Wreck and Sally Morgan, which happened to be during the washing of the breakfast dishes.

"The three-wheeled wonder," said Charley, "has become known to the family."

The Wreck's towel paused in the middle of a polishing movement.

"No, Henry; not through me," added Charley. "It was discovered as a result of unmanly curiosity on the part of the boss's son. He hammered the padlock off the door."

"Well?" inquired the Wreck.

"The news havin' been communicated to the old man, and both havin' examined the hidden party, there is a sort of notion—not positive, but leanin' in that direction—that this particular flivver was met before."

Sally and the Wreck both looked at Charley and waited.

"The discovery bein' put up to me," continued Charley, "I violated a considerable part of my principles by denyin' any knowledge. The reason ain't important. The main thing is, I come out of this conversation lookin' like one of two things—either a durned fool or a *particeps criminis,* which means one of the same gang, that bein' the proper learned way of puttin' it. Accordin' to this conversation, I didn't know any more about that flivver than if she had come droppin' out of the sky."

He paused and studied the pair. Sally was pink in the cheeks and was biting at her under lip, a sure sign of doubt. The Wreck was inscrutable.

"Well?" he repeated.

"We're gettin' to the point," said Charley. "The point is, I reckon I'm the only person on the ranch who can tell the sheriff of this free and independent county just where it might pay him to head in."

"Well?"

"You have a disappointin' way of shootin' that word, Henry. I reckon we've got to decide how we're goin' to proceed with the discussion. Are we goin' to show all hands on the call, or are we goin' to proceed hypothetical?"

The Wreck looked at Sally, who was wrinkling her forehead into furrows. She seemed willing to leave the decision to him.

"There ain't any objection to givin' the gang five minutes for consultation," said Charley.

"Nothing to consult about," said the Wreck.

"Meanin'?"

"Meaning we don't get you."

"H'm. It looks like the case was hypothetical."

Sally stirred restlessly. She did not like beating around bushes.

"Can't we talk right out in meeting?" she asked, suddenly.

"Thank you, ma'am," said Charley.

"Wait," said the Wreck.

He tossed his dish towel on the drain board and edged himself into a seat on the table, from which his legs dangled loosely.

"What are you going to do about it?" he demanded.

"I figure that I'm goin' to hang on to the cook and dish-washer that was handed to me by Providence."

"Blackmail?"

"I'm shocked," said Charley.

"What is it, then?"

"I figure coaxin' is a better word."

"Are you getting the idea you can keep us here as long as you damned please?"

The Wreck was beginning to display nervous symptoms, and Sally gave him an anxious look.

"In a way, it's out of my hands," said Charley, mildly. "Suppose I was to say to you, 'Honey-mooners, climb right into flivver and help yourself.' That don't necessarily get you anything at all. The first person that climbs into that three-legged critter and tries to drive off in it is goin' to set the boss prancin' in pursuit. You don't seem to get the idea. She's bad medicine, that flivver. It ain't safe to acknowledge even a passin' acquaintance. She's tainted. Mind you, Henry, I ain't accusin' her of anything. I'm merely recitin' the suspicions of others."

The Wreck was making an effort to be judicial.

"Suppose," he said, "that I was to tell your boss how you happened to get a cook and a kitchen helper?"

"That would be sinkin' us all in the same ship," admitted Charley. "It would be a kind of community suicide. But you ain't goin' to tell him, on account of Mis' Williams here, who's got rights of her own in the matter."

The Wreck could see that, but he did not like to acknowledge it.

"Every idiot on the place," he said, "seems to be chasing around with the idea that somebody committed a crime. Suppose it happened that there was no crime at all?"

"I'm open-minded," observed Charley.

"Suppose," continued the Wreck, as he glared

through his spectacles, "that you happened to be stranded with your wife out in the middle of a county that's so big there isn't any sense to it. Suppose you didn't have a drop of gas. Suppose somebody came along who had plenty of gas, and you offered in a decent manner to pay for a few gallons if they'd let you have it. And suppose a big hog sat back in his seat and gave you the laugh and told you to get busy and push your car out of his way, so he could drive on. And suppose you had to have that gas or stay there until God knows when. Hey?"

His voice had shrilled itself to an edge and he was making gestures with both arms.

"All right; I'm supposin'," said Charley.

"Well, what would you do?"

"Speakin' hypothetical, you mean?"

"Speaking any way you like," barked the Wreck.

Charley rubbed his chin and appeared to consider the problem.

"I reckon," he drawled, "I'd try to get me some gas."

The Wreck waved an arm to indicate that all doubts were resolved.

"That's all there was to it," he said.

"Mind, now," said Charley, cautiously, "I'm not sayin' that I'd feel drove to committin' unlawful acts. Gettin' gasoline, you might say, is meetin' one of the demands of nature, and I reckon it can be justified by powerful arguments. But when it comes to takin' people's watches and jewelry and—"

"They lied!" interrupted the Wreck.

"I'm only repeatin' what was told the sheriff."

"I say they lied."

"I guess we're showin' all hands on the call," mused Charley.

"I'm getting tired of all this lying," said the Wreck, sliding off the table. "I can stop it in three minutes."

He was headed for the door when Sally detained him with a firm hand.

"Henry, are you crazy?"

"I'm sore."

"You stay right here. I don't care whether you're sore or not. You're not going near Mr. Underwood."

"Why doesn't he stick to the truth, then?"

"I haven't the least idea. I don't particularly care. But you keep away from him."

The Wreck shook himself loose from her grip and went back to the table. Charley McSween nodded his approval.

"There ain't any occasion to get excited," he said. "You might go up there and tell him he's a liar and bust him in the eye. But that wouldn't be no compensation for sittin' in jail over at the county seat, waitin' for 'em to give you the rest of your natural life."

"I'm not going to stay here for the rest of my natural life," growled the Wreck.

"There ain't any need."

"How long are you figuring on?"

"I figure I'm goin' to need you and Mis' Williams so long as the boss and his family are here."

"How long is that?"

Charley seemed to be calculating.

"Not more'n a month, it ain't likely."

Sally gasped.

"A month!" she cried. "Why, we won't dream of it!"

"I'm sure sorry, ma'am. But he 'most always stays a month."

"We've stayed longer now than we had any business to."

"We're all creatures in the guidin' hands of Providence," observed Charley. "A month ain't much in the lives of young folks."

Sally was showing plain signals of alarm. She fell to clasping and unclasping her hands and moistening her lips, while her eyes blinked with bewilderment and consternation. Finally she began walking to and fro.

"I won't do it!" she exclaimed. "A month! Not another day, if I can help it. You haven't any business to keep us here. Do you think I'm going to stay here and be turned into a slave, cooking your meals and doing the kitchen work for a lot of able-bodied men who are too lazy to help themselves? Yes, and doing the housework, too. I won't stand for it!"

Charley looked interested, and so did the Wreck.

"Just because I've been good-natured about it," stormed Sally, "is no reason why I'm going to let anybody rub it in. I don't care what happens. I'm through! I'm going to find out—"

The Wreck was patting her on the arm.

"Ss-h, now," he said. "Go easy."

She flung his hand aside and turned on him with a look of amazement.

"Henry Williams, are you a worm?"

"That's all right," he said in a voice that tried to be soothing. "You're not going to go running yourself into trouble."

"You mean to say you're going to submit?" she demanded.

"There, now; you mustn't get excited," said the Wreck.

For an instant she was without speech.

"Excited? You say that *I'm* excited? *You?* Why—why—"

She sat in a chair and burst into hysterical laughter. The Wreck turned to Charley and shrugged his shoulders.

"Sometimes she gets a little nervous spell," he explained. "She'll be all right in a minute or two."

Sally listened in amazement as she laughed. It was almost impossible to believe. Henry Williams said she was *nervous!*

"Now I reckon we're all normal again," remarked Charley, with a satisfied nod. "There ain't anything in the world like matrimonial teamwork, ma'am. When Henry busts loose, you soothe him down. And when you bust loose, Henry jams his foot on the brakes. It sort of keeps you both steady and makes for a reasonable amount of peace and quiet."

"But we're not going to stay a month," said the Wreck. "Don't make any mistake about that."

"No," said Sally. "We positively won't stay."

"Well, maybe it won't be a month, ma'am. The family might take a notion to clear out in a couple of weeks."

Sally and the Wreck shook their heads. They were calm again, but they had not changed their minds.

"The main point," said Charley, "is what in blazes can you do? You ain't goin' to navigate very far on three wheels, and anyhow, you're goin' to get hopped on the minute you try. That's the practical side. Now, personally, I'm disposed to be reasonable. I ain't givin' any indorsement to the habit of highway robbery. Bein' law abidin' myself, it may be I'm prejudiced; but that's the way I feel. At the same time, I ain't sayin' but what there may be occasions when it's justifiable to make use of gasoline wherever it can be found handiest. That, I reckon, is the sentimental side. They sort of balance off, as near as I see it."

"Get down to cases," advised the Wreck.

"I'm comin' to it. I'll put it brutal, maybe, but I'm sincere, as always. I'm not going to let you young folks go diggin' out of here just because you feel restless. I've got a duty to my boss and a duty to myself. I ain't goin' to say anything to him, mind. I've done considerable lyin' up to now, which is a sort of guarantee that I'll perform such other lyin' as may be necessary. I've even gone so far as to get myself looked upon with suspicion. But if you try bustin' loose out of here and leavin' me flat, with no cook and no dish-washer, and takin' your flivver with you as a sign of guilt, the whole durned temple is due to be pulled down sudden and ruthless."

He eyed them both with great gravity.

"It may be, Henry," he added, "that when she comes down the foreman of this God-fearin' establishment is goin' to get buried along with them that starts the wreckin' job. But she's comin' down, just the same. I ain't hankerin' for ruin, but on the subject of cooks I'm a desperate man."

CHAPTER XVI

FIND THE WHEEL

THE breakng point had come, and Sally and the Wreck both admitted it. They spent all forenoon planning the getaway. Charley McSween committed an error in applied psychology when he mentioned the probability of a month at the Underwood ranch. To the Wreck, who was merely West for his nerves, it might have been no great matter, although he did not fancy his environment. But to Sally it was a prospect of unutterable dismay, and the Wreck was there to serve her. She should have been in Chicago before this; Ma Morgan ought to be getting the first letters. In the absence of news, there would soon be panic at the Bar-M. Dad Morgan would be rousing the county, or starting for Chicago, or gunning for the Wreck, or doing something else desperate and foolish.

"We've just got to get away from here," said Sally.

"Sure. Don't worry. I'll get you on the train all right."

"Um-m. I don't know about the train. I may want to go back home."

"You haven't got your trousseau yet," he reminded her.

She gave him a speculative look, not sure whether he was serious. But he was.

"Perhaps I can fix up a trousseau out of some things I've got home," she said. "At any rate, it's not important now. It's not even important just where we go. The point is to get started."

"It's easy," nodded the Wreck.

It was not easy, however. There was a flivver wheel to be found, and neither of them had even encountered a clue. They devoted part of the morning to searching for it, and tried to be systematic about it. Sally took the house, which she ransacked from top to bottom, while the Wreck gave his time to a close inspection of all the outbuildings and such other possible hiding-places as suggested themselves to him. Both shook their heads when they met to report.

They discussed the big Underwood car. The Wreck had never driven the like of it, although he was confident of his ability, as always. But Timothy had all the valves out, and with a prospect of idle weeks ahead of him, was puttering over the grinding job, in no hurry to complete it.

"I could make him put the valves back," said the Wreck, "but I couldn't give him any good reason for it. I suppose I'd have to lock him up after he did it, to keep him from telling."

Sally dismissed the idea with a wave of her hand.

"If we can't find the wheel to our own car," she said, "what do you say about trying to make it on horses?"

"Perfectly simple."

She was doubtful about that.

"I'm not sure about you," she said.

He began ruffling with familiar symptoms.

"Henry, there's no need for you to be sensitive about it. You're not supposed to be a good rider, any more than I'm a good chemist. You haven't had the training. I think you'd make a beautiful rider in time, but you're a very bad one just now. You suffer agony every time you get on a horse."

"You haven't heard me squealing," he said, sharply.

"No; I haven't. You wouldn't squeal if you were dying. But so far as making a getaway goes it's not a question of squealing. It's a question of falling off."

He flushed painfully, but she could see no use in dodging the facts.

"I've seen you fall off four times," she said; "three times in one day."

"But the second ride I only fell off once," he declared, stubbornly. "I showed improvement, didn't I?"

"You fall off any time the horse stops suddenly, Henry."

"All right, I admit it," he said. "But after we get started we're not going to do any stopping, are we? And after we've made the getaway, what difference does it make if I do fall off?"

There was something about his stubbornness that secretly delighted her, but she did not mention it.

It was true that he had a bland habit of claiming to be able to do anything, and to some it might have sounded like the talk of a braggart. But Sally knew it was otherwise; it was merely an expression of his sincere beliefs. Besides, he was always making good, in some haphazard, unexpected way, and making good was meeting the acid test.

"Well, we may have to try it," she said, "if you really don't mind falling off."

"I don't mind."

They decided, if it came to a question of horses, that the Wreck would take Charley McSween's big bay, while Sally would take the rangy animal that Jerome Underwood rode.

"They're the two best horses on the ranch," she said, "with the exception of that ugly roan that one of the boys rides. But he's out riding fence somewhere, so we can't get it. If we're going to steal horses, we want good ones."

"Sure. The best," affirmed the Wreck, speaking as a connoisseur.

"We'll have to leave most of our baggage behind, of course. We'll have to travel light and fast —as fast as we can, anyhow."

"Don't you worry about me. I'm all right so long as they keep going."

"And of course we can't start until it's dark and everybody is asleep."

"Suits me."

The vision of getting away, even though it was not beyond the rough planning stage, brightened her wonderfully. She became as cheerful as though she were already far on the road. Of course, she knew, it would be an awful ordeal for the Wreck, but he was so willing, even eager, to undergo the torture that it reconciled her to the prospect. Whatever befell him, she knew that he would take it standing up, like a man—except, of course, when he happened to fall off.

The Wreck, despite his brave front, was not looking forward to the exploit with joy, even though it might bring discomfiture to their enemies. He would never love a horse. He knew too well what they did to him. But with Sally determined to make an early departure, he was the last person to interpose any objection as to method. If it became necessary to crawl all the way to the Bar-M on hands and knees, or even to Chicago, he would have taken the same attitude. It was his business to see that Sally reached her destination, whatever it was, and he proposed to attend to it.

"I'll put up all the grub that we can carry," said Sally. "That'll be more important than spare clothes. It will be mostly sandwiches, I'm afraid. What kind do you like?"

"Any kind."

"But you must have some preference."

"I'm not particular."

She beamed at him, and he did not know why.

"You're not fussy about your cooking, are you, Henry?"

"Not that I know of."

"It's not the main thing in your life, is it?"

"No."

"And if you were marrying a girl that isn't the first thing you'd think about?"

What in thunder was she driving at, he wondered? Was she making fun of him? He was not marrying cooks or anybody else. Why couldn't she let him alone?

"No; I wouldn't think about it at all," he answered, rather stupidly. "Would I be supposed to?"

She laughed without restraint; he was such a queer, awkward person.

"No; it would be rather nice not to think about it," she said. "But, just the same, I'm going to put you up the nicest sandwiches I know how to make."

"All right. Anything at all."

"And I may even expect you to praise them."

"Sure. I will."

She laughed again, but there was not the least hint of teasing in her eyes.

"Henry Williams," she said, "sometimes you can be perfectly lovely. No; I know you don't understand. It makes it better because you don't."

He had no answer for that, and was uncomfortable. For some reason he could not explain, he was red in the face; he could feel it. He could not stand women, and he would never learn how.

"I guess I'll have another look for that wheel," he mumbled.

"All right. Good luck, old timer."

She watched him go, a half-amused, half-puzzled look in her eyes. There was a hint of motherliness in the smile on her lips; but it was not all motherliness, either.

"Honestly, he's a dear," she told herself. "But he hasn't the least idea of it. Poor thing! He's going to have an awful time riding Charley McSween's bay. But he'll never whimper. He'll be horribly cross, and he'll bark at me every minute —but he won't whimper. And he thinks he's a nervous wreck! I wish Daddy Morgan could have seen him the night he whipped Mort. H'm. I'd better start on those sandwiches. I wonder what kind he *really* likes?"

The Wreck was making another search of the outbuildings, still bewildered in mind about the conversation. Of course, she was teasing him about something, but he could not figure it out. He was quite certain that he had never expressed any opinions about eating in the presence of Sally Morgan; he always took whatever they set before him and ate it without comment. Of course, there was no doubt she was able to cook. But was that anything extraordinary?

Yet he was not displeased, now that he had a chance to think things over, even though he had been embarrassed at the time. He had an idea that her intentions were the very best. He never knew Sally to do anything mean; he did not think she even practiced the feminine cruelty of making men squirm— that is, intentionally. She had called him "old timer." It gave him the same sensation as when she first called him "Henry," which was a name that he never got from any woman except his sisters. He had a pleasant sense of being admitted into the comradeship of his new country. He had not yet picked up very much about the West, but he knew that "old timer" meant that you really belonged. It made him feel less like a stranger. Unconsciously, he squared his shoulders as he poked around among the outbuildings, squinting through his spectacles at places where the wheel might possibly be.

He was still engaged in this occupation when he ran into Charley McSween. For an instant he contemplated trying to choke the secret out of him. Getting away in the flivver would be much easier than stealing Charley's horse. But he kept the impulse in check, letting his undercurrent of caution have sway, for there was the chance that Charley would remain stubborn, even in possible defeat, and then matters would be worse than before.

"I reckon you're huntin' for the wheel," observed Charley, who could put two and two together.

"Maybe."

"Tryin' to thwart Providence is a job only for them that are reckless, but I can't say as you're lackin' any of the main qualities. But you're wastin' time, Henry. She's hid safe and sure. I figured all the places you'd look before I put her away, and then I sequestered her elsewhere."

"I'll find it," said the Wreck.

"In which case I'll only have to bury it again,"

said Charley. "Why not be reasonable? Why can't you and the bride stay the month out and go peaceful? As sure as shootin', if you pull out of here in that flivver while the boss is still at the ranch, you're a marked man."

"And if I let it stay there, they'll confiscate it anyhow, won't they?"

Charley rubbed his ear.

"Hadn't thought of that," he admitted. "I reckon they might. But that's one of the risks in playin' the stick-up game. I figure there'd be more profit in losing a flivver, of which there is plenty more, than in ridin' herd on your sins while you're sittin' and lookin' out through one of them little winders they build high up in the wall."

"You needn't worry about me going to jail," said the Wreck.

"But I am. I kind of like you, Henry. You're awful wild for these parts; I reckon if you was to settle down here the county would become real lively, instead of pursuin' its peaceful ways. But you ain't without your good points. And you've gone and picked yourself a nice wife, which ought to start you turnin' over a new leaf. There ain't any permanent prosperity in stickin' folks up, even for gas. It's against law and morals, and your wife won't like it after a while. Right now I'm takin' long chances shelterin' you. But havin' made the resolve, I'm seein' it through, mostly because I like the Williams family."

"Bet you I find the wheel," said the Wreck.

"I'm not a gamblin' man."

"Ten to five."

"You're talkin' immoral."

"I'll make it fifteen to five."

Charley made a gesture of helplessness.

"I've got human failin's," he said. "Most of my life is an open book, but I ain't no St. Anthony. Fifteen to five goes. Want to double it?"

"Sure."

"Then she's thirty to ten. It ain't right I should take such odds, but you drove me to it. I'm tryin' to cure you. You ain't got a Chinaman's chance, which is nothin'. But I'm wishin' you luck."

The Wreck continued his search, not so much because he wanted to win Charley's ten dollars as because he wanted to avoid riding Charley's horse. He had looked in all the likely places, so far as he could remember; now he tried looking in the unlikely ones. The part that puzzled him most was his patience and lack of temper. Ordinarily, he ought to have been fuming, with his nerves raw and his muscles twitching with irritation. But a stolid mood seemed to have settled upon him, and he continued his task with a phlegmatic calm that astonished him.

He saw Chester Underwood emerging from the shed where the flivver stood on its crutch, but took no notice of him. There was nothing that Chester could contribute in the way of information, and he felt that it was politic to let him alone. The more he searched the more probable it seemed that he would ride away on Charley McSween's horse. He would not allow the small matter of a bet to detain him, although he would have found pleasure in triumphing over the foreman of the Underwood ranch.

Sally informed him at lunch time that the sandwiches had been made and put away, and that she hoped he would not complain about them. He merely shrugged. She also told him that she was going for a little ride in the afternoon with Chester. He shrugged again, but there was a scowl that went with it.

"Don't be silly, Henry," she said. "We've got to play the game right up to the last minute."

"I didn't say anything. I'm playing it."

"He's just a kid," she added.

"Oh, go on and ride."

She did. He saw them ride away toward the hills, and then spent part of a miserable afternoon in further quest for the missing wheel. It was none of his business, of course, but it did not seem to him that a girl who was engaged to the sheriff, or anybody else, ought to be galloping over the range with any young man who happened to come along.

The afternoon of Jerome Underwood was equally unpleasant. He wanted to get hold of Bob Wells and acquaint him with discoveries, but the sheriff was somewhere on the road and could not be reached by telephone. It seemed to Underwood that the whole system of suppressing crime was unnecessarily primitive. He saw the situation entirely in terms of New York; he expected metropolitan service.

He fumed and exploded, and he shot grim innuen-
does at Charley McSween, who maintained his calm,
although he began to be sorry that he had ever
bothered himself about obtaining an emergency
cook.

Sally came back from her ride, flushed and charming. She told Chester that it had been delightful,
every foot of the way, even saying it in the presence
of the Wreck, who happened to be in the vicinity
of the corral, apparently still looking for an essential part of his flivver.

Back in the kitchen again, she became serious and
restless. She waited awhile for Henry Williams;
she had something to say. But the Wreck was evidently minded to keep aloof. He did not appear
until after she had sent Timothy to find him, with a
message that she wanted to talk to him. He came
into the kitchen with a sullen look on his face and,
without a word, began putting on his apron, grimly
resigned to the performance of at least one more
hateful task.

"Never mind the apron yet," she said. "There's
something more important."

He waited for the explanation.

"We may not have to ride horses," she whispered,
after a cautious glance to make sure there were no
eavesdroppers.

"Huh?"

"Chester has found the wheel."

He merely stared.

"I knew he had something on his mind," she said.

"That's the main reason I went for a ride. He was all puffed up with importance. He has the idea that he's going to put something over on the sheriff."

"Where's the wheel?" demanded the Wreck.

"He wouldn't tell me."

"Well, what did he tell you?"

"In the first place," said Sally, lowering her voice, "he told me all about his wonderful discovery of the flivver, and all about what happened between his father and Charley McSween. He's terribly proud of what he has done. He thinks he's a sort of detective. So, having found the car and stirred up a lot of excitement, he thought the next thing to do was to find the wheel. He told me that he found it inside of ten minutes."

The Wreck had a twinge of chagrin. He had spent whole hours on the job, without obtaining so much as a trace.

"Of course," added Sally, "it wasn't for me to show that I was especially interested. I wasn't going to stir up any suspicion. I got just as interested as I could afford to be, but not any more. I told him I thought he was wonderfully clever, and I even asked him where he found the wheel. But he said he was not going to tell anybody until he caught the hold-up gang—not even his father. He has an idea that if he doesn't say anything about the wheel it will help him to find the people who own it."

The Wreck considered the information.

"Anything else?" he asked.

"Nothing else, except—" She hesitated.

"What?"

"Well, I thought if Chester knew where the wheel was, that perhaps you could find out, too."

There was an interchange of glances.

"I think I get you," said the Wreck.

"I think you do, Henry."

"Much obliged."

"But not till after supper," she warned him. "We've got to wait for dark. And, of course, I'll help any way I can."

"No need for you to get mixed up."

"But it's my affair, too."

"Oh, all right."

So Chester Underwood had discovered the wheel, had he? The Wreck began to study the situation, and became absorbed in it.

"It was all right for me to go riding, wasn't it?" interrupted Sally.

He came out of his reverie and looked at her as if he did not get the point.

"All right?" he echoed. "Why not? I guess anything you do is all right, isn't it?"

"It all depends, Henry Williams. You're so awfully queer."

CHAPTER XVII

RECKLESSLY THOROUGH

IT was after dark when the Wreck sneaked his ridiculous little grip out of the bunk house and carried it up to the shed where the flivver stood. He tossed the grip into the car and placed an unlighted lantern where he could easily find it. Then he walked back to the kitchen. Sally was there, pretending to be busy, but her mind was not on her task.

"Go up-stairs and throw your grips out of the window," he said. "I'll be waiting for 'em."

"I've been thinking," said Sally. "Suppose he won't tell?"

"He will. But I want your gun."

"You've got to be careful, Henry."

"I'll be careful."

She saw that his mood seemed to be wholly calm, and it reassured her.

"The gun will be in the small bag," she said, as she went out of the kitchen.

But before she tossed her grips out of the window, down into the shadow where the Wreck stood, she took the precaution of emptying the cylinder of the six-shooter. She was thinking less about the safety of Chester Underwood than she was of the welfare of the Wreck.

The man who waited in the shadow picked up the
grips as they thudded on the ground and hastened
away in the direction of the shed. He had several
things to do before he was ready to recover the
missing front wheel. That would be the final detail,
he decided. He was not assailed by the smallest
doubt that he would find what he sought.

He went over to the shed where the big Underwood car was kept and found a couple of five-gallon
cans. Two big metal drums, filled with gasoline,
stood outside, and a hemisphere of moon supplied
light enough for his work. He filled the cans and
returned with them to the tool-shed, where he
flooded the flivver's tank to the brim. Then he
made a second trip, refilling his cans and putting
their metal tops firmly in place. This gave him a
ten-gallon reserve, which he lashed firmly to the
running-board of the flivver.

A third trip to the place where the big car stood
carried him inside the shed, where he fumbled for
a minute in the semi-darkness, found something on
the work bench and slipped it into his pocket. Outside, he paused in front of the gasoline drums and
considered the idea of emptying the remainder of
their contents. He decided it was not necessary.
Back to the tool-shed, he seated himself on the
ground outside and waited. As he sat there it
occurred to him to examine Sally's six-shooter. The
empty cylinder brought a scowl to his face, then a
grin. He believed that he understood. After all,
it made no real difference.

It was nearly ten o'clock. There were lights upstairs in the ranch house, a light in the kitchen. But the bunk house was dark. He hoped that Charley McSween was in bed; the affair would be better for no complications. But he wished that Sally would hurry up. He was not at all certain she would be able to fulfil her part of the undertaking. Minutes passed and he grew restless.

"I suppose my nerves will be all shot to pieces," he grumbled. "It's always the way. Keep me waiting long enough and I'm not fit for anything."

A sound of voices reached him and he rose softly to his feet. Presently he could see two figures in the dim light. They were approaching the tool-shed, strolling, all too slowly to please him. The Wreck was tense and jumpy. He could hear what Sally was saying.

"But I think it was awfully clever of you to find the car, Chester. And then to find the wheel, too. Why, it's a lot more than the sheriff has done."

Chester laughed pleasantly.

"All you've got to do is to use a little common sense," he said, modestly. "Of course, you've got to have a sort of instinct for it, I suppose."

"Indeed, yes," declared Sally, heartily. "Where did you say you found the wheel?"

"I didn't say," replied Chester, shrewdly. "I'm just going to wait until I see whether somebody else can find it."

They were close to the tool-shed.

"But I wouldn't tell anybody," said Sally.

Chester laughed again. They were sufficiently close for the Wreck to see that he was trying to make a captive of Sally's fingers, and she did not seem to be resisting.

"Perhaps I'll tell you to-morrow," said Chester. "At any rate, I'll tell you first."

The Wreck stepped briskly out of the shadow in which he had been standing.

"Stick 'em up! Quick!"

There was a smothered exclamation from Chester. Sally stepped aside as the Wreck advanced.

"Up, I said," snapped the Wreck. "This is business."

Slowly the young man's hands went up, as he stared through bewildered eyes at a six-shooter whose muzzle was within a foot of his stomach.

"Y-you!" he gasped.

"Me," affirmed the Wreck. "Talk low and only speak when you're told to. Sally, take the gun."

She stepped forward and he slipped it into her hands.

"Keep it on him," he commanded. "If he makes a queer move, you know what to do."

He moved behind the prisoner and ordered him to lower his hands behind his back. With a piece of heavy cord he bound them tightly, until Chester squirmed. Then he relieved Sally of the gun.

"You—you're the hold-up man!" spluttered Chester, when he found his voice again. "Sally, are you—"

"Shut up," said the Wreck, sharply.

"You're both in it! Now I know—"

The muzzle of the six-shooter was pressed against a tender spot between his ribs.

"Cut out the comment and listen," said the Wreck. "Where's the wheel?"

Chester's glance went appealingly to Sally, but he did not find any encouragement in her face.

"Where's the wheel?"

"I—I don't know."

"That's a lie. Where is it?"

Chester drew a deep breath.

"I won't tell you," he answered.

"Give you half a minute to tell," said the Wreck. "And remember: I'm desperate and I'm nervous. What happens to you is nothing in my life. If you don't tell me where it is, I'm going to beat you to a finish. And if you don't tell then, I'm going to shoot you."

Again Chester made an appeal with his eyes in the direction of Sally.

"Better do what he says," she advised, coldly. "He's mean when he has a gun in his hands."

"Sally! I didn't think—"

"Don't talk to me. Talk to him."

"Where's the wheel?" repeated the Wreck.

Chester glanced toward the ranch house. There was no hope of help from there, even if he shouted. And something in the tense figure of the Wreck warned him not to shout.

"You give me a fair chance to fight and I'll show you," he said.

"Not a chance," observed the Wreck. "I'm not fighting to-night. Fifteen seconds gone. Come through."

"I—I—"

Chester was not a coward, but he knew when the cards were against him.

"Time's up," said the Wreck, significantly. "Now!"

Chester sighed, and his figure sagged.

"It's in the back of the car," he said.

There was a smothered exclamation from the Wreck, who ordered Sally to take the gun. He went to the flivver to investigate. The rear compartment, where baggage was usually stored, was never locked, and he lifted up the lid and thrust a hand inside. He could feel something under an old piece of tarpaulin that he had used at odd times for a tent. It was the wheel.

As he hauled it into view he muttered something about Charley McSween. It angered him to think of the hours he had spent in searching. But he would have time to reflect upon the iniquitous ingenuity of Charley later on.

"Got it?" called Sally.

"Yep. Keep him there until I light the lantern."

The lantern lighted, he placed it in a far corner of the tool-shed, where it would throw an illumination light on the work he had to do.

"Bring him inside," ordered the Wreck.

Chester, with Sally following, walked into the

shed and the Wreck closed the door behind them. He motioned Chester to a place against the wall.

"Keep the gun on him," he told Sally. "I'll be through in five minutes."

Working briskly, he kept his word. It took less than two minutes to slide a jack under the front axle, lift it and kick the soap-box aside. He slipped the wheel into place, adjusted the lock nut, carefully inserted the cotter pin and spread the ends. When the hub cap was screwed on and the jack removed, the flivver stood on four wheels again.

"You wait till they get you for this," said Chester, grimly.

The Wreck laughed, threw back the door and began rolling the flivver into the open. He did not dare to start the motor, knowing that it would split the night with its clamor. Once he had the thing clear of the shed, he went inside again and ordered Chester to sit on the soap-box. Then he tied his feet together.

"We're going to lock you in here," he said. "You're lucky it's no worse. We're not going away just yet. One of us will be outside. If you do any yelling, I'll come back and gag you. Maybe I'll shoot you. I don't know which. Come on, Sally."

She joined him outside and watched him close the door of the shed and slip the padlock into place. He had already extinguished the lantern.

"If he hollers," said the Wreck, loud enough to be heard within the shed, "shoot through the door."

He winked as he spoke, then hurried off in the

direction of the ranch house, leaving Sally to stand guard, with the gun in her hand.

There was still a light in one of the upper windows and he moved as cautiously as possible as he neared the house. He remembered exactly where a ladder lay, alongside the wall, and went directly to it. Carrying it to a corner of the building and raising it, he rested it gently against the clapboards. Then he mounted cautiously. Nearing the eaves, he groped overhead, found something with his fingers, then reached into a hip pocket. The jaws of the pliers were sharp and the telephone wire parted with a thrumming sound.

The Wreck did not wait to learn whether anybody within heard the noise, but slid down the ladder and hurried away. Twenty yards distant from the house he began groping in the grass and presently found what he sought. As he began walking again he was coiling wire in his hands. The telephone line, until it reached the spruce several hundred yards distant, was carried on a row of poles. He followed it as far as the first pole, cut the wire again, then hurried in the direction of the tool-shed, with the coil over his arm.

Sally, nervous at the delay and not understanding the cause of it, was standing guard at the door. Without a word of explanation, he tossed the coiled wire into the bottom of the car.

"Now help push," he said, in a low voice. "I don't want to wake the dead unless I have to."

Together, they got the flivver into reluctant mo-

·tion. Without her, the Wreck would not have essayed the task, for it would have been far too slow; but Sally was strong, and between them they got the machine moving at a fair walking pace. Fifty yards distant from the shed they cut into the wagon tracks that marked the trail, and for a while the going was somewhat easier.

"Keep heaving at it," he said, to encourage her.

"I am," panted Sally.

They were some two hundred yards from the ranch house when the flivver began to encounter a slight up-grade. It seemed to become suddenly heavy. Presently, despite their utmost efforts it came to a stop.

"Good enough," gasped the Wreck. "Climb in."

She was in the seat when he laid hold of the crank. The first half dozen pulls brought no response. He paused an instant to recover breath, then set his teeth and yanked again. There was a furious bellow from beneath the hood and the flivver quivered like a frightened horse.

"Better hurry," urged Sally, with an anxious look toward the house.

He was leaping into the seat as she spoke, advancing the gas lever until the flivver roared and trembled appallingly. Then the lights switched on and the car plunged forward, up the grade toward the sheltering spruce.

Sally, her eyes turned in the direction of the ranch house, saw another window up-stairs suddenly illuminated. Somebody carrying a lantern ran out of the kitchen doorway. The Underwood ranch was awake. She told the news to the Wreck, but it did not seem to interest him. Sitting rigid behind the wheel, he was glaring at the trail as he guided the bouncing flivver.

In a minute they made the turn that shut the house from view. The road became winding, but he did not permit the fact to interfere with speed. Sally held fast to the seat, trying to realize that they were actually in flight. She knew better than to offer a word of caution; when the Wreck was driving he resented suggestion. Besides, she was just as anxious as he to put distance between the flivver and the ranch.

After a mile of going he brought the car to a sudden stop and leaped out, leaving the engine running. She saw him rush off among the low trees and thought for half a minute that he must have lost his mind. Then she caught sight of his figure outlined against the moonlit sky. It was perched at the top of a slender pole that rose above the tree-tops. Before she could conjecture what he was doing, he slid from sight again. Bursting back into the trail, he swung aboard again and they were off.

"Just wanted to cut the wire some more," he said, between gasps. "Makes it a little harder for 'em."

"You'd better not waste much time cutting wire," she warned him, with another look backward.

"Why not, Mrs. Lot?"

"They've probably got the big car out now."

He reached into the pocket of his coat and drew

forth something that fell clinking into her lap. She picked up two metallic objects and tried to examine them in the dim light.

"What are they?" she asked.

"One of 'em's an intake valve, the other's an exhaust. Timothy's been grinding them."

"And they can't run the car?"

"Not particularly," said the Wreck.

"And how are you going to get them back to Timothy?"

He took them from her hands and tossed them into the bushes at the side of the trail.

"Let 'em send to New York for new valves," he answered, in a tone of savage satisfaction. "They expect to stay a month, don't they?"

"You're only piling up trouble for yourself, Henry Williams."

"Nope. Only playing safe."

And to emphasize the safety of his play, he stopped the flivver again and ascended another pole, from which he cut the wires with two vicious snaps of his pliers.

"Don't forget they can make time over this trail with a horse," said Sally. "If I were you I'd keep moving."

"I hid the saddles," said the Wreck, grinning.

"You what?"

"Took all the saddles and bridles and carted them out back of the corral. Dumped them into a gully. They won't find them till morning, anyhow."

As the broad scope of his precautions to forestall

pursuit dawned upon her, Sally experienced a feeling of awed admiration. She already knew that he had a way of doing things on impulse; but it was a discovery to learn that the Wreck could be coldly calculating.

"In that case," she said, "you might slow down a little until we reach the main road. There's no use breaking our necks until we get off the Underwood property."

He adopted the suggestion and drove more slowly, although he did it with reluctance. He had a sort of affection for the dusty flivver, and the touch of the steering wheel inspired him. He was in a mood to make the machine fly, if it would.

A third time he dismounted, as they reached the end of the private road, and threw open the gate. He even took the trouble to close it, after they passed through. Then, once more taking the wheel, he looked at Sally. The main road lay just in front of them, running at right angles.

"Which way?" he demanded. "I suppose you're headed for the train, aren't you?"

CHAPTER XVIII

THE WRECK SUPPLIES A COOK

SALLY was not certain whether she was headed for the train or the Bar-M. She had not attempted to plan anything beyond the getaway, which loomed so large in her vision that it blocked off any glimpse at the future. But now she was confronted with the need to make a decision. She had no desire to go to Chicago. She was not in a mood to contemplate the purchase of a trousseau. She had certain annoying opinions on the subject of good cooks, and they persisted in thrusting themselves into the problem.

But it might be easier to go to Chicago, even if she did not buy a trousseau there. There were difficulties in the way of an early return to the Bar-M; it would entail explanations that she did not want to make, not so much on her own account as on that of the Wreck. She felt that if worst came to worst, she could justify her own course fairly well. But she did not know whether she could clear Henry Williams. Every unlawful thing he had done was on her own account, she knew, and not for all the world would she let him take the consequences single-handed. If they went back to the Bar-M she did not see how she could invent a story that would cover the situation. Certainly, she did not propose to tell the truth. She believed in truth, and she did not like inventions—but there was Henry Williams to be considered. And the welfare of Henry Williams rose above ethical considerations.

"Let's take the road back the way we came," she said. "I don't mean all the way. But we'll try to hit a branch road which will take us to the railway line. I think you spoke about Mr. Underwood saying they drove around by way of Duncan. I've never been to Duncan, but I think it's on the railroad. Why not try it?"

"It's Duncan," said the Wreck.

The flivver turned left into the highway and hurried on through the night. It was running beautifully and noisily and the Wreck listened to the beat of the motor with a sense of keen satisfaction. Never had it hit on all four cylinders with more boisterous regularity. The rest had done it good. It was both rhythmic and raucous, which was the way a good flivver ought to be.

"If I make the train," asked Sally, after a long break in the conversation, "what are you going to do?"

"Oh, I'll drift down to the Bar-M."

"But how will you explain being away so long?"

"I'll say I took my time. Camped."

"But it's going to hang you up at the Bar-M longer than you figured, isn't it?"

"How?"

"I thought you had to get back to Pittsburgh."

"No hurry. I'm not traveling on schedule."

"But I thought you were just out here to rest your nerves," she mused. "And they're all right again, aren't they?"

He shook his head violently.

"Bad as ever," he said. "Fierce."

"Henry, that's nonsense. You eat like a horse and you sleep like an old cat. I don't believe there's a thing the matter with your nerves."

"What do you know about it?" he demanded. "I'm the person that knows. I can *feel* 'em. If you had my nerves strung through your system you'd be jumping around like a grasshopper. You'd be just what I am—a wreck."

"But you're not a wreck. That's just one of your silly ideas."

"You're always arguing."

"Oh, you can be disagreeable if you wish," said Sally. "But when you talk about needing a rest for your nerves you make me tired."

"Oh, well, I don't have to rest them at the Bar-M, if that's what you mean."

"I didn't mean that. You know I didn't. You can rest them at the Bar-M from now until dooms-day, if you like."

"I'll go somewhere else," he said, stubbornly.

"Don't be silly."

That was as near as she would go to telling him exactly what she thought. If he was bound to rest his nerves in Montana, she did not know of any better place than the Bar-M. In fact, she did not know of any place which would serve so well. Even if he became a sort of permanent boarder, she did not see that the family would be inconvenienced. There was plenty of room.

"Oh, I'll bother somebody else for a while," he assured her.

It sounded to Sally as though he regarded his nerves as so many toys, and that if she did not like his toys he would take them to some other place and play. So she laughed.

"We're always getting into some absurd controversy, Henry. And here we are, right in the middle of an escape. By rights, we ought to be serious. Are you sure that you hid all the saddles?"

It was a change of subject that lasted them until the conversation again died into monosyllables, and then wholly ceased for miles. The night was cool and Sally buttoned her coat. The Wreck never seemed to feel heat or cold; she could not remember that he ever made a comment on the weather, not even on the day he arrived at Dad Morgan's ranch. There was a wiry constancy and equanimity about his bone and flesh that often amazed her. Only his nerves gave him the least concern.

"Hungry?" she asked.

"Sure."

She unwrapped a package of sandwiches and handed him one. He made three bites of it. He accepted another, then a third, and they vanished in the same fashion.

"Like 'em?" she ventured.

"They're great."

"Wonderful! At last you admit I'm a cook, Henry. I even baked the bread, you know."

He gave her a quizzical glance.

"What's all this business about cooking, anyhow?" he asked.

"Never mind. It's something like a joke, I think. Perhaps I'll tell you some day."

"All right. Can I have another one?"

She was smiling as she gave him the fourth sandwich and watched it disappear.

The flivver was snorting along famously, and Sally propped herself back in the seat and enjoyed herself. It was good to feel free again on the open road. She would even have been willing to try cutting across the range, if there was need for it. The Wreck's mood was exhilarated. He laid it to a nervous exaltation from which he would presently react, in all probability; but while it lasted he proposed to make the most of it.

Lights ahead brought them back to a sharp sense of realities. Sally clutched his arm instinctively. The lights appeared suddenly, around a turn in the road, twin points that signaled the approach of a car.

"Henry! It can't be—"

"He was riding a horse," said the Wreck, knowing instantly of whom she spoke.

He slowed the flivver down as the lights came nearer. Somebody would have to turn out; for it was a one track road. Presently he came to a dead stop and waited. The other car approached cautiously, maneuvered, wrenched itself out of the wheel ruts and took to the level stretch of grass that paralleled them. Abreast of the flivver it came to a stop.

"Good evening," said a voice. "Can you tell us where we are?"

"Montana," replied the Wreck, cautiously.

There was a laugh from the darkness. Sally could discern two figures sitting on the front seat. The rear of the car seemed to be piled with a mass of stuff that was probably camping material.

"I know it's Montana." A man was talking. "We've been in Montana for five days, and we've kept right on driving. What I'm trying to locate is some place where we can stock up with a little grub. Getting tired of bacon and flapjacks."

Sally was relieved. They were not tenderfeet, unless tenderfeet come from the Pacific coast as well as the Atlantic. There was a Western twang in the man's voice, but she knew that it came from beyond the Rockies.

"Like eggs and chickens and vegetables and stuff like that?" asked the Wreck.

"*Do* we?" Two voices blended.

"Well, there's a good ranch two or three hours up the road," said the Wreck. "You turn off to your right when you come to a gate. Can't miss it."

"And then what?"

"Close the gate after you and follow the road until you come to the house. You'll just about make

it by daylight. Tell them you'd like to have breakfast. Ask for a man named Charley."

"Yes?"

"He'll let you cook your own breakfast."

"Sounds great," said the voice. "We're just a
bit tired of driving."

"That so? Well, Charley will be glad to have
you stay for a while."

"They always told me Montana was hospitable,"
the voice declared. "Much obliged, stranger. Good
luck to you."

"Good luck."

The flivver moved ahead and Sally, glancing backward, saw the other car pull into the road again.
She turned to the Wreck and stared at him under
frowning brows.

"Henry Williams, that was an awful thing to do.
You know what Charley is likely to do to them."

"They said they were tired of driving, didn't
they?"

"But he'll try to keep them a whole month!"

"Charley isn't such a bad lot. I think we owe him
a cook."

"And it's just the same as telling him which way
we went," said Sally.

"What's the difference? Nobody 'll catch us
now," remarked the Wreck, with optimism in every
syllable.

A minute later she was trying to smother a laugh.
Every day she learned something new about Henry
Williams. It was a mean trick to play on a stranger;

it was reckless, too, from their own standpoint. It seemed, in fact, nothing short of malicious mischief. But there was something irresponsibly boyish about it and she could not force herself to scold him, as she knew she ought to have done.

After a little they began discussing trains going East. Sally, still somewhat doubtful as to whether she was really destined for Chicago, said that she did not believe they would make the railroad that night. The Wreck, strangely enough, agreed with her. He was less concerned about their goal than about the fact that they were in motion, going somewhere.

"When it gets to be daylight," she said, "I'm afraid we're likely to find the main road risky."

"You mean the sheriff?"

"Yes."

"How big is the posse?"

"Don't tell me you're dreaming of making a fight if we meet them," she exclaimed.

"I was only wondering how big it was."

"It doesn't make any difference. Even Bob Wells, alone, is big enough."

"Is he?"

She shook her head impatiently.

"You don't understand. I'm not saying you're not able to fight. What I mean is that we mustn't meet them at all. Of course, Bob wouldn't do anything to *me*. But we can't afford even to let him see us. And besides, we'll be dead for sleep by daylight."

"Oh."

"So it seems to me that the sensible thing to do is to turn off the road before it gets light, if we can find a place, and hide until it gets dark again."

They discussed it for a while, and he agreed with her. He had no doubt of his ability to skip a night's sleep if necessary, but there was no need to ask the same hardship of Sally. So they decided to find another hide-out as soon as it seemed wise to desert the road. Meantime, the flivver steadily left the Underwood ranch farther and farther behind.

Sally sat wondering what Charley McSween was saying, what Chester was doing, what everybody was thinking. She was afraid that Charley was having a difficult time of it with the boss of the ranch, and there were points about Charley that she admired. Of course, he had no business to kidnap them in the beginning, and it was intolerable for him to talk about detaining them for a month. But in other respects she found Charley McSween rather agreeable.

The Wreck was not thinking about Charley at all. He was not thnking of anything in particular, for that matter. He was in a mood of unusual content, his conscience clear, his mind restful, his optimism unshaken. All he asked was to keep on driving, indefinitely. Even the presence of a woman passenger did not disturb him. The sex still bothered him, of course; but Sally was less a trouble than any of the others. There was no foolishness about her, and if it came to a pinch she could be relied upon to do things. In fact, she was just about as good as a man, he admitted to himself.

"We mustn't forget to look for a turn-out," she reminded him, after she glanced at her watch and studied the stars. The moon had already dipped below the horizon.

Each watched their own side of the road, the bobbing beam of the headlights spreading itself sufficiently wide to illuminate any turn-out they might reach. Sally discovered what appeared to be a regular wagon road on her own side, but after an examination they decided against it. There were signs of recent use and she feared that it might belong to another ranch. They were not in a hurry to meet any more ranchers.

Considerably later, when the sky behind them was growing paler with the coming of a day, the Wreck stopped the car and called attention to what looked like a trail, branching off to the left. Sally got out and examined it. There were wheel ruts, but they were much overgrown. Wherever it led, it presented every aspect of abandonment. The country about them, as they could gather from the rough skyline and the pitching of the road, was broken and probably wooded. Sally did not remember it at all; she had been asleep when they passed that way before.

"Shall we try it?" she yawned.

"Get in."

He turned the flivver at a sharp angle and they left the main road. The new route began climbing a rise, immediately, then dipped into a gulch. The Wreck found himself forced to drive with care, for there were sharp turns every few yards. The road merely followed the natural contour, no effort having been made to grade it or to shorten the distance between points.

"There are lots of these old roads in this part of the country," commented Sally. "Most of them lead to mines that never panned out."

After some ten minutes of slow, but thrilling travel, she suggested a halt.

"This ought to be far enough," she said. "There are two ridges between us and the main road."

The Wreck stopped the car. The abrupt silencing of the motor left them in a stillness that was fairly startling. The place was dark, too, for there was a heavy growth of trees all about them, and the spreading light in the eastern sky did not reach them. As they sat for a minute trying to get the feel of their environment, Sally's hand crept over and sought the Wreck's arm. She was not nervous, exactly, but the touch of him reassured her.

Then her fingers clutched him with sudden fierceness, and she could feel his muscles tense under the grip.

"Did you hear that?" she whispered.

He had heard. It was the soft neigh of a horse.

She sprang to her feet, steadying herself against his shoulder, and her eyes began searching in the gloom. An instant later she bent her head.

"There's a little fire off through the trees—to

the right," she said, in a low voice. "We have run into somebody's camp."

"Let's go," said the Wreck.

He was climbing out to crank the motor, when she clutched him again.

"Wait! I can hear somebody coming. You'll never be able to turn around in this place."

He, too, could hear footsteps off in the brush. Reaching forward to the dash, he switched off the lights.

"Turn them on!" commanded Sally. "We're caught anyhow, and I'm not going to be pounced on in the dark."

He turned the lights on again, and they waited. The footsteps were cautious, but they were still approaching.

"Put the gun away," she whispered, as she saw him fumbling with it. "It's not loaded and you'll only get us into trouble. You can't run that kind of a bluff on Bob Wells, anyhow."

"Who?"

"Who else? Why, it's almost certain. Oh, of all the luck! We've run plumb into him! You let me do the talking, Henry Williams."

The footsteps were nearer.

CHAPTER XIX

CAPTURED

JUST as Sally's fingers were digging into his arm until he was ready to growl a protest, a voice came from the bushes beside the car: "You better get 'em right up in the air—quick."

Sally raised her hands promptly, and the Wreck followed suit, after she commanded him.

Into the back glare of the headlights stepped a man who carried a rifle that looked ready for work.

"One of 'em's a woman," he called, evidently addressing somebody behind him.

There was no answer from the rear. It seemed that the matter of conversation had been left wholly in his hands.

"We'll take the pedigree," said the man with the rifle. "Any relation to the sheriff?"

"Plenty of relation," said Sally, promptly. "We want to see him."

There was a chuckle by way of answer.

"Sure you're lookin' for the sheriff?" he inquired. "I kind of figure he's asleep and don't want to be disturbed."

"You lead me to Bob Wells," said Sally. "I'm going to step right out of this car, and if you start anything with that gun you'll wish you'd never been born."

The Wreck followed her, and they stood beside the flivver, with a rifle muzzle not more than a yard distant from them.

"The lady speaks first," said the man with the gun. "And be careful about your hands."

"I'll talk to Bob Wells and nobody else," declared Sally, firmly.

"Are you speakin' serious?"

"I certainly am. And I'd advise you not to argue about it."

He muttered something that she could not hear, yet it conveyed the idea that his mind was in doubt. The Wreck remained passive during the colloquy. He did not need Sally's caution. Whatever might be required of him, he felt that the time was not yet. Beside, he was sure that Sally had the right idea. There was no need for dealing with subordinates when Bob Wells was on the ground. He was quite willing to face the sheriff.

"Lead me to the sheriff," said Sally.

There was a suppressed laugh from the figure that held the rifle.

"I'll lead you," he said. "Come to think of it, I figure you'd better lead yourselves. You just head for that camp-fire and I'll keep walking behind you. And don't forget I'm carrying a gun. Not that it makes any difference to me, but it might make a heap of difference to you."

Sally set off in the lead, stumbling through the brush in the direction of the camp. She was angry enough to shout what she wanted to say to Bob

Wells, but she would not spoil the dramatic effect of a face-to-face meeting. The Wreck followed in her wake, grim, yet somewhat out of countenance. They had blundered into something they did not expect, but they would emerge with banners flying, he knew in his heart. In fact, there was a real advantage in having everything settled here and now.

It was a very small, disorderly and informal sort of camp, Sally discovered as soon as she put foot within the glow of dying embers. There was no tent; there was no sign of an establishment that contained even ordinary comforts. But there were two men with rifles in their hands, sitting up in their blankets and studying the strangers with hard eyes.

"Well, who you got there, Lefty?" inquired one of the men on the ground.

"Parties lookin' for the sheriff," observed Lefty, with a somewhat exaggerated wink.

"Just the two of 'em?"

"Just them."

The asker of questions arose to his feet for a better survey of the visitors. He was a large man and his most conspicuous feature was a broken nose. Sally and the Wreck came to learn that his companions called him Nosey.

"Where is the sheriff?" demanded Sally, but this time she did not say it with any confidence. A sudden misgiving had assailed her.

"We ain't figurin' to meet up with the sheriff to-day," remarked Nosey.

"This is not his camp, then?"

"No; you might say it isn't."

Sally glanced at the Wreck.

"Well, Henry, I suppose we'd better be going," she said.

He nodded and was turning to lead the way, when he found the muzzle of Lefty's rifle sticking into his ribs.

"You two better set down awhile," said Nosey, who seemed to be a person of authority. "Lefty, you just keep your eye on the lady and gent. Denver, I wanta talk to you."

The third man climbed out of his blankets and followed Nosey. They went beyond earshot. The guard motioned Sally and the Wreck to seats on the ground and placed himself opposite them at a little distance, his back against a tree. The rifle lay ready in his hands.

"I'm afraid we've blundered," whispered Sally.

"What do you make of this bunch?" asked the Wreck.

"Pretty tough, I'm afraid."

"Might have been worse."

"How?"

"Might have been the sheriff."

"That's so," nodded Sally. "But I was all ready for him. Now I don't know just what we're up against."

Daylight was coming rapidly in the untidy camp, and the more Sally saw of the place the less she liked it. There was only one inference, of course; they had stumbled into some kind of a gang, very likely the same gang for which Bob Wells was searching. Fine luck!

Nosey and Denver rejoined the group.

"What's the idea?" demanded the Wreck. "Prisoners?"

"Maybe," said Nosey, who looked thoughtful.

"Well, if it's robbery, you don't stand to win very much."

"What's the game, comin' in here askin' for the sheriff?" asked Nosey. "You friends of his?"

"We know him," said Sally, cautiously.

"That's plain enough. You were callin' him by name awhile back. You workin' for him?"

Sally and the Wreck said "No" together.

"I ain't so sure," mused Nosey. "He might think it was a smart trick, gettin' a woman to help play the game. I reckon you know the sheriff's out around here somewheres with a posse?"

"We heard so," admitted Sally.

"Do you know who he's lookin' for?"

"I suppose he's looking for you, isn't he?"

"Well, you might say so."

"You won't find us the least bit of use to you," said Sally. "You might as well turn us loose. And if we run into the sheriff we won't say anything."

Nosey shook his head incredulously.

"How come you're off the main road, up in here?" he inquired. "What fetched you? No; I figure we ain't goin' to turn you loose right yet."

The Wreck, who had been wonderfully patient through it all, was thinking whether it would pay to claim a community of interest with Nosey and his friends. He suggested it to Sally in a low voice, but she shook her head.

"They probably hate a rival gang worse than the sheriff," she whispered. "Besides, we don't look like a gang. They'd never believe it."

Denver had stirred up the fire, tossed a few fresh sticks on it and was getting breakfast. The leader of the party went off in the direction of the flivver, evidently to make an inspection. Lefty, still acting as guard, sat impassive against his tree, apparently not even indulging in thoughts.

"They can't keep us forever," said Sally.

"But perhaps long enough for the sheriff to catch up," suggested the Wreck.

"That would be bad, although I was resigned to it awhile ago. Now I feel as if we had a chance again."

"We'll make a break whenever you say."

Sally shook her head.

"This outfit would shoot you if it had to, I haven't the least doubt," she said. "And besides, Henry, do you know that right now I haven't the least desire to make a break? I'm horribly sleepy. I'm not a bit excited over this; I'm too tired. So long as I thought it was Bob Wells' camp I was mad, and that woke me up. But now I'm drowsy again. I'm not going to make any break from here until I get some sleep, and I don't care if the sheriff walks right in on us."

Denver motioned that they could help themselves

to breakfast. It was not very inviting. All that
Sally wanted was a cup of coffee. The Wreck, however, ate heartily.

Sally found a fairly comfortable spot under a
tree and stretched herself for a nap. She advised
the Wreck to do the same.

"I'll sit alongside of you," he said, "and keep an
eye on things."

"Better get some sleep yourself."

"I'm not sleepy. I can't sleep. I'd like to
bust—"

"Ss-h," said Sally.

In three minutes she had dozed off and in ten
her slumber was deep. The Wreck propped himself against the tree, drew up his knees, folded his
arms across them and directed a surly stare at Lefty.
The latter, with his rifle at his feet, did not seem to
be disconcerted. He did not, in fact, appear to display much interest in the prisoners, beyond an eye
to their security.

The Wreck was determined to keep a vigilant
lookout for opportunities. After a little while he
observed what struck him as a singular phenomenon.
The figure of Lefty was undergoing some strange
distortion. It shrank, it swelled; sometimes it
seemed to float in the air, again to sink into the
ground. The image trembled and danced before
his eyes, in a queer yet fascinating manner. There
were moments when it vanished entirely, only to
reappear with illogical abruptness, three or four
times as big as it was before. He had been calculat-

ing the possibilities of a sudden dash; he believed that Lefty would succumb to swift attack, if only Denver were not hovering about as a potential rescuer. Yet when Lefty began to assume a variety of shapes and sizes he was not so certain. His elusiveness to the eye was disconcerting.

Then he was conscious that Lefty had assumed normal proportions again. He was strolling around the camp, his rifle drooping from the hollow of his arm. Sally was sitting up, doing her hair with the aid of a little mirror that proclaimed the advance of the feminist movement in Montana. She was smiling at the Wreck.

"Have a good sleep?" she asked.

"Huh? Sleep? I haven't been asleep. Maybe I closed my eyes a minute, but I was just resting 'em."

"Then they've had a good rest, Henry. I've been awake for an hour and they've been closed all that time."

"What time is it?"

"Almost sundown."

He stirred himself and grinned sheepishly.

"What's been going on, anyhow?" he asked.

"I don't know, except that the ones they call Nosey and Denver aren't here. I asked Lefty where they were and he said they'd been gone for hours, and that it was none of my business, anyhow."

The Wreck studied Lefty with an appraising eye.

"We might jump him," he whispered.

Sally shook her head.

"Not with that gun in his hands. I think we'll have to wait awhile."

Later, they asked their guard if they might go to the flivver and get some sandwiches. He seemed interested in the sandwiches and signified that they could go under escort. They went, returning to camp with Sally's parcel of provisions. Going and coming, Lefty followed them. He accepted a couple of sandwiches with a grunt of acknowledgment, ate them with apparent approval, but did not relax his vigilance.

It was dusk when Nosey and Denver rode into camp and dismounted. Lefty grumbled something about being left alone all day and was told to shut up. Then there was a conference. The Wreck and Sally missed most of it, but gathered that Nosey had decided that it would be safer for all hands to remain where they were for another night. Something was said about the sheriff, but they could not catch that part.

"I'll be doggoned if I'll stay here another night," said the Wreck to Sally.

"Ss-h. We may have to."

"But what do they want with us?"

"I've no idea. I think they're just afraid to turn us loose."

The Wreck addressed himself to the leader.

"What's the idea?" he demanded.

"Shut up."

The Wreck glowered and moved uneasily, but

Sally laid a hand on his arm and warned him with
a look.

"Any reason my wife and I can't be driving on?"
he asked.

"And notify the sheriff?" sneered Nosey.

"Damn the sheriff."

"Sure. Only I don't figure you're goin' to drive
on for awhile yet. Besides, we may be wantin' to
use the car ourselves."

"And how long do you think we're going to stay
here?"

"Just as long as I see fit," said Nosey. "And if
you don't keep your face shut, I'll shut it for you."

Again Sally restrained her partner in captivity.
The only thing that had a soothing effect was her
plea that if anything happened to him she would
be left there alone with three unpleasant strangers.
They talked things over in low tones while Nosey
and his companions busied themselves with getting
supper.

"They're worried about the sheriff," she said.
"That's plain enough. Bob must be right in the
neighborhood somewhere. They don't even dare
go out to the main road."

"Well, they're not going to steal my car. That's
certain."

"What are you going to do about it, if they make
up their minds?"

He was not certain, but he had an idea there
would be noise and excitement.

"And a few shots," added Sally. "And then we

won't worry about flivvers or anything else. You keep your head on your shoulders, Henry Williams. I'm not in any great hurry to lose mine."

He growled a complaint about hanging around and doing nothing.

"We'll find a chance yet," she whispered. "They're just as much fussed about this as we are. They don't want us around here, but they're afraid to let go of us. They don't know that we're running away from the sheriff, too, and we'd never be able to make them believe it. We're a pair of white elephants on their hands, but they can't find the answer."

Lefty, who had relinquished guard duty to Denver, brought them some greasy bacon and coffee.

"You'd better fill up," he advised. "You can't tell when you'll be feedin' again."

He did not suffer an explanation of this remark, and Sally and the Wreck had a fresh sense of uneasiness. Then the trio of captors entered upon a long consultation. The only person who paid even casual attention to the prisoners was Denver, who sat where he could keep an eye on them and whose rifle was too handy to encourage an attempted break.

Darkness came again, and Sally and the Wreck were ordered to move closer to the fire, where they could be watched more readily. Nosey took the added precaution of tying their feet together. He did not bother about their hands as yet; he merely wanted to be sure that they could not break and run on an instant's notice.

The consultation of the trio continued, at a little distance from the fire, where they were beyond earshot of the prisoners. Although it was conducted in undertones, Sally and the Wreck sensed disagreement, and even acrimony. Finally, Nosey brought it to an end with a peremptory gesture.

"You stay here and watch 'em," he ordered Denver. "Lefty and me are goin' down by the main road for awhile. And the first crack they make, let 'em have it."

Denver grumbled about being left behind.

"Somebody's got to do it," snarled Nosey, "unless you're for hittin' 'em over the head now. You do as you're told."

Denver sullenly seated himself by the fire, his rifle between his knees, and watched his companions as they disappeared among the trees. Then he fell to glowering at Sally and the Wreck.

CHAPTER XX

THE STORM

PROBABLY an hour elapsed before anybody spoke. The Wreck's soul writhed under the torture of inactivity. Time after time he calculated the chances of a spring at Denver's throat. Even with his hobbled feet he believed that he might achieve a success; but he could not be absolutely sure. On his own account, he was willing to try and abide by the break of the luck; but with Sally to be considered he could not conscientiously bring himself to the point. If anything went amiss with the attempt, she would be in a worse predicament than her present one.

Denver was watchful. Sitting across the campfire from the two prisoners, he did not permit their least movement to go unnoticed. And the rifle was always at his hand. The Wreck hoped that he might become drowsy; even an instant's nod would be sufficient. But Denver was apparently a person who could dispense with sleep when he chose, and this was obviously one of the occasions. He was a black-haired, saturnine person, apparently rather stupid, yet smart enough to devote himself single-minded to the vigil that had been ordered by his chief.

Sally and the Wreck made an effort to pass time

in conversation, but they felt no freedom of speech in the presence of Denver, who listened but offered to take no part. His presence discouraged talk, particularly, as the one subject they wished to discuss —escape—was prohibited because of his inevitable eavesdropping. But they boggled along for awhile, half-heartedly, because there was nothing else to do, until a deep-toned rumbling noise interrupted Sally in the middle of a sentence.

"Thunder," she remarked, casually. "Wouldn't wonder if we caught a storm."

"Uh-uh," said the Wreck, gloomily.

He could imagine nothing more uncomfortable than sitting there in a downpour. The camp did not even boast a tent.

There was more rumbling from back in the hills, and twice there were flashes in the black skies. Denver added a couple of sticks to the fire and huddled back again, still with the rifle between his knees.

"I suppose we'll get wet," remarked Sally, in a resigned tone. "Well, there's nothing on me that will get hurt."

"Let it rain," said the Wreck.

There was a stirring of leaves on the topmost branches of the trees, followed by an atmospheric sluggishness that became oppressive. The lightning was growing more brilliant and frequent, while the noise from the skies was multiplying itself. Just one more discomfort to be endured, the Wreck reflected; they seemed to have encountered nothing but bad luck since they left the Bar-M.

A fresh roll of thunder, and a second later Sally touched his arm. He glanced toward her, and found that her eyes were watching Denver across the fire.

"What?" he asked.

"I didn't say anything," answered Sally.

There was a faint frown on her forehead which he interpreted as an order not to ask questions. Yet he knew there was something she wanted to say to him. She was still looking at Denver, and the Wreck also looked. The study brought him no enlightenment. Denver sat stolidly and watched them without interest, yet with a diligence that was admirable. Presently the Wreck's attention wandered.

More thunder and another touch of his arm. Sally was still staring at the man on the other side of the fire. What did she mean? The Wreck also fell to staring, although he tried to do it in an unobtrusive manner. Apparently it had something to do with Denver.

An instant later he had a glimmer of understanding. There was a brilliant flash, then an interval of three or four seconds, then a deep bellow that echoed heavily through the woods. Denver's head twitched, his glance lifted itself for an instant toward the tree-tops, then he huddled back and glared again at his prisoners. The Wreck settled himself to watch.

He had not long to wait. A vivid play of light in the skies, a series of rolling crashes. Denver's head twitched again in involuntary accompaniment, his shoulders stirred and there was a restless movement of one hand. Once more his eyes sought the blackness overhead, only to wince when it was gashed with a white, irregular streak.

Sally and the Wreck exchanged glances, the latter making a faint movement of his head, to signify that he understood. Denver was afraid of a thunderstorm. It seemed so absurd that for an instant the Wreck wanted to laugh. Stolid, insensitive to human contact, with a jaw fashioned perfectly for a heavy-weight champion and a physique that matched it, Denver was the ideal bully and bad man. Habitually he wore an expression that told of his inurement to violence. Without fear, he would take his chances with a sheriff or anybody else. But he was afraid of thunder and lightning.

The heavens crashed again, flaring in two different directions. Denver responded automatically, with a twitch that affected his whole body. The pair of watchers saw him tighten a quivering lip. He favored them with a look of defiant suspicion— a warning that they would better keep out of his private affairs. Sally turned her eyes upward.

"It's getting nearer every minute," she told the Wreck.

"Yes; we're going to catch it."

"I only hope it rains, too," said Sally. "The dry storms are the worst."

"You bet they are," agreed the Wreck. "I don't know why, but it's always so."

"And it's always worse in the woods, on account of the trees. Why, I remember—"

The sound of her voice was swallowed up in a
roar. Something had been struck, and not very far
distant; they could feel a tremor in the ground.
Denver's head seemed to shrink between his shoulders and for a second his eyes closed tightly. Then
they opened with a jerk of terror as he remembered
his prisoners.

"That was close," said Sally, in an awed tone and
with a meaning glance at the Wreck. "I'm afraid
we're going to be right in the center of it. If it
would only rain!"

"Well, we've got to take our chances," declared
the Wreck, solemnly. "What can we do?"

"Nothing," she sighed. "Only—"

Denver was biting savagely at his under lip and
the fingers of one hand were drumming nervously
on the ground.

"Does it hit much in the woods?" he asked, suddenly. There was a sort of emptiness in his voice.

"More than anywhere else," answered the Wreck.
"But it doesn't do any good to run. If it's going
to get you it'll get you, as sure as a gun."

"I'm—I'm afraid I'm getting nervous," whim-
pered Sally.

The skies flared and detonated again and, with a
little shriek, she threw her arms around the Wreck's
neck.

"Henry!" she cried.

His eyes were stealthily watching Denver and his
hand was creeping cautiously toward a stick of split
wood that lay near the fire.

"Not yet—wait!" Sally was whispering with her lips close to his ear. "Give him a minute or two more. He's slipping fast."

The Wreck waited. He found it difficult to believe what he saw with his eyes. Denver's big body had sagged loosely and his shoulders were trembling. He was a man on the verge of a panic, but nerveless. His lips twitched grotesquely, his eyes seemed to be staring at nothing. He wanted to shut them, but he did not dare.

"I—I don't like it," he mumbled, in a petulant voice. "I—"

"It's awful!" cried Sally.

"God help us!" groaned the Wreck.

There was a lull, a sudden blast of wind in the trees, then a fresh onset of fury from the skies. Flash and crash were blended in a terrifying ensemble. Sally, still clutching the Wreck, kept her eyes on the man beyond the camp-fire.

His body swayed, his hands clasped themselves in a sudden paroxysm and there was a dull agony in his eyes.

"I can't stand it!" he whined, in a high falsetto.

Suddenly he crossed his arms on his knees and buried his head. He was sobbing.

"Now!" whispered Sally.

The Wreck's fingers had closed on the split stick. He rose swiftly to his hobbled feet, balanced himself, took aim and flung it furiously at Denver's head. Instantly he followed it, leaping clumsily across the fire and hurling himself on the huddled figure.

Denver went over on his back and the Wreck clutched for his throat.

"Grab his gun!" he cried to Sally.

She was scrambling toward it when she saw him roll off the recumbent figure, hitch himself into a sitting posture and begin the task of untying his feet.

"No hurry," said the Wreck. "He's out cold. I don't know whether it was the stick of wood, or whether he just fainted. Get your feet loose before we do anything else."

Sally went to work at the cords that hobbled her. The Wreck cast a contemptuous glance at the flabby inert form of Denver, the bully.

"The big simp!" he said, as he shook his feet free.

"Oh, I don't know," said Sally, working feverishly. "It's horrible when you're afraid like that. You can't help it. I've seen ma when she was just as bad. And we had a cowpuncher once who was even worse, although he was a terrible fighter. And—"

The bellowing storm obliterated the remainder of the sentence. As she stood up, free of her bonds, she shook her head, as though to throw off an unpleasant sensation.

"You can say what you like," she declared, "but it's a pretty mean storm, just the same. I'm not claiming to enjoy it myself."

The Wreck had rolled Denver over on his face and was tying his hands behind his back. He worked

quickly and roughly, but he made the job thorough.
Then he reached for the cord that Sally held and
began tying the big creature's ankles.

"But look what it did for us," said the Wreck,
as the storm shrieked at them again.

"Is he hurt much?"

The Wreck began exploring the skull of his victim.

"I can't even find blood," he said. "He had a
hat on when I hit him. There's a big welt on top
of his head. When he comes to he'll think he was
struck by lightning."

"You don't think he's dead, Henry?"

"No!" answered the Wreck, scornfully. "I can
feel him breathing. Come on, now. We'd better
get out of this."

He picked up Denver's rifle, examined the breech,
then threw it across his shoulder. Sally bent over
the loose figure and stared at it curiously.

"We all have our weak spots," she said, solemnly.
"I'm honestly sorry for him."

"We did him a kindness," averred the Wreck.
"He won't worry about the rest of the storm. Come
on!"

"Where?"

"We're going to get the car, of course."

He seized her hand and they plunged into the
brush that surrounded the small clearing where the
camp lay. As they did so, the rain came. It did
not begin gently, with widely scattered drops, but
came in an abrupt rush, with a roar that resembled

the voice of a cataract. Even through the trees it beat down on them from the darkness, carried on the wings of a squall that fairly howled. Almost as abruptly the electric phase passed, so that now the flashes were fewer and dimmer.

They blundered forward, clinging to each other. They stumbled over roots and vines, floundered blindly into trees, forced their way through underbrush that seemed to claw at them. Both were drenched to the skin and gasping for breath before they had gone a hundred yards.

"Seems to me we've gone far enough," panted Sally. "It was only a little way from camp."

"It's right around here somewhere," said the Wreck. "Come on."

He dragged her forward again.

"If we could get some more lightning we could see something," she complained.

"We'll find it," he promised, confidently.

But they had not found the flivver in five minutes, or ten, although they steadily groped their way through the dripping woods, trying to shield their faces against the beating rain.

"We've been going uphill too much," said Sally, who had a sharp misgiving concerning their quest. "The ground was almost level between the flivver and the camp."

"Then we'll go downhill some," declared the Wreck.

They went downhill for awhile, but it was still a blind scramble through the trees and underbrush, with no touch of a flivver to greet their outstretched hands. It was very dark. They could hear distant thunder, but the lightning they could not see. And it rained as though determined never to stop.

"I don't see that that rifle is doing you any good," observed Sally, as they paused to rest. "It's only so much more to carry."

"We may need it," he said, stubbornly.

Half an hour passed. The rain was lessening, although the fact made little difference; neither Sally, nor the Wreck, nor the woods could get any wetter.

"I'm afraid," she said, "that we started in the wrong direction when we left the camp."

"We'll go back to the camp and start over again."

"But you'll never find the camp now, Henry."

"Sure."

There was no use in arguing or trying to discourage him, and Sally knew they might better be moving than standing still, so she suffered herself to be led on another journey through the darkness. The Wreck seemed to be tireless. He plodded and stumbled onward, scorning difficulties, picking himself up whenever he fell, clinging to the rifle, and doing it all with an amazing optimism and even a show of patience.

"Any time you want to rest, just holler," he advised.

Sally promised that she would, but she kept going.

They did not find the camp. Even if they passed within a few yards of it the chances were against discovery, for long ago, Sally knew, the rain must have obliterated the last vestige of glowing embers. But the Wreck searched stubbornly for hours, it seemed. He would not admit that he was lost, although Sally would have conceded it without hesitation. He seemed to proceed on the theory that groping through the woods was like walking the streets of Pittsburgh—even if you happened to be in a strange neighborhood you would locate your street at last.

"Let's rest awhile," he suggested.

Sally was willing. Her skirt was heavy with moisture and her legs were tired. They found a fallen tree and sat for a long time, during which the moon came out. It did not give them much light, but it had a cheerful aspect. They did not talk much. She felt that the Wreck was chagrined about their failure to find the flivver and did not refer to it. Nor did she even speculate on what they were going to do next, although it seemed to her that their plight was more unfavorable than ever.

"We ought to be getting some daylight in an hour or so," she said.

He agreed with her and suggested that they walk again. There seemed to be no end to the woods. How far they had traveled, or in what direction, Sally had not the smallest idea. She felt quite helpless. The one thing that gave her a measure of confidence was the demeanor of the Wreck. He was undaunted; everything would be all right as soon as it got light enough to see what they were doing.

They were resting again when a noise made by something that moved stirred them both to alertness. It was not far distant, and Sally held her breath as she clung to the Wreck's fingers. Several times the noise was repeated; it was as if some heavy body were forcing its way through the brush.

"Maybe it's one of the gang, she whispered.

"Maybe. Do they have bears here?"

"Not many, I reckon. I never saw one."

"You stay here," he said. "I'm going to see what it is."

"No."

"I've got a rifle, haven't I?"

"I don't care. You'd better stay here."

They heard the noise again.

"I'm going," said the Wreck. "Sit still."

"Henry!"

He was gone, trying to be stealthy about it, but making a din as he plunged forward into the gloom. Sally gritted her teeth and followed him. What was he blundering into now?

She was several yards behind him when she heard a scuffle, then a muffled exclamation from the Wreck. Something was plunging around in the brush ahead of her.

"Henry!" she called sharply. "Henry!"

Then his excited voice floated back to her.

"I've got hold of a horse," he cried. "What'll I do with it?"

"A horse!"

"Yes, a horse!"

"Hang onto it; I'm coming."

She went forward at a run, tripped, fell headlong, picked herself up and resumed.

"He's rearing around," complained the voice of the Wreck. "The damn fool, he's just—"

"Well, you hang onto him," said Sally grimly. "I'll be there in a second. Darn these woods, anyhow."

CHAPTER XXI

THE SHERIFF'S HORSE

WHEN she reached him, the Wreck was still struggling with a dark shape that was making desperate efforts to back out of the encounter.

"Let me see," said Sally, pushing herself to the front. "What are you holding him by, anyhow? Why, he's bridled!"

It had not occurred to the Wreck that a horse roaming the woods at night did not usually wear a bridle, but to Sally, who knew about things, it was an oddity.

"Easy now, boy." She had hold of the bridle and was talking in a soothing, professional tone. The effect of her voice and her practised hand was almost immediate. "That's it; gentle, now. And who turned you loose in the woods?"

An instant later she made a second discovery.

"Saddled, too! That's queer. He's broken loose from some place. I suppose the storm scared him. There now, boy; steady. Well, can you beat it? Saddled and bridled, all ready to hand."

She stroked the animal's neck, patted his shoulder and talked gently to him. Presently he responded with a nuzzling against her arm, and then she knew she had him.

"We can't be far from the camp, Henry. He must belong to Nosey, or one of that crowd, of course. A horse might get frightened in a storm like that, but he wouldn't run very far in the woods. Listen!"

The Wreck had not heard anything, but Sally's quick ear caught a familiar sound.

"There's another one roaming around here somewhere," she said. "Listen again."

After a short interval both heard it—a faint whinny from off among the trees.

"Don't move," said Sally. "This one will answer in a minute. They'll get together, or else I don't know horses."

Presently her prediction was realized, but it took another call from the distance before the bridled horse answered.

"Stay right here, Henry. The other one will come to us. You might have that rifle ready, just in case— There may be somebody riding it, you know, looking for this one."

The second horse was advancing more rapidly now. There was another interchange of calls and Sally clung more tightly to the bridle of their captive. The Wreck stood tense, ready to shoot at anything that looked like a man. Sally cautioned him not to be too quick; she did not want any bloodletting unless it was a final alternative.

Out of the brush and into the dim light came a second riderless horse.

"Hold this one," said Sally, giving the bridle to the Wreck.

An instant later she had a second captive.

"Bridled and saddled like the first one!" she exclaimed. "Did you ever hear of such luck?"

"What do you make out of it?"

"They must belong to Nosey and Lefty. I suppose they left them standing somewhere, maybe, while they got out of the storm themselves, and the poor things got scared and ran away. I don't blame them."

"Well, what are we going to do with 'em?"

Sally peered at him through the gloom, as if trying to see whether he was serious.

"Do with them?" she echoed, in amazement. "What do you usually do with a horse? Kiss it? You big silly, we're going to *ride* them."

The Wreck made a grimace.

"How about my car?" he demanded. "Aren't we going to look for that?"

"No, we're not. Are you crazy? So long as we've got their horses let them keep the car. We don't want to go messing around that camp again to-night. We're liable to get ourselves into trouble again. Don't try to push your luck too far, Henry Williams. We're in big luck now—we've got their horses, two of them, anyhow. And we've got one rifle. What more could we ask?"

He pondered the proposition gloomily. Of course,

he could not expect her to understand how anybody could become attached to a flivver. He could not treat the idea of abandonment so lightly; not that it was particularly valuable to him in dollars, but there was a bond of sentiment to be considered. Yet he could see the sound sense at the bottom of her verdict. After all, he was primarily responsible for getting Sally Morgan either aboard a train or back to the Bar-M. The flivver would have to take its chances.

"Oh, all right," he growled.

"Why, of course," said Sally.

"Then which way do we go?"

"We ought to try to hit for the main road, I suppose. That seems the most sensible thing to do. We'll probably be able to get our bearings then. I'd wait till daylight, only I don't think we ought to. I'm afraid we're too near the camp. They'll be out looking for these horses. They can't afford to lose them."

"They've got my car," he reminded her.

"But maybe they can't run it, Henry. It's one thing to ride a horse around this country; but when it comes to exploring it in a flivver, well, you've got to be an expert."

He merely grunted at the compliment, for he suspected that she was only joking.

"You'd better ride the one that you caught," she added. "He's all quieted down now. Can you mount him?"

"Certainly I can," snapped the Wreck. "But what are you going to do? You haven't any riding skirt."

Sally laughed in the darkness.

"Don't you worry about me, old timer. I'll ride him. Wait till I shorten his stirrups a bit."

The Wreck had scaled the side of the first captive and was trying to find a comfortable place in the saddle, when Sally made a flying mount of the second.

"You'd better let me go ahead," she said. "We'll just walk while we're in the woods. And don't get yourself knocked off by a branch. Come on."

They set off at a slow pace, Sally giving her animal its head, save for occasional guidance in the direction she thought they ought to follow. The Wreck's horse followed, determined not to be isolated again so that all that his rider had to do was to balance himself in the saddle and fend off branches with the rifle.

Sally had but a vague idea of whither they should go to seek the main road. It was, in fact, little more than an arbitrary guess; but she stuck to it because it seemed to give them a definite route, if nothing more. She was weary of aimless wandering, and particularly weary of wandering afoot. The Wreck, having no ideas of his own as to their course, was content merely to follow. Given the flivver, he would have developed positive convictions as to whither they should go; but riding a horse confused him—it forced him to concentrate on the problem of not falling off.

One consideration in Sally's mind was to avoid the camp at all costs, and apparently she was succeeding in that, for after half an hour of riding in a direction that was generally straight they saw no trace of it. The country was rather broken, but she did not mind that, if they could only get out of the woods. With the first faint coming of dawn she was pleased to discover that the trees were becoming more sparse. They had already left most of the brush behind them. A few minutes later, as they rode out into an open space, the light about them was visibly increased.

The Wreck's horse ranged alongside Sally's mount without urging and nipped gently at the shoulder of his companion.

"G'long there," said Sally, good naturedly. "Mind your—"

She broke off into a little cry and reined her horse sharply.

"Henry Williams!" she cried.

"What now?"

She was staring at the Wreck's horse.

"Look—look what you're riding!"

"Huh?" He squinted down through his spectacles at the top of the animal's head, as though expecting to discover, perhaps, that it was an elephant or a camel, rather than a regulation Montana mount.

"It's Bob Wells's horse!" said Sally, in a voice of awe.

And indeed it was, as the Wreck could now see,

with a fair amount of early morning light coming over the hills. It was the big black animal that even he, to whom most horses looked alike, had come to associate with the sheriff.

"I'll be doggoned!" he muttered.

Sally sat rigid in her saddle, as though the sight had petrified her. It was Bob's horse, Bob's saddle, Bob's bridle—the whole outfit was there. No wonder she had been able to soothe the frightened animal, back in the darkness. He knew her.

"We've stolen the sheriff's horses!" she gasped.

"Found 'em," corrected the Wreck.

"Oh, Henry!"

"Well, what of it?"

"But— What in the world does it mean? I'm all mixed up."

The Wreck did not have any very clear idea of what it meant, but the discovery was rather pleasing to him. Unconsciously, he assumed a more jaunty pose in the saddle.

"One horse is the same as another to me," he remarked. "You thought they were good enough when we found 'em in the woods. What's the matter with 'em now?"

"But Bob—his horse—and— Why he must have been right close to us!"

"Well, he didn't find us, did he?" remarked the Wreck, triumphantly. He even risked his seat by leaning forward and stroking the neck of the black horse.

Sally glanced at her own mount. She could not

remember ever having seen the animal before. It was a medium-sized bay, rather easily gaited, but evidently not built for speed.

"We must have all been pretty close together in the woods," mused Sally. "Think of that. Of course, Bob didn't know about us; he couldn't have. But he must have been pretty hot on the trail of that gang. I suppose that's what Nosey was worried about last night, when he and Lefty went down to watch the main road. What I don't understand is Bob losing his horse. He must have been doing some scouting on foot and didn't figure on any storm messing things up. This one I'm riding, of course, must belong to somebody in the posse."

The Wreck grinned down at his mount. In some measure, the black horse compensated for the loss of the flivver.

"I'll bet Bob's just crazy," said Sally.

"Sure."

"Why, if anything happened to that horse— whew! He'd sooner let the whole gang get away than lose his horse."

"Well, he can have it back when I'm through with it," said the Wreck with an airy tone. "I'll exchange it for a flivver any time."

"And the humiliation of it," continued Sally, talking half to herself. "Think of a sheriff going out to catch somebody and having somebody else run off with his horse. Can't you see it, Henry?"

"I can see it fine."

"And there he is, back in the woods there somewhere, with nothing to ride, and probably the gang laughing at him."

"Well, it's a good laugh," agreed the Wreck.

"Why, it's awful!"

"Is it?" He looked at her sharply. "What's the idea? Do you want to go back and hand him his plug and say, 'Here we are. Take us to the hoosegow'?"

Sally shook her head impatiently.

"Of course not. We can't. But I'm just trying to make you understand what a frightful fix it is for a sheriff to be in. Oh, he must be simply wild! Just imagine yourself in his place."

"Say, are you trying to get me nervous about this?" demanded the Wreck. "Because you're wasting time, if you are. I can just eat this."

Sally eyed him with a speculative look as he began running his fingers through the mane of the black horse. She had never seen the Wreck looking quite so buoyant. Presently she began to laugh.

"I wish Bob Wells could see you," she said.

"Yes?"

"Oh, you needn't get belligerent. I'm laughing at Bob. He'd just die of mortification. He'd either curl up and die or shoot you, I don't know which."

The Wreck shrugged and eased himself in the saddle. Then he began laughing himself.

"Well, what do we do next, Sally?"

"Keep moving, I suppose."

"Which way?"

It was getting to be a fine morning as she swung

about in her saddle and began studying the country.
There were hills all about them, partly wooded,
while the open spaces were mostly surfaced with
rock. The little valley into which they had ridden
was green and lush, but showed no signs of having
been used for grazing stock.

"I confess I don't know where we are," said
Sally. "There doesn't seem to be a trail in sight and
I haven't any idea which way the road lies. But
I'm certain we didn't cross it in the night."

"Which way are you headed—Chicago or Bar-
M?"

"You're simply bound to ship me off to Chicago,
aren't you?"

"Me? I don't care which way you go. Only I
thought you wanted to buy—"

"Forget it," said Sally, almost sharply. "Do you
expect to get me talking about trousseaus out in
the middle of nowhere at all?"

"Well, when people start out to do things—"

"Henry, don't be disagreeable."

"All right, I'll never say another word about it."

"And don't be silly, either."

"After this, you can change your mind as much
as you darn please," said the Wreck.

"I wonder now," said Sally, regarding him with
a half-amused look. "Do you know I'm awfully
patient with you, Henry Williams—and I'll be
switched if I know why."

"Excuse me," he said, awkwardly. "It's my
nerves again."

She burst out laughing.

"What do you say we ride up to the top of one of those hills and have a look-see?" she said.

"All right."

She led the way again, across the meadow. The Wreck felt suddenly miserable. Somehow, he was always making an idiot of himself, getting her into arguments, irritating her, saying things he had no business to say. Yet he could not understand the philosophy with which she regarded their situation. In her place, he would have been in a frenzy of restlessness, due to thwarted plans. He would have wanted to get to Chicago, even over the dead bodies of sheriffs and hold-up men, if necessary, do his buying and finish up what he started out to do. But here was a person who did not seem to care whether she completed her errand or not. Probably she could not help it, being a woman; but it struck him as peculiar.

Not that he really wanted her to go to Chicago. He thought it was all right for her to be in Montana, so long as he was there, at any rate. He could get along with her better than he could with most people. She was the first person who had called him "Henry," and she had called him "old timer," too—twice. He had an idea that she wanted to be kind to him; she was kind, no mistake about it. In fact, she was mighty good to him. She tolerated a lot of his nonsense and she put up with his nerves, and he was not insensible of the fact. Take her by and large, she had a lot of common sense—nerve, too. And she was cheerful about it, always. He felt mean and ungrateful. Why was he always breaking out with remarks that upset her? He was sorry.

Before he knew it he was saying so, almost shouting it at her as she rode on ahead.

"I'm a crab and I know it," he concluded. "So you'll have to excuse me."

She swung around in the saddle and looked at him in astonishment.

"A crab?" she repeated. "Why, you're not a crab, Henry. I don't think so at all—not one bit. You're all right, old timer."

There! She had said it again. The Wreck squared his shoulders and snatched smartly at the reins.

"Giddap," he said, recklessly. "Get a move on."

They broke into a trot and he did not mind it in the least. What did he care if he fell off?

Soon they were climbing a hillside, the horses slowed to a walk again. It was steep going and rocky, but the sheriff's animal knew his business. As for Sally, she did not seem to be conscious of any difficulties in the ascent. Her head was turning from side to side, as she studied the landscape; she let the bay pick the trail.

When it became too steep for the horses, they dismounted, still some little distance from the summit.

"We'll leave them here," said Sally. "Just throw

the reins over his head and he'll stand. I think we ought to go up to the top for a better look."

"Sure," said the Wreck.

"And by the way, Henry, look in Bob's saddle bag and see if there's anything to eat. Unless I'm mistaken—"

The Wreck discovered two bars of chocolate.

"Thought so," nodded Sally. "Bob's never without it. Bring it along."

They set off up the rocky slope toward the summit.

CHAPTER XXII

THE WRECK SURRENDERS

IT was not the highest of the hills, but it was bare at the top, so that it afforded them a panorama that boxed the compass. Sally and the Wreck spent a long time studying the country. There was a gentle morning breeze and the sun was already warm, a combination of advantages that favored the drying of their clothes. Eventually they found a flat rock and sat there, eating the sheriff's emergency ration.

"I'm sure that streak off to the north," said Sally, "is the main road. You can get three different glimpses of it if you follow the way I'm pointing."

The Wreck nodded his agreement, although he was not certain that he saw what she meant. Sally could see a lot farther than he could.

"So I suppose that's where we ought to make for," she continued, "as soon as we get under way again."

"But we don't want to run into anybody else," he reminded her.

"No; of course not. So I'd suggest that we keep more to the west of the route we took coming in. There's a sort of valley that we ought to be able to get through. It's broken in a couple of places by

269

ridges, but I reckon we can get over them. We'd better keep out of the woods as much as we can; they slow you down."

The Wreck agreed to everything. He was resolved to have no more arguments. If Sally decided they ought to sit on top of the hill for a week, he would agree to that. He even decided to say nothing more about the flivver, unless she brought up the subject herself.

"I've about made up my mind," said Sally, "to go back to the Bar-M."

"Yes?"

"Of course, you won't approve of it. You like to see people finish what they start."

"I don't object," said the Wreck. "It's all right for you to do anything you please."

She studied him speculatively.

"I don't want you to think I'm a quitter, Henry. But I'm not sure that I have any errands in Chicago. Not now, at any rate."

"That's all right."

"And besides, I could hardly go the way I am, without my baggage or anything."

"Oh, I guess you look all right."

She smiled.

"Thank you, Henry. But I look like a fright, just the same. And if you don't mind my saying it, so do you."

"I don't mind. I know it."

He had emerged from his night in the woods with his trousers torn at the knees, a sleeve half

ripped from his coat, a hat missing and a general
aspect of dishevelment.

"Saddle sore?" she asked.

"No!"

"I think if you could always ride the sheriff's
horse, Henry, you'd overcome your prejudice—provided the sheriff happened to be wanting it."

He grinned and munched his chocolate bar.

For a while they talked about Charley McSween
and the Underwood ranch, wondering how long it
had taken to reëstablish communications. They
even drifted as far east as Pittsburgh, the Wreck
idly speculating as to the doings of the assistant
chemist, whom he had left in charge of the laboratory. He was glancing in the direction where he
thought Pittsburgh lay when his eye was attracted
by a movement of something in the meadow below
them.

"What's that?" he asked, pointing.

"Two horses, with riders," said Sally promptly.
"And they're following our trail, I do believe."

"I left the rifle hanging on the saddle," he said,
sheepishly.

"Let's hustle down and get it. Besides, we want
our own horses."

Half running, half sliding, they started down the
steep hillside. Sally kept a watch on the meadow,
which the two riders were crossing at a brisk pace.
It was too far for her to make an identification,
but whoever they were, they were unwelcome.

"Keep behind the rocks and trees as much as

you can," she advised. "We don't want them to
see us if we can help it."

They dodged into cover wherever they could find
it, working downhill in a zigzag course toward the
spot where they left the horses. When they had
gone as far as seemed necessary she called a halt.
The horses were not in sight.

"I'm afraid they've drifted down toward the
meadow," she said, "where the feeding is good.
What do you think we'd better do?"

"Keep going."

"But if they reach the horses first—"

"We've got to take a chance. Maybe it's nobody who'll bother us, anyhow."

She had misgivings on that score, but followed
him as he took the lead. A few minutes later when
he was several yards in advance, she saw him stop
abruptly and make a signal for caution. As she
joined him he pointed to an opening in the trees.

"It's your friend and somebody else," he whispered.

The Wreck was right. Bob Wells, dismounted,
had recovered his own horse and was subjecting it
to a critical scrutiny. He was also examining the
rifle that hung at the saddle. With him was a man
whom Sally had never seen before, evidently one of
the posse.

"Out of luck again," she groaned.

"Oh, they haven't got us yet," said the Wreck,
confidently.

"But they will. They know that somebody is on

this hill and they'll never give up till they find us."

Presently the sheriff began examining the ground and Sally pinched the Wreck's arm.

"He'll get the trail now, just you see. There— he's looking up. Duck!"

There was a big boulder handy; they stepped behind it and flattened themselves on the ground.

"What'll we do?" asked Sally. "No use going back uphill again. They'll nail us to a certainty."

"We might work around to the side," he suggested. "But—they're coming now."

Up the steep slope they could see the sheriff advancing, his head turning quickly from side to side as he searched for something. There was a gun in his hand and Sally knew exactly how well he could use it. Close at his heels followed the other man. Both were walking.

"Well, I guess this is the finish," she said, grimly. "They can't say we haven't given them a good run for it, Henry."

"Huh. Maybe we're not through yet."

"I'm afraid so. No fighting, Henry. You haven't a chance."

The Wreck was chagrined, but he was not yet in despair. So far as his own case was concerned, it did not matter. He hated to surrender to Bob Wells; he would sooner be a prisoner at the Underwood ranch. But in either case, his own fortunes were relatively unimportant. It was Sally who counted. He could understand exactly how she must feel. Here was the man she was to marry, coming up to place her under arrest—and without being aware of it! The Wreck felt that he had failed at last, unless he could think of something within the next minute or two. If he could only get Sally out of the way—

They could hear the sheriff's voice, saying something to his companion. It had a peculiarly irritating effect upon Sally, who gritted her teeth and scowled. She was not frightened—merely angry.

"Listen," whispered the Wreck, "you stay here."

"Where are you going?" She seized his arm.

"I've got a scheme. Leave it to me. Promise, now."

"We're both in this together. Henry—"

"Let me go," said the Wreck, fiercely. "I know that I'm doing. Are you going to let me go?"

She stared at him earnestly, then released his arm.

"Please be careful, Henry. Please!"

"Sure." He spoke almost jauntily.

Rising suddenly to his feet, he patted her on the shoulder and winked reassuringly.

"So-long, Sally. You stay right here until you're sent for."

He stepped out from behind the boulder. She did not know what he meant, but she watched him with wondering eyes. Why—he was surrendering!

The Wreck's hands were lifted in the air as he strode down the trail. He had not gone half a dozen paces when the sheriff's gun covered him.

"Heigho," said the Wreck, frivolously. "Looking for anybody?"

Bob Wells stared, and as he stared his mouth opened wide.

"Well, I'm a son of a gun!" he gasped.

"Uh-huh," assented the Wreck. "What's the idea?"

"It's the four-eyed dude!" said the sheriff, in a voice of wonder.

"Sure."

From her place of concealment Sally watched, too astonished to move. What in the world was Henry Williams trying to do now?

The second man joined the sheriff, and both stared incredulously at the spectacled Wreck.

"So it was *you* who stole my horse," said Bob Wells, still in a tone of unbelief.

"Just utilized him," said the Wreck. "He was running loose."

"And *you've* been running a stick-up game!"

The Wreck seated himself comfortably on a rock and grinned. Obviously, he was enjoying himself.

"I decline to answer, on the usual grounds," he remarked. "You needn't keep that gun on me unless you're nervous. I'm not armed. I left my rifle on the horse."

The sheriff was staring in growing amazement.

"Well, I'll be damned," he muttered. "A stick-up man! I used to think there was something queer about you, but I never guessed that. Did you stick up all three parties?"

"No answer, on same grounds," said the Wreck, with a smile.

"I'll have plenty of witnesses, I reckon," said the sheriff. "But, doggone it, you've certainly sprung something on us."

"It's a nice day," remarked the Wreck, gazing up at a white cloud.

The sheriff's eyes wandered and his glance roved the hillside.

"Where's your gang?" he asked, suddenly.

"What gang?" The Wreck's tone was innocent.

"The bunch that are in on this with you?"

"Who said there was anybody in with me? I didn't."

"It happens we know about the rest. Where are they?"

"Well, if I was a sheriff," drawled the Wreck, "and if I thought there was anybody else I wanted, I'd go and look for 'em."

"You may as well come through," said Bob Wells, sternly.

"There's nobody here, at any rate."

"You're a liar."

The Wreck grinned pleasantly and yawned.

"Maybe," he assented. "I suppose they'll say I'm a liar if I tell them about your horse."

The sheriff flushed.

"Who rode the other horse over here?" he demanded.

"Nobody."

"That's a lie, too."

"Some day I'll lick you for that," observed the Wreck, genially.

"What would you be doing with two horses if you didn't have somebody else with you?"

"I'm a trick rider."

Bob Wells stood glowering.

"You're a fresh bird," he muttered. "You're the only four-eyed hold-up I ever saw. And to think of you living over at the Bar-M for a week—two weeks! Pretty smooth, Henry Williams, which I don't reckon is your name."

"Pretty smooth," agreed the Wreck, with a nod.

"What is your name, anyhow?"

"You wouldn't believe me."

"I dunno. I'm pretty nearly ready to believe anything. If I heard you'd done a couple of murders I'd believe that."

The Wreck began playing with a handful of pebbles.

"We'll get your gang anyhow," said the sheriff. "It's only a question of a little while."

The Wreck was humming a tune. Even Sally could hear him from her hiding-place, and it astonished her. Henry Williams had never done anything like that before.

"So you may as well come through," added the sheriff.

"You're repeating yourself," the Wreck reminded him.

Suddenly Bob Wells remembered something.

"Where's that flivver of yours?"

This was news to the Wreck. He had supposed that the flivver was also captive.

"She's in Montana," he said.

"Where?"

"I told you."

"You worked both ways, didn't you?" observed the sheriff. "Flivver and horseback."

"I'm hearing you say it," said the Wreck.

"Well, you're in for about life, Henry Williams, unless they happen to get you away from me. And in that case—" The sheriff made a significant gesture.

The Wreck smiled again and reached for another handful of pebbles. And just then Bob Wells remembered another thing, and it startled him.

"What became of Sally Morgan?" he demanded.

"Miss Morgan? Oh, she got her train."

"When?"

"Same day she started for it."

"Sure about that, are you?"

"I ought to know, hadn't I?"

The sheriff regarded him doubtfully.

"If I had the least suspicion she didn't," he said, slowly, "I'd shoot you where you sit."

"Uh-huh. Well, she got it, all right."

"I ought to wring your neck, anyhow, just for luck. The nerve of you, passing yourself off for a tourist on decent people, and riding around the country with *my* girl!"

"Some joke," admitted the Wreck.

Bob Wells turned for a whispered consultation with his companion. Together they subjected the

Wreck to a long, puzzled scrutiny. It did not appear to annoy him.

"Well, no more nonsense," said the sheriff. "Lead us to your gang."

"Nobody around here, sheriff."

"We know better."

"No," said the Wreck, shaking his head. "I know better."

"Going to make us take a look, are you?"

"I'm not making you. But if you want to waste your time, go ahead."

The Wreck was disappointed. He had been trying amazingly hard to appear convincing, but evidently he had failed. He did not think he had protested too much; he thought he had been doing it about right. But somehow he could not put it over.

His only hope now was that Sally had managed to disappear. He wanted to keep her out of it, at any cost. He had figured that if he went along with the sheriff there would be a chance to escape later. Then he could come back for her. It was not much of a plan, but at least it gave her another chance.

"We'll take him along with us, Jim," said the sheriff. "You keep a good eye on him. And you, Williams—" He paused to give his words effect. "If anybody fires on us, you'll get yours, first of all."

"You're a big fathead," said the Wreck, irrelevantly.

"Get up," ordered the sheriff.

The Wreck obeyed. For an instant he stood contemplating a dash downhill. They might not be able to hit him if he kept dodging, and if he could once make the horses there was no telling what sort of a chase he could lead them. It would give Sally an opportunity, anyhow. But he never had a chance to test the idea.

Out from behind her boulder stepped Sally Morgan, her eyes very bright and her cheeks red under the tan. She walked briskly into the group.

"Hell!" said the Wreck. "Now you've done it."

Bob Wells fell back a pace and gaped at her.

"Sally!" he cried.

Courtesy of White Studio, N. Y.

THE WRECK SURRENDERS.

Scene from the Play.

CHAPTER XXIII

GETTING ENGAGED

A BREATHLESS interval of silence followed, during which the mental processes of the sheriff strove desperately for equilibrium. He felt that he was staring at an apparition. Sally had taken her stand beside the Wreck, whose attitude was one of grim dejection. His plan had failed; everything had crashed. Why hadn't she kept out of it?

"Sally Morgan!" The sheriff's voice was unsteady.

"Certainly," said Sally.

Bob Wells took a step forward, reached for her, hesitated. Something in her look stopped him.

"But he said—" The sheriff glared at the Wreck. "He said—"

"I heard what he said," remarked Sally, a coolness in her voice that found no counterpart in the color that surged in her cheeks and neck.

"He said he put you on the train!"

"Stage play," said Sally.

"Then he—"

The sheriff's eyes narrowed as he studied the Wreck.

"Sally, you've been kidnapped!" he exclaimed.

She laughed.

"Don't be a fool, Bob."

He seemed poised for a spring.

"And don't finger that gun," added Sally. "Get down to earth. Kidnapped? Do I look like a person who could be kidnapped? You'd better not make a fool of yourself."

"You never took the train," muttered Bob Wells, staring at her. "And you never went back to the Bar-M. And you—"

He broke off for sheer inability to carry his thoughts to a conclusion. Again he turned to the Wreck.

"If you've kept her a prisoner," he said, "you'll never get out of the State alive."

"Maybe," agreed the Wreck. "I suppose I didn't have any business to do it."

Sally turned a look of amazement toward him.

"Henry Williams!" she cried. "Don't *you* be a fool. And you, Bob Wells, put that gun away. There isn't going to be any shooting, not for one minute. Kidnapped! Prisoner! I never heard such nonsense in my life."

The Wreck sighed. He had tried to keep her out of it, but she would not stay out. He had no idea what folly she might commit now. But he had a vivid impression that Sally Morgan had never looked so wonderful—and he had seen her often when she was pleasant to gaze upon.

"I—I don't get it at all," said the sheriff, helplessly.

"Well, you'd better get it!" Sally exclaimed. "It's

about time. What do you mean by chasing me all over the country?"

Bob Wells stared.

"You heard me. I said chasing me. Do you think I'm a criminal? Do I look like one? Can't I do what I like without having a posse on my trail?"

"Sally!"

"I mean exactly what I say. How dare you go pursuing me all around Montana?"

The sheriff was dazed.

"I wasn't pursuing you," he faltered.

"Yes, you were. You pursued me up here, didn't you? And you pursued me yesterday, and the day before, and probably the day before that. I won't have it, Bob Wells. You wait till I tell Dad Morgan."

"Sally, you're all wrong."

"No, I'm not. I'm right! I know what I'm talking about. I reckon I know when there's a posse after me. How *dare* you chase me?"

"But I didn't! I hadn't any idea."

"Oh, didn't you?" said Sally, contemptuously. "You mean to tell me the sheriff of this county goes out chasing people without knowing who he's after?"

"I was out after a gang," said the sheriff. "How did I know—"

"It's your business to know. What did the people elect you for? Did they elect you to go galloping around the country after a girl you've known all your life?"

"I didn't know it was *my* girl. I didn't know it was any girl."

"*Your* girl!" said Sally. "Bob Wells, you're a whole lot stupider than I thought you were."

The sheriff shook his head in a weary way. He did not understand anything. Nor was it very clear to the Wreck; but he kept out of the conversation, hoping for enlightenment.

"I'm all mixed up," said the sheriff. "What's it all about, anyhow?"

"You listen," commanded Sally.

She told it, from the very beginning. She told it rapidly, but she did not leave out many of the essential parts. She told it with gestures and high inflections, but she kept it all in orderly sequence. Bob Wells listened, at first in sheer amazement, then with a look of incredulity in his eyes. Frequently his glance traveled to the Wreck, but the latter was paying no attention to the sheriff. He had eyes and ears only for Sally Morgan.

"So that's what happened and that's why I'm here," concluded Sally. "And any sheriff who had half an allowance of brains ought to have found it out long ago."

Bob Wells considered it for a minute.

"Why didn't you telephone home?" he asked.

"If you can't understand, it's not worth while trying to make you."

"Well, then, why didn't you telephone me?"

"Because I didn't see fit."

"It's mighty queer. I don't see how you can explain—"

"What?" cried Sally.

"A lot of things. You go running around the country with this man—God knows what kind of a record he's got—and you seem to think it's nothing at all."

"Stop!"

But the sheriff was recovering poise. He was a man whose rights had been trifled with. His bewilderment was giving way to resentment.

"What kind of a position does it leave you in?" he demanded.

Sally rested her hand on the Wreck's arm and regarded Bob Wells with a blistering stare.

"Henry Williams," she said, slowly and distinctly, "is a good sport and a gallant gentleman, and I'm not ashamed or afraid to go anywhere with him. Is that clear to you?"

"And you're engaged to me," said the sheriff, with a grim finality.

"Am I?" Sally was holding herself steady.

"Well, aren't you?"

"I think you've said so several times, Bob Wells. Probably I let you think so. Probably I thought I was myself. There didn't seem to be any reason why I shouldn't be. It just—well, it just drifted. Thank Heaven, it didn't drift too far."

The sheriff was becoming uneasy again.

"Maybe you can explain everything yet," he suggested.

"So that's your attitude," she observed, calmly. "Having explained already, you want me to explain some more. You've got a fine lot of trust in me, Bob Wells."

"Haven't I a right to an explanation?"

"Possibly—if we were engaged. But we're not."

"Sally!"

She waved the protest aside with a gesture.

"Oh, it's not just because you don't trust me," she said. "I've changed my mind about a lot of things. I've decided, for instance, that I don't want to be somebody's cook."

Bob Wells made a sign of bewilderment, but the Wreck began to prick up his ears.

"I reckon you know what I mean," said Sally.

"But I don't."

"Well, if you want an explanation, I heard everything you said to Mr. Underwood, while you were eating supper. Yes; I listened at the door. I can remember it, too. 'When you get a good cook the thing to do is to rope her and brand her and don't let her get outside the corral.' Remember that? I do. 'I'm going to marry one.' Remember that? 'Out in this country a girl that can't cook isn't worth a hoorah.' Do you remember that? 'When it comes to cooking I don't have to take off my hat to anybody.' Perhaps you remember that one, too. You told him all about the wonderful cook you were going to marry. It wasn't a wife you were marrying —it was a cook. Do you deny it?"

The sheriff swallowed and turned a dull red.

"We just happened to be talking about meals," he said.

"Meals—and cooks. That's what you think about and talk about the most, Bob Wells. I never realized it until I listened at the crack of the door. I'm not ashamed for listening. I'm glad. It was mighty lucky. Perhaps you'll marry a cook some day, Mr. Sheriff, but her name won't be Sally Morgan."

The Wreck listened with a queer intermingling of triumph and dismay—triumph because Bob Wells was losing something, dismay because Sally's romance had ended in a crash, with himself the cause of it. The sheriff took the news with a dull sense of chagrin and resentment.

"I reckon it's lucky on both sides," he remarked, in a surly tone.

"Yes," affirmed Sally.

"I'm not hankering to marry anybody who goes running around—"

"Easy on that!"

The Wreck was speaking, and there was a fine edge in his voice.

"Why, back at Underwood's they told me they had a married couple working for them," blurted the sheriff.

"That was simply Henry's idea to cover a situation," remarked Sally, in a composed voice. "It was mighty considerate of him."

The Wreck stood glaring. He did not want to hear very much more from Bob Wells.

"Wait till your old man gets the news," said the sheriff, with an accusing look at Sally.

"When Dad gets it he'll get it all," declared Sally. "What's more, he'll believe it, too. He won't go into any cross-examination and he won't have any doubts that a man ought to be ashamed to have. And if he wants to know if I'm engaged to anybody, I'll tell him 'Yes.' I'm engaged to Henry Williams."

The sheriff's jaw dropped. The Wreck almost swallowed his tongue. The other member of the posse, who had been standing stolidly throughout the conversation, widened his eyes and observed Sally with a new interest.

"I am engaged to Henry Williams," repeated Sally, in a clear voice. "So that settles that."

"Is—is that true?" demanded the sheriff, looking at the Wreck.

It seemed to Henry Williams that the universe was crashing about his ears, that this was the magnificent end of all things. But he rallied gamely.

"She said it, didn't she?" he cried.

"Yes; she said it," admitted Bob Wells.

"Well, what more do you want?"

The sheriff could not think of anything more for half a minute. He was stunned. He was angry, too. He felt that he was the victim of some grotesque joke. It seemed plain enough that he had lost Sally Morgan, but the idea that she was going to marry a near-sighted, goggle-eyed, jump-nerved —well, there were a lot of things he could say

about the Wreck and none of them was in his favor.
Besides that, he was a crook, a bad actor, a stick-up
man, with a record already established for himself
in Montana and the Lord knew how much outside
of it.

"I feel sorry for you, Sally," he said.

"Don't bother," she advised.

"You won't marry him very soon, anyhow."

"No?"

"He's got a lot of time ahead of him."

"You mean you're going to take him to jail?"

"I'm the sheriff," Bob Wells reminded her.

She was incredulous for an instant. It sounded
absurd.

"Then, of course, that means you're going to take
me to jail, too," she said.

He shook his head.

"You don't belong in this case," he said. "We'll
just leave you out of it. I—I'm not aiming to take
a girl to jail."

"Well, you'll not take him without me, Bob
Wells."

"Don't talk foolishness, Sally."

"Foolish or not, I'm talking facts. If he goes,
I go."

"No; I reckon you're going home," said the
sheriff.

"Not unless Henry goes," she said, with finality in
her voice.

It seemed to the Wreck that he was merely a
bystander; that the situation had slipped out of his

hands and into those of Sally Morgan and the sheriff. Whatever game she was playing, he wanted to play also; but he could not yet grasp it. She did not mean what she said, of course, about going to jail. And as for the other part—being engaged to him—that was just wild nonsense. But what did she really mean?

"As soon as I get to a telephone, I'll send for your father," said Bob Wells.

Sally flared.

"I'm no child; I know what I'm doing," she cried. "I've told you the truth about the whole business, but you're too stubborn to believe it, or too stupid, I don't know which. You mean to stand there and tell me you think Henry Williams is a hold-up man?"

"Did he deny it?"

"No. But that was because he was trying to keep me out of it. Now I'm in it, and I'm in it to stay. Why, you haven't got a case that will hold water for five minutes, Bob Wells. Do you think anybody's going to blame him for taking a few gallons of gasoline?"

"What about the other stick-ups?"

Sally shook her head impatiently.

"I didn't know a sheriff could be so dense. What are you wasting your time with us for? Why don't you go and find the real people?"

"Doesn't look like I'd wasted this morning," remarked the sheriff, glancing at the Wreck. "Where's the rest of his gang?"

The Wreck was not paying much attention to the

conversation. He was wondering what an engaged man was supposed to do and how he would ever play such a preposterous part.

"Henry Williams hasn't any gang at all, unless it's me," declared Sally. "Why don't you go out and find Nosey and Lefty and Denver?"

"Who?" asked the sheriff.

"Nosey and Lefty and Denver, I said. Do you mean to tell me you never heard of them?"

"Not that I know of."

Sally looked at the Wreck and laughed.

"What do you think of that, Henry? Here's a sheriff with a *real* gang in his county and he never heard of them."

She turned to Bob Wells.

"Maybe you can't find them, but Henry and I did. You needn't look so astonished. We did, I tell you. We spent all day yesterday and part of last night with them. I didn't tell you that part before, because you're so bent on making a fool of yourself about Henry that you'd have said he was one of them. But it's a fact, although I don't suppose you'll find it out until Henry and I are in jail and the hold-ups keep right on happening."

"Maybe you can show me this gang," remarked the sheriff.

"Maybe we can," said Sally. "Henry, shall we show him the gang?"

The Wreck shrugged.

"What's the use?" he asked. "What would he do with 'em if he got 'em?"

"Still, we might point them out," said Sally. "He might want to scold them for spoiling his county, or something like that."

"They might talk back," objected the Wreck.

"Not if he was polite to them," said Sally.

"Well, maybe not. But I wouldn't be sure about Nosey."

The sheriff decided it had gone far enough.

"It may look funny to you two," he said, "but if there's any gang around here that I haven't met up with, I figure it might be healthy for Henry Williams, so called, to produce the evidence."

"Well, we don't guarantee they're going to wait for you," observed Sally, "but we'll try to show you the place, anyhow."

"Come on, then."

The sheriff turned to his companion.

"Keep your eye on this man," he said. "He's liable to try to put something over on us."

They started downhill toward the horses, Sally walking beside the Wreck. She gave his arm a reassuring squeeze.

CHAPTER XXIV

THE WRECK COMMANDS

IN single file the sheriff's cavalcade rode across the meadow, back toward the broken woods from which Sally and the Wreck had emerged at dawn. Sally was in the lead, because she was supposed to remember the trail. The sheriff's companion followed. Then came the Wreck, swinging awkwardly in his saddle. Bob Wells took the rear place, mounted again on his own horse. He rode with a heavy, sullen air, his gaze fixed on a spot between the Wreck's shoulder blades.

Sally had carried a bold, contemptuous front in her colloquy with the sheriff, but she was not light-hearted. Now that she rode alone, she found that her mood was rather serious. If the sheriff persisted in making trouble for Henry Williams there was no doubt of his ability to create it. On the surface of things, the Wreck's case presented unpleasant possibilities. If Jerome Underwood wanted to push matters, as she was afraid he would, the Wreck might find difficulty in getting himself clear. There was no doubt he had broken laws. He had piled one thing atop of another; sometimes he carried things too far. All this worried her, despite what she knew of the motives that prompted him.

But it did not concern her so much as another matter—her declaration to Bob Wells that the Wreck was to be her husband. She had said it in a moment of defiance, although she had a reason that went beyond that. She was thinking of Dad Morgan and Ma. She felt that an engagement would cover a multitude of doubts; that it would offset possible shock in the minds of persons who viewed things from the conventional standpoint. But how about the Wreck? What did he think of it? What was his opinion of a girl who said things like that off-hand, just to make matters a little easier for herself?

The opinion of Henry Williams was important, as Sally saw it. She was anxious about it. It was much more important than the opinion of anybody else, as she now realized. What would he do? What was he thinking, 'way down underneath? Suppose he failed her—what then? No; he would not fail her, she knew that. But even if he did not fail her, what might he really feel? She was glad to be alone at the head of the column; she did not feel like talking to anybody, particularly the Wreck.

The Wreck's thoughts ran along a different line. He understood why Sally Morgan had made her astonishing statement. It went back to the same reason that prompted him to claim her as his wife, at the Underwood ranch; it was a concession to certain things that society expected of its members. It meant nothing beyond that, of course. But that was the least part of what he thought about. He was disturbed because Sally's real romance had crashed. He did not like Bob Wells; never had and never would. But if Bob meant happiness for Sally, the rest did not count. He wanted Sally to be happy. He felt that she had wrecked things because of a mere angry impulse, and he was not sure they could be repaired. Worst of all, he identified himself as the cause. He would never forgive himself.

The prospect of going to jail did not disturb him. He did not take it very seriously. There might be a flurry, but it could not last long. The main point was getting Sally back to peace and happiness, for that was his clear responsibility. Whenever they got through with him he would go back to Pittsburgh, where he might forget about things—or might not. But before that everything must be made straight and smooth for Sally Morgan, so that he could look his own conscience in the face, even if for no other reason. Engaged to her? He laughed at himself. Not that there was any mirth in it, but it was a form of self-mockery for which he was in the mood.

The cavalcade was in the woods, where Sally found it easier to follow trail than she expected. There were the tracks of their own horses, and the tracks made by the sheriff in pursuit, and there was a good deal of wet and trampled underbrush that served as a guide. The party rode briskly, even the Wreck managing to keep his place in the line.

Presently they came to a splitting of the trail

and Sally could not be certain of her course. It
marked the place where the sheriff and his man had
converged with their own tracks. Bob Wells
straightened it out in a jiffy. He remembered exactly where he had picked up the trail, while he
was hunting for his own horses, and he showed her
that the other trail must have been made by herself
and the Wreck, riding through the night. Sally accepted the information with a cold nod and set off
in the lead again. If she could stick to their own
trail they would arrive somewhere in the vicinity of
Nosey's camp, and they would then be within a
stone's throw of the flivver.

She came to a second spot where there was a
confusion of footprints and hoofprints, and this
she knew to be the place where she and the Wreck
had discovered their mounts. She explained the situation in a few words and gestures, the sheriff
nodding as he studied the ground. Then they un-
dertook to trace the wanderings of the fugitives
in the storm. This did not prove so easy, for humans
do not leave so clear a trail as horses. But Bob
Wells proved to be a help. When it came to finding
tracks, there was no doubt of his efficiency. Even
Sally was forced to admire it. Time and again they
lost the trail, where the storm had beaten it to the
vanishing point, but through some instinct that he
possessed, backed by a general sense of locality, the
sheriff always managed to pick it up again.

In the end, all this retracing of a wandering trail
brought them to a place that Sally and the Wreck

instantly recognized. It was the camp of the three-man gang. There was little left but soaked embers, but there was no opportunity for mistake.

The sheriff dismounted and examined the place attentively. He listened closely while Sally explained everything, including the affair of Denver and the thunderstorm. If she seemed to stress the part the Wreck had played, she did it, nevertheless, with a strict adherence to truth; she merely gave it from her own viewpoint, in which Henry Williams loomed like a giant.

The Wreck left the telling all to her; he did not even interrupt when he felt that she was giving him too large a part. He chose the part of a listener and an onlooker. When the sheriff began walking to and fro, studying the deserted camp, the Wreck found himself side by side with Sally. It was their first proximity since they had mounted the horses at the foot of the hill, miles back. He moved uneasily in his saddle. He neither knew what he was expected to say, nor what he ought to say.

He glanced at her, because it seemed difficult not to do so. Sally smiled encouragingly. But the smile robbed him of his wits.

"It's a nice day," he said.

She glanced up at the sky, through the tree-tops. It was blue and laughing now.

"Beautiful," she answered.

"Not so warm as yesterday."

"No; not so warm."

He made a nervous gesture that meant nothing in particular.

"But it's likely to be warmer to-morrow," he blurted.

"Yes," said Sally.

"And it probably won't rain."

"Probably not."

He felt like a fool. The conversation had exhausted everything he dared to say. So he fell to glaring at the sheriff, and pretended to be preoccupied. But she would not let him alone; she was still smiling at him.

"I think," she said, "that the rest of the summer won't be quite so hot. It gets cooler at night, you know."

"Uh-huh."

"But, of course, we can't tell. We might have a hot wave."

He looked at her suspiciously.

"Still, we might not have it," she added. "It's all luck."

"Yes; luck," he nodded.

Now she laughed outright.

"Henry, *please* don't be absurd. Scold me for something; jump all over me. I won't mind."

"You're all right," said the Wreck, lamely.

"That's not much, but it's better than the weather," said Sally. "You're terribly angry with me, I imagine."

"Who? Me?"

She nodded.

"You're crazy," he snapped.

"Still better," said Sally, in a contented tone. "You're perking up."   •

"Are you kidding me?"

"Who? Me?" she echoed. "Why, Henry!"

He shook his head irritably. He was miserable at heart and he knew he was ridiculous. Why couldn't a woman let a man alone?

The merriment faded from Sally's face; the look in her eyes softened. Poor Wreck! She was not really trying to tease him; she was only trying to talk to him. But he insisted on holding himself aloof. He did not want her to make any advances.

"Just forget it," she said. "I didn't mean anything."

"Oh, that's all right."

"Thanks, old timer."

From the deserted camp the quartet, captors and prisoners, rode over to where the flivver had been left. It was so ridiculously easy to find it by daylight that the Wreck wondered how he had ever missed it, even in darkness and storm. He ceased puzzling over that matter, however, when he saw the car, and went into a black rage, instead.

The flivver was lying on its side in a clump of bushes, with two wheels in the air, and a chipmunk sitting on one of them, just to add an ironical touch. It was plain enough that Nosey's gang had been trying to make use of it. They had undertaken to turn it around and head it back toward the main road, but the turning room was limited, and the surface was a hillside, and the thing had gone over for want of a skilled hand.

The Wreck climbed down from his horse and walked all around his beloved car, furious but saying nothing. All he wanted at that moment was another meeting with Nosey's gang. Yet so far as he could see, there was nothing radically wrong with the flivver. Front and rear mudguards on the under side were crumpled and the wind-shield was shattered; but the running gear seemed to be intact and he knew that there was nothing the matter with the motor. Most of the gasoline, of course, had spilled out of the tank; but through some freak of precaution the gang had removed the extra cans from the running board before they tried to turn the car. The cans were standing near the car, and he discovered that they were still full.

"Is it very much damaged, Henry?" asked Sally.

"No," he answered, shortly.

"Will it run?"

"Of course."

They were still examining the flivver when two men came down the abandoned road and hailed the sheriff. They were the other half of Bob Wells's posse. It was evident they had something on their minds which they regarded as important, for they did not waste much time in a study of Sally and the Wreck or the overturned car.

"Good thing you got them horses," said one of them to Bob Wells. "We need 'em. Bill and me have been scoutin' around while you was gone and we've hit a hot trail. But there wasn't any use tryin' to foller it on foot. If we're quick we'll nail 'em before sundown."

"I've nailed one of them already," said the sheriff, with a glance at the Wreck.

"Who, him?" The newcomers stared briefly. "Well, maybe. Only he don't belong with this bunch we've got located. They've only got three horses. We better get started, Bob."

But the sheriff was not ready to start. The news from the dismounted half of his posse put him in a quandary. He asked many questions, to which he got emphatic answers. It was plain enough that what Sally and the Wreck said about the gang was true. But what about the Wreck himself? The sheriff glanced at him speculatively from time to time as he talked with his men. He was beginning to have his doubts, but it was hard to overcome a stubborn streak. He related what he knew about the Wreck and asked for an opinion. Sally he left entirely out of the narrative, just as though she were not there.

One of the sheriff's assistants was a middle-aged man of stolid appearance. He studied the Wreck with shrewd eyes.

"Well, I don't know anything about *him*," he said, "but I know we've got some other folks located that we want bad. And you're missin' the chance of your life, Bob, if you don't get started."

Bob Wells was rapidly reaching the same conclusion. But what was he going to do about the

Wreck? He could not take him along on a man hunt, for there was no spare horse. He could not leave a guard behind, for he felt that he needed all his men. He did not believe that he really wanted him after all, but he hated to let him go, particularly when he looked at Sally Morgan. It seemed like a humiliating surrender. But it also looked like the inevitable course. His men were restless; they did not seem to take much interest in the Wreck. Even the man who had been with him during the hunt on the hillside acted as though he did not regard Henry Williams as a person of particular importance, so far as the law was concerned.

"Sally," said the sheriff, suddenly, "I'm going to make you a deputy."

"What for?"

"I'm going to put this man in your custody."

Sally shook her head.

"Oh, no, no you don't," she said. "Henry Williams is his own boss, so far as I am concerned. You're not going to drag me in on your foolishness, Bob Wells. I wouldn't be one of your deputies for a million dollars."

The sheriff reddened, but made no reply. He consulted again with his posse and reached a decision.

"I'll need those horses for my men," he said, with a nod at Sally and the Wreck. "We'll try to come back and give you a lift later."

Sally dismounted. She was elated. She had never believed from the beginning that Bob Wells would risk taking the Wreck to jail. But the Wreck remained in his saddle, staring at the sheriff.

"What's the idea?" he demanded. "Expect to leave us here with an upset car?"

"I said I'd try to come back," the sheriff answered. "We're in a hurry and I want that horse."

"You'll get this horse when I get my car running, and not before. Think you can leave a lady stranded out here in the woods, do you?"

"Get down," said the sheriff, advancing.

"Wait," remarked the Wreck. "And listen."

He indulged in a deliberate pause, during which he glared steadily through his horn-rimmed spectacles.

"Sheriff," he said, "I'm a nervous man and I'm apt to be impulsive and do things without considering. But I've got this particular thing all figured out to a hair, and I was cool and calm when I figured it. Just as sure as you go off and leave Sally Morgan and me stranded in the woods I'm going to make the State of Montana too small to hold you. It may be the third largest in the Union, as Sally says, but it won't be big enough for you.

"I'll start campaigning this county, and when I get through with it I'll take the next one, and I'll go through every county in the State, if it takes me the rest of my, life. All I'll do is to tell the truth— the whole of it. I'll tell them how you chased your own girl for days and days and didn't know it. I'll tell them that when she needed a horse she took yours and left half your posse on foot. I'll tell them how you let a real stick-up gang go about its business under your nose while you went off chasing your own friends and acquaintances. I'll tell them about the cook you were going to marry, but didn't. I'll tell them every little thing, from start to finish."

He paused again, for it was an exceptionally long speech for the Wreck. The sheriff glowered at him. The posse looked at the sheriff.

"And if you figure you can keep on being a sheriff in the State of Montana after I get through," concluded the Wreck, "then I'll give you a chance to find out by running for sheriff myself."

Bob Wells hesitated. After all, he was a pretty good sheriff, as Sally always said, and when there was a gang loose in his county he knew his duty. But he was human, too. He did not like to be laughed at.

"And of course," said Sally, speaking up in a clear voice, "I'll back up every word that Henry Williams says."

The sheriff swallowed his pride.

"What do you want me to do?" he asked, looking at the Wreck.

"I want you and your men to get busy and put that flivver on her feet and help get her out of here, so that Miss Morgan and myself can go on about our business."

"Yes," affirmed Sally.

Bob Wells turned to his men, and caught one of them grinning.

"We'll have to hustle," he said. "It won't take long."

CHAPTER XXV

—AND THE FLIVVER ROLLS

THE Wreck bossed the job. He took an arrogant tone, particularly toward the sheriff, and Sally was glad; not because she wanted to humiliate Bob Wells, however. Her anger had faded and there was nothing vindictive about her, although she had a sweetly unreasonable resentment against having been pursued, even though she had been anonymous to the pursuer. She was glad because the bossing job gave the Wreck something to do, and in its performance he forgot his embarrassment about other things, at least temporarily.

He was terse and confident in his commands. Not a finger would he lift himself; he had four men working for him. It took their united strength to put the flivver on four wheels, and they did it exactly as the Wreck said it should be done. Bob Wells threw his muscle into the task as though it were a welcome substitute for conversation. He wanted to get it over with and be on the trail again. There was gloom in his mind and he did not want to dwell upon the subject of a shattered romance.

"Not that way!" called the Wreck, sharply. "Want to buckle a wheel for me? You can't push her sideways. Cut the front wheels; no, the other way. That's it. Now shove her backwards. Easy! Now cut 'em the other way, and push her forward. You work like a gang from an old ladies' home. That'll do. Now cut the wheels back again and push her in the other direction. What? You've got to get her back on the road, haven't you? Well, keep on doing what I tell you and don't ask questions. I'm the brains department. You're the birds who do the work."

Sally listened to all this with a sense of satisfaction. She did not pretend to understand the mechanical demands of the task; she was merely gratified to see that the Wreck was normal again.

The flivver was back in the abandoned road, but Henry Williams was not through with his helpers. They expected that he would fill up the gasoline tank, turn the crank and say good-by. But he said it would have to be rolled for quite a distance, perhaps all the way to the main road. The sheriff scowled.

"You ran her in here, didn't you?" he inquired. "Why can't you run her out?"

"Ran her in here in the dark," said the Wreck. "Didn't know what chances I was running. Won't run 'em again. Roll her."

"We haven't time."

"No? Well, I have. I've also got enough time to campaign the county, if it comes to that. Roll her!"

So they rolled her. The Wreck condescended to sit in the flivver while they rolled the thing up a heavy grade, with Bob Wells sweating and cursing under his breath and the members of his posse silently bending themselves to the humiliating task.

On the down grades the Wreck dismounted and let the posse do the steering. Then it was that he found himself walking behind, with Sally Morgan at his side. Proximity gave him a queer thrill. He stole glances at her, when he thought she was unaware of it. Engaged! He blushed whenever he remembered it. Of course, it was all a mere makeshift. He did not intend to permit himself any illusions. But there was no illusion about the breaking of her engagement to Bob Wells, if it had ever really existed. And with that broken, Sally was free, affianced to nobody, except theoretically to himself. Suppose it advanced from a theory to a condition? Oh, no; he had no illusions. But suppose it did? He did not know whether such matters could be dropped in an offhand way; he had no experience whatever. Perhaps it would be necessary to have a formal talk about it. He dreaded the thought. He was not a coward in most things, but in this he was an utter craven.

It made matters a great deal worse because he had achieved a discovery—he did not know how he was going to get along without Sally Morgan to take care of him. In a most subtle way she had become a part of his routine, and despite the fact that she was a woman! It was one of those insidious influences that fasten a grip before you are aware of it. He leaned on her. She might not know it,

but he did. Of course, he might shake it off after
he returned to Pittsburgh; but he could not be sure.
What appalled him most was the knowledge that he
did not want to shake it off. It was bothersome;
intensely embarrassing. But it was fascinating, too.
He walked behind the flivver in a pleasant but for-
bidden dream, with Sally walking at his side.

"Hey, you boneheads!" He would rouse himself
like that. "Keep her in the road. What are you
trying to do; put her up a tree? Somebody get in
there and keep a brake on her. Keep her in the
road, I'm telling you. Isn't there *anybody* here with
human intelligence?"

Then he would look at Sally, his mood would
soften and the old embarrassment would descend
on him like a shroud.

"We'll get out of here all right, Sally. Don't
you worry."

"I'm not worrying."

"I mean about—" He caught himself.

"About what, Henry?"

"About afterwards."

"Oh!"

Sally had long silences herself. But her own case
was more troublesome than the Wreck's because
she had no flivver job to boss.

She wished it were all over; that Bob Wells and
his posse would hurry up and take themselves off
and vanish absolutely out of the picture. It was
embarrassing to have Bob around. She even thought
that the Wreck might navigate the flivver himself,

for she had seen him perform feats more difficult.
She found no joy whatever in the peonage to which
the sheriff and his posse were subjected; she believed
that most of it was unnecessary, even from the standpoint of punishment. But at the same time she did
not want to be left alone with Henry Williams.
That was the woman of it.

"Don't you worry," repeated the Wreck, suddenly bold. "You don't have to—Hey! Don't
you know which way to turn the wheels on a curve?
Want to upset her again? Want to wreck her?
Want me to tell everybody in Montana what a set
of clumsy fatheads—No; the other way! Oh, you
get the idea, do you? All right. A little pep, now.
Hi, you sheriff, are you loafing?"

Sally looked at the Wreck.

"I don't have to what?" she asked.

"Oh." He was caught unawares. "Why, you
don't have to—That is, unless—That's not it,
either. What I mean is, you're not really engaged."

It was a reckless speech and he felt instantly that
he ought not to have made it. Sally was looking
straight ahead.

"Of course not," she said, in a low voice.

The Wreck cursed himself. He knew that he was
clumsy, and yet he was desperately groping for an
understanding. The prospect of an early departure
of the posse disturbed him as much as it did Sally.

"What I mean," he said, "is that it's working
backwards, if you can understand. First we were
supposed to be married. Then that's off. Then

we're supposed to be just engaged. And then that's—For the love of Mike! Don't put your shoulder against that mudguard. You'll bend it! Get hold of the body. And shove. Shove! Don't they grow *any* brains in Montana?"

The sheriff and the posse glared—and shoved.

"And then?" remarked Sally.

The Wreck remembered that he had started something.

"Why, then the engagement's off, I suppose," he said, as he glared at the posse. "Which leaves everything exactly where it was at the start. That's what I meant about things working backwards."

There! He had reached the subject at last. He had dealt with it boldly, perhaps roughly; but he had not dodged it. Sally's eyes had a queer, uncertain look. She did not glance in the direction of the Wreck, for she was afraid of a meeting of glances. Besides, she was not sure that she would get a clear vision of him. There was something blurring, even when she looked at an object as plain and familiar as the flivver. Silly, of course; but she could not get the blur out of her eyes unless she rubbed them, and she scorned that, with the Wreck at her elbow.

"Backwards of course," she said.

"Sure," said the Wreck. "You see—well, you see— Let go of that steering wheel! Can't you see that she'll stay in the ruts? All you've got to do is to get busy and shove. You act like you were pushing a five-ton truck. No. *No!* The other way.

Are you trying to bust a spring? That's the way; now shove! If you haven't got any brains, can't you have a little beef?"

He came back from the bossing job with a glance in the direction of Sally. What? She wasn't crying? He could feel his soul squirm. She *was* crying, but it was so unobtrusive, so nearly tearless, that the Wreck knew he was not expected to observe it. Well, why shouldn't she cry, he thought? Her whole world had collapsed. Her romance was gone. He knew that she was through with Bob Wells, but what else was left? He raged at himself again. All he had done was to destroy things. Yes, he alone was responsible. And it was a wreckage beyond his power to repair.

"I'm sorry everything has gone busted," he said.

"Oh, nothing much is busted," said Sally, quickly. "That's all right."

"Oh."

He stole another glance. She was not crying, after all; at least, not now. Strange people, women. You never could tell how long they were going to stick to one thing. That was one reason they disconcerted him. Still, if there was anything he could do for Sally Morgan, all she had to do was to say the word. He would even try to anticipate it.

"Of course, we don't need to tell the sheriff it's all off," he said, suddenly.

"No?"

"What's the use of giving him the satisfaction? We could just keep on—"

He broke off in a cry of rage. The flivver was diving into the brush again and the posse seemed unable to stop it. He leaped to assist, slammed on the emergency brake, brought the cantankerous thing to a halt and fired a broadside of denunciation. He excoriated them severally and collectively, shaking his fist under the nose of the sheriff and behaving in such a threatening manner that Sally stood and marveled at the fact that four able-bodied gentlemen of Montana should endure it. But it was more amazing to see that they not only endured it, but followed his directions about putting the car back on the road.

When he came back to her she hastily smothered a laugh. Not for the world did she want him to know that she amused her.

"They don't get anything right," he complained.

"Still, I think they're trying," she said generously.

"But they don't understand."

"Lots of people don't understand things."

"Huh?"

She meant something; he felt certain. He could tell by an odd note in her voice. Did she mean that there were some things that *he* did not understand? Well, if so, what were they? As for Sally, she was in a tremulous mood, not sure of herself. Mirth and gloom struggled within her, which was exasperating, to say nothing of the embarrassment.

"What don't they understand?" demanded the Wreck.

"Things."

"What kind of things?"

"All kinds."

"Now you're just talking nonsense—in circles."

"I suppose so," said Sally.

"Do you mean me?" he asked, sharply.

"Oh, don't let's quarrel again."

"I'm not quarreling. I never quarrel. My nerves may get on edge, but I'm always pleasant. I'm always—"

They were doing something wrong with the flivver.

"Damnation!" he yelled, and sprang to the rescue.

Eventually they got it right again and once more resumed painful progress toward the main road. They were not far from it now; almost to the top of the last rise. When the Wreck returned to Sally he was mopping his forehead.

"Excuse me," he said, "but they get me all worked up. Once we get to the main road, we're all right. Plain sailing then. We'll be almost at the end of this foolishness."

"Yes," agreed Sally.

"I bet you'll be glad."

She bit her lip until it made her wince. He was probably the most impossible person in the world.

"Get you home in no time after we hit the road," he added.

She flared without a warning symptom.

"Stop talking to me, Henry Williams!"

"Now what have I said?" he asked.

"N-nothing!" She almost shouted it.

"Then what are you sore about?"

"I—I'm not sore. I just think you're the biggest idiot in the whole State of Montana—that's all."

He puzzled over that, got no sense out of it, but became suddenly contrite.

"I suppose so," he said. "I can't ever seem to do things right. Only I thought you were in a hurry to get home, and—What?"

She had mumbled something, but he did not catch it.

"What did you say?"

"You're always putting words in my mouth!" she exclaimed. "I never said I was in a hurry to get home. I never said I'd be glad. I never said—"

The tears were in her eyes again and she made an angry effort to dash them away with her hand.

"Oh, stop it!" groaned the Wreck. "I didn't mean anything. Honestly, Sally. I'm just a bone-head. I don't know the right thing to say, that's all, or what to do. But I would if I was different."

She gave him a look of inquiry.

"Different how?" she asked.

"Different every way. I wouldn't be afraid to say anything to you if I was different. I'd take my chances against anybody. I'd show 'em. But what's the use? I'm a near-sighted, goggle-eyed mutt. I'm all nerves. I'm a wreck. I've got a rotten temper and a mean disposition, and I know it."

"Do you really believe all that, Henry Williams?"

"Certainly I believe it."

"Would you let anybody else say it?"

"No!"

"Neither would I," said Sally.

The Wreck stared. He swallowed hard. His taut nerves, it seemed to him, were vibrating a million times to the second. He felt as though he were soaring far above the common things of earth. Did she really mean—No! *Yes!* He was scared —absolutely appalled—yet triumphant. How was it that everything hit him so suddenly? For he saw light at last. But the light was so dazzling that it did not show him the way. It blinded him. It confused him horribly. It fairly made him dizzy.

"Sally!"

"Yes, old-timer?"

"Sally Morgan! Honestly, could you—"

There was a surly interruption from the voice of the sheriff.

"We've rolled this darn thing as far as we're going to. There's the main road in front of you. If you can't manage yourself from now on, you can stay here for the rest of the summer, for all I care."

The Wreck came back to earth, but he touched it very lightly. He shook himself, blinked, grinned, laughed aloud. His chin was up and his shoulders were back. He was awake, because he saw a flivver, and four men, and other familiar objects. He also saw Sally Morgan, very pink in the cheeks and with a queer, incredulous expression in her eyes. He strode forward like a champion. He swaggered a little. He was ragged, a trifle absurd—but kingly.

He made a sweeping gesture that belonged in

melodrama, but with the Wreck it was intense realism. It was a dismissal.

"On your way!" he commanded. "Get out of here. You're all through. Beat it!"

The middle-aged, solid-looking man, who stood wiping his face and breathing heavily, spoke up from the heart.

"Last time I'll ever go out on a posse with you, Bob Wells," he said. "I don't mind performing the reasonable duties of citizenship, but I'll be doggoned if I'll ever roll a flivver again—not if it stands between me and the gates of Heaven. When I get through with this job I'm going back home and I'm going to stay there. If you want a justice of the peace, you know where I am. But if you want a garage hand—"

The Wreck interrupted him by walking briskly forward and tapping him on the breast with a rigid forefinger.

"Justice of the peace, did you say?" he asked.

"Justice of the peace," said the middle-aged man.

"Issue warrants, try cases, send people to jail, and all that?"

"All that and other things, young man."

The Wreck beamed at him.

"Can you marry people?" he demanded.

"Not only can, but do," answered the justice of the peace.

The Wreck whooped.

CHAPTER XXVI

A MODERN DOCUMENT

HE made a rush at Sally, seized her by the hand and began dragging her forward.

"Settle the whole business right now!" he cried.

Sally was startled, dismayed. Her cheeks were fiery.

"Come on!" shouted the Wreck. "Meant what you said, didn't you?"

"I—I didn't say anything," stammered Sally.

"Yes, you did. I understood it. Took me a long time, but I woke up. ‹ Come along!"

They were facing the justice of the peace.

"Marry us!" commanded the Wreck.

The magistrate grinned at them, particularly at Sally. But now she was defiant. She nodded her head peremptorily.

Bob Wells emerged from a trance.

"You can't get married without a license," he said. "And I don't believe you've got any."

"How about it?" demanded the Wreck.

"Well," said the justice of the peace, "I guess that's about right. Haven't you got a license?"

"Where would I get a license?" retorted the Wreck. "Pick it off a tree? What's the good of being able to marry people if you can't do the whole job? Can't you dig up a license?"

The magistrate scratched his ear and looked at the sheriff. Bob Wells shook his head.

"You can't marry them," he said. "You ought to know it. Besides, when she gets over her excitement maybe she'll think different."

Sally's eyes blazed at him.

"I'm not excited and I know exactly what I'm doing, Bob Wells. Don't you try interfering, unless you want me to make you the silliest looking sheriff in ten counties."

The Wreck gazed at the sheriff and grinned widely. He felt like dancing, or doing something utterly irresponsible.

"I'm a justice of the peace," mused the possessor of the title, as he looked sympathetically at Sally and the Wreck. "I've got a good deal of legal authority. Wouldn't wonder if I could write licenses on a pinch. Never tried it, but—"

"You'll get yourself into a jam," warned the sheriff.

"Oh, I've been in all kinds of jams, Bob. Just got out of one." He eyed the flivver. Then he turned again to the pair in front of him. "Well, if you young folks want to take a chance, I'm game."

The Wreck squeezed Sally's arm until she winced, but she smiled at him.

"I wash my hands of it," said the sheriff.

"No, you don't. You'll be a witness," said the Wreck. "And, for the love of Mike, judge, get a move on. I'm so nervous I'm liable to go crazy."

The justice of the peace was fumbling in his pockets and presently drew forth a folded and tattered document.

"This ain't a regular license," he explained. "It ain't anything but a road map. But if I can find a clean space on the back I'll see what I can do."

He found a clean space after search, discovered a lead pencil and began to write.

"I know how the language goes, anyhow," he said. "That part of it will be just as regular as if it was printed. I've seen a whole lot of licenses, including my own. There ain't anything very complicated. There. Now, just sign where I'm pointing."

The Wreck signed. Sally signed. And the justice of the peace signed.

"I reckon that's a good enough license," he said, with a touch of pride. "It reads straight as a string. It's kind of smudged, maybe, and hardly fit for a frame, but on the main points it's just like a printed one. Only you owe me a dollar, which 'll be duly turned over to the county. Thanks. The ceremony's free. Here she goes."

He rattled it off with a speed born of experience, and it was all over when Sally and the Wreck thought it was just started.

"You're married, all right," said the judge. "I always do it quick. It holds just as tight as a long one. It's like a short affidavit; it puts you in jail just as sure as if it was a regular indictment. And

I tell you what: if anybody makes any kick about that license, all you've got to do is to pay another dollar and get a printed one. There ain't any question about being married. The only point is whether we broke any laws doing it. But I reckon that won't worry you."

The Wreck roused himself from a daze.

"How do we get from here to the Bar-M?" he asked.

"Easy," said the judge. "Hand me that license for a minute."

He unfolded it and turned it over.

"See. Here's where we are," he explained, putting a forefinger on the map. "You just follow the main road from here, going left, until you come to this road. Wait; I'll mark it for you. Then you follow the other road. It's a little twisty, but you can't miss it. Keep right on the way I'm showing you until you come to this turn. You keep bearing to the right. That fetches you to another pike, and you follow that to the left. And there's the Bar-M, right in there."

The Wreck nodded and the judge folded the document again.

"It ain't over seventy miles at the outside," he added. "And most of the road is fair. Just hang onto that paper and you're all right. If you want to know whether you're married, read one side of it. If you want to know which way to go on your honeymoon, turn it over. That's what I call a modern and improved public document, useful in more ways than one. Ain't that so, Bob?"

But the sheriff was striding down the trail in the direction of the horses.

"Well, good luck, folks," said the judge, as he shook hands. "The posse's got official business on its hands. I reckon it ought to be easier than rolling flivvers."

Sally and the Wreck were left alone. They stood silently until the last member of the posse disappeared. Then the Wreck looked at her awkwardly, coughed, reddened and kicked at a stone that lay in the trail. Suddenly he walked over to the flivver and cranked it.

"Get in," he said.

She got in, settled herself in the seat and stared ahead of her.

They followed the pike for nearly an hour, until they came to a road that crossed it. Not a word was spoken. The Wreck did not know what to say, while Sally was certain that he would have to say it first. He fumbled with the dog-eared document, unfolded it and found the license uppermost. Hastily reversing it, he studied the map.

"This is where we turn off," he said.

Sally merely shrugged.

He turned the flivver into the new road and drove on for awhile. But with every mile he grew more restless. He was conscious of a burdensome sense of shortcoming. Yes; he was a failure. Sally was offended; she would not speak to him. He was always blundering, and now he seemed to have achieved the greatest blunder of all. Yet what it was he did not exactly know. He ventured a sidewise glance at her. She looked queer, remote, yet bewilderingly serene. She did not seem to be aware of him.

The Wreck grew desperate. He shut off the engine and jammed the brakes. He began to gesticulate. He became abruptly voluble, without any clear idea of what he was saying.

"Now, don't you worry a particle. It's my fault, every bit of it. Of course, I hadn't any business to. But—but—I just couldn't help it, that's all. I was dreaming, I guess. I got crazy notions. I thought maybe—Well, anyhow, it's my fault. And I'm sorry; that is, if you're sorry. If you're not— But what's the use of talking about that? I'll do my best, you just see. I'll work my head off for you. I'll do anything. Who wouldn't? You give me a chance, that's all. I'll go back to Pittsburgh and I'll make a million dollars for you. I'll give you anything in the world you want. All I want is a chance, I tell you. You just watch me. And I'll make good, too. I've *got* to make good. You're the finest—Well, anyhow, I'm going to make you happy, if it breaks my neck. And maybe, after awhile—Just try me, that's all. I'll make good, as sure as your name's Sally Morgan."

She turned to him with a faint smile on her lips.

"But my name isn't Sally Morgan," she said.

"Huh? Why—that's right. I forgot." His speech became lame again.

"Well that's how I feel, anyway."

She studied him for several seconds, then laid a firm, warm hand over one of his, where it rested on the wheel.

"Old-timer," she said, gently, "you don't need all those words to say it in."

"But I wanted you to understand—"

"Perhaps I do."

"But you *don't*. What I wanted you to understand was—was— It's foolish, but—" His voice suddenly rose to a shout. "Well, anyhow, I love you!"

Sally's fingers closed around his.

"Now you're talking, Henry Williams," she said, contentedly.

The Wreck swooped on her.

It was minutes afterward when Sally freed herself, half laughing, half crying. There was a strange, wonderful look in her eyes as she surveyed him—a look of proud, absurdly happy, possession. There he was, with his horn-rimmed spectacles, his squint, his old challenging air of defiance—Henry Williams, of Pittsburgh, Pa., Nervous Wreck—but all hers.

"And I *do* love you," he was saying, belligerently.

"Of course," said Sally. "But it took you so long—"

He swooped again, expertly, for the Wreck was a quick student.

"There!" exclaimed Sally. "Now you'd better

get out and crank the flivver, or we'll never make the Bar-M to-night."

"But I want you to understand—"

"You dear idiot, I understood long ago."

The Bar-M lay before them, almost at their feet. The ranch buildings huddled close to the ridge on the eastern side of the wide coulée, and the flivver was poised at the top of the ridge. Into the hills beyond the sun was dipping. To the north lay the summit of Black Top. Nearly home.

"I'm afraid we ought to have stuck to the road," said Sally.

The Wreck had insisted on cutting across the range, when they reached a point opposite the Bar-M coulée.

"Miles around the other way," he said. "And here we are, almost there."

"But it's pretty steep, Henry."

She looked down the long green slope with a calculating eye.

"It's nothing," said the Wreck. "Just watch."

The flivver dipped into the grade, slowly at first, then with growing speed. Half way down it was traveling like a wild thing. Sally set her teeth and clung to the seat. She braced her feet against the floorboards. She closed her eyes.

The Wreck had the service brake jammed down as far as it would go. He hauled back on the emergency brake. The flivver plunged onward, her brake bands screaming and smoking.

"We're going to hit something!" cried the Wreck.

Sally opened her eyes.

"Don't hit the kitchen!" she cried. "Ma's in there! Hit the corral!"

He could at least steer, and he did. They hit the corral. A section of fence flew into kindlings and the flivver charged onward. The sorrel horse, directly in its path, lifted his head, snorted, wheeled, lashed out with his heels and missed it by inches. The fence on the farther side loomed. The Wreck still fought with the brakes. There was a second crash, a lurch, a splintering of various things. The flivver stopped.

Dad Morgan, who was leaning against the fence a few yards distant, removed his pipe from his mouth and examined the situation with interest.

"I see you made good time gettin' back," he remarked.

"Dad!" cried Sally.

"Howdy, Sally? Howdy, Wreck?"

He strolled near for a better look at the flivver. One of the wheels was crumpled, both mudguards were curled up, the wind-shield was gone and there was a rivulet of steaming brown water dripping from the radiator.

"I reckon," said Dad, "that her nervous system is kind of shot up."

"Oh, Dad!"

Sally leaped clear of the wreckage and had her arms around his neck.

"Git the trousseau?" he asked, when she let go of him.

"Trousseau!" cried Sally. "Why, I—I'm married!"

"Well, I'll be durned!"

"Where's Ma? I want to tell her."

"Well, I'll be durned," repeated Dad. "Your Ma's over to the house, I reckon. Where's Bob?"

Sally began to laugh.

"I'm not married to Bob. I'm married to Henry Williams!"

Dad Morgan's glance wandered to the Wreck, who was still sitting in the flivver, gloomily surveying his work.

"Now I *will* be durned," he said, thoughtfully. "Come to think of it, I reckon I'll be damned."

"You'd better be nice to him," warned Sally, in a whisper. "He's the dearest thing in the world."

She raced away in the direction of the house, where the slight figure of Ma Morgan stood framed in the kitchen doorway.

Dad watched her go. Well, women were queer folks. But if Sally said it was all right, that settled it. Married, eh? The Wreck was his son-in-law! Fair enough, he mused. Sally always insisted the Wreck was game. His own course of conduct was clear.

"Wreck," he said, "providin' it ain't necessary for you to sit there watchin' the remains, there's a bottle up at the house."

"Sure," said the Wreck, as he climbed down. "Only don't grin at me. Hear me? Don't grin! It makes me nervous."

THE END

www.ingramcontent.com/pod-product-compliance
Lightning Source LLC
Chambersburg PA
CBHW032238010726
47494CB00002B/543